MOONSHADOW

THE NIGHTMARE NINJA

MOONSHADOW
THE NIGHTMARE NINJA

by **SIMON HIGGINS**

LITTLE, BROWN AND COMPANY
New York   Boston

To the memory of my father,
Major Aubrey Higgins,
Royal Engineers, 1914–2007,
the gentle samurai who raised me.

Little, Brown and Company

Hachette Book Group
237 Park Avenue, New York, NY 10017
Visit our website at www.lb-kids.com

Little, Brown and Company is a division of Hachette Book Group, Inc.
The Little, Brown name and logo are trademarks of Hachette Book Group, Inc.

The publisher is not responsible for websites (or their content)
that are not owned by the publisher.

First U.S. Paperback Edition: June 2012
First U.S. hardcover edition published in June 2011 by Little, Brown and Company
First published as *Moonshadow: The Wrath of Silver Wolf* in Australia in 2009 by
Random House Australia Pty Ltd.

Library of Congress Cataloging-in-Publication Data
Higgins, Simon, 1958–
[Wrath of Silver Wolf]
The nightmare ninja / by Simon Higgins. — 1st U.S. ed.
p. cm. — (Moonshadow)
Summary: Battling a power-hungry warlord in medieval Japan, teenaged Moonshadow,
an orphaned ninja in the shogun's secret service with the ability to see through the eyes of
animals, encounters a weaponless assassin who enters the mind of his victims during their sleep.
ISBN 978-0-316-05533-8 (hc) / 978-0-316-05534-5 (pb)
[1. Ninja—Fiction. 2. Orphans—Fiction. 3. Supernatural—Fiction. 4. Japan—
History—1185–1868—Fiction.]—I. Title.
PZ7.H534964Ni 2011 [Fic]—dc22 2010043177

10 9 8 7 6 5 4 3 2 1
RRD-C
Printed in the United States of America

THE FURUBE SUTRA

(the "Shrugging Off")

Preparation Verse

Gather, tidy, and align your ways,
for they bring karma

Facing Self Verse

Cleanse any lies made this day,
scatter not one grain of life

Verse of One Resolved

To end this path in happiness,
seek peace within your mind

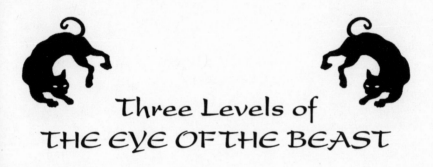

Three Levels of
THE EYE OF THE BEAST

1. Beast Sight
To link your mind to a creature and use its senses

2. Dual Sight
To see with your own eyes and those of a
linked animal

3. Sight-Control
To both see through and command a beast,
making it your spy or weapon

THE BRAVE NEW EDO

The midnight temple bell gave a final hum, masking the sound of Moonshadow's landing. Its voice declared the halfway mark of the Hour of the Rat.

He crouched low on the roof, scanned the moonlit horizon ahead, and listened. Before the echo of the bell died away, the tiles behind him creaked.

Moonshadow turned without a sound to the ninja who had landed behind him. His tightly bound night cowl showed only his eyes, but he offered her a smile anyway. The willowy silhouette of Snowhawk, his trusted friend and mission partner, promptly returned a nod. She adjusted the sword on her back and then stretched out to press an ear to the cold, curved tiles.

Snowhawk bobbed up, drawing an iron right angle and a small crowbar from her backpack. While she silently worked the first large tile loose, Moonshadow rotated slowly on the spot, checking their surroundings for any hint of movement.

His sharp eyes probed the darkness, ears strained to pick up any hint of trouble. Moonshadow felt his mouth turn dry. It wasn't due to anything he saw or heard. He always grew tense just around this point in a mission. The cloth covering his nose and mouth trapped a taut sigh. Tension and fear, though never pleasant, were actually friends. They kept a spy sharp, cautious, attentive to detail, improving the chances of surviving a mission.

He knew that, as usual, his status as a secret defender of the Shogun would offer no protection. If he and Snowhawk were caught spying on a lord like this, that nobleman's sentries and bodyguards would instantly unleash a hail of arrows or sword cuts upon them, no questions asked. Moonshadow finished his sweep of their dark, undulating surrounds. There was no hint of movement, but any surrounding rooftop could still be hiding loyal, watchful guards, themselves scanning every nearby shadow. One hasty, eye-catching move or careless sharp sound and the mission would be ruined. Worse still, the hunters would suddenly become the prey.

Slowly Moonshadow began a second circle. Such caution was essential! He and Snowhawk might not be that far from home, but if they were detected, ambush and death could swoop as quickly here as in any far-off valley or castle. There was only one place in all the world where he could relax: the walled monastery of the Grey Light Order.

But that lay on the opposite side of this massive, fast-growing city.

He studied the jagged Edo skyline as he turned. So many new, unfamiliar buildings and, thanks to the rising foreign influence, even a few with flat roofs.

A minor lord, Akechi, owned the mansion they were breaking into tonight. It stood in the center of the aristocratic quarter of Tsukiji. It was a whole new district, perched on reclaimed land that had once been the lowland marshes of the Sumida River delta. To the northwest lay mighty Edo Castle, the Shogun's home, stark in the moonlight, its tower's whitewashed walls shining.

What a twist! By draining the marshes, the Shogun himself had created Tsukiji and now here, beneath Moonshadow's very feet—if their intelligence was right—a nobleman was plotting treason against their ruler.

Moonshadow braced himself. They must stop him.

On the horizon, black mountains carved the wide sky, and the distant snowy cap of Mount Fuji glowed like an upturned white bowl, faint in the moonlight.

He stared southeast to Edo Bay. Tiny lights bobbed in the harbor where samurai guarded their lords' coastal ships.

At first, Moonshadow heard no sounds but the usual: cats fighting here and there; far off, the short-lived barking of a startled dog, quickly followed by its owner's rebuke; a shrill seabird, calling its mate to the northern fork of the bay. Then noises from the mansion below made him hold his breath and listen hard. *Footsteps, muffled voices.* Did they belong to Akechi's guards? What if one of them had *shinobi* training and, therefore, animal-sharp ears?

A gentle breeze swept the roof. Moonshadow pulled down the edge of his cowl's face-bindings, cooling the sweat on his upper lip as he drew in the soft wind's salty tang.

A tap on his shoulder made him turn. Snowhawk

had finished lifting tiles and it was time to descend. They had recited the *furube* sutra together just before this mission, but its mind-clearing effect, at least for Moonshadow, was proving short-lived. The shrugging-off sutra was uttered each dawn and sunset and prior to going into action. It was supposed to help a spy remain calm and able to concentrate, but now he felt tension rising, knotting his stomach. His thoughts were speeding up too.

Once inside the attic, they would be especially vulnerable to ambush. A spy's worst nightmare was being cornered in a small space. There, swords were nearly useless and most tricks and illusions wouldn't work. *Shuriken*, the star-shaped iron throwing knives that *shinobi* used with deadly effect, were badly hampered by roofing beams. Any light at all, and eye-tricking night suits lost their power.

Growing up, Moonshadow had heard many awful stories from his trainers about agents who were detected and then trapped in cellars, drains, or attics. Attics just like this one.

The nastiest tales all involved an enemy retaliating with fire. Moonshadow pictured the face of an agent who had once visited the Grey Light Order monastery, a man with only one eye and a horribly scarred face. That spy, Brother Eagle had later told him, had been cornered in a stable by a line of guards, doused with oil, then set alight even as he fought wildly to escape....

Moonshadow glanced down at their square black entry point and tried not to picture flames roaring below. He had just fought off the image when a muffled sound made him shudder. His eyes darted to the left.

What was that? Movement across tiles. Very faint, but close. Up on the next roof? Whoever it was had an incredibly light step. That meant a high level of stealth training.

His hand glided to the grip of his back-mounted sword.

Snowhawk saw the motion and instantly slid backward into a band of shadow, her long fingers creeping between the lapels of her jacket, probing for a *shuriken*.

Moonshadow pointed up at the next roof's visible face, its gentle slope looming over them. The roof capped a mansion one story higher than the one they were entering. The pale wall under its dark tiles was bland and, luckily, windowless.

He listened intently. More sounds. Someone was definitely moving up the roof's opposite slope, heading for that nobbled ridge-cap at the apex. The erratic footfall grew a little louder. Snowhawk drew a *shuriken* from a concealed pouch in her jacket, gripping the black iron throwing knife carefully so its star points wouldn't cut her hand. Moonshadow knew that, like him and unlike normal folk, she too could hear the sounds—but only now that they'd intensified.

Snowhawk's hearing was sharper than Moonshadow's, developed from a lifelong special *shinobi* diet, sensory focus training, and years of listening for the *swish* of a weapon that might slay her.

She and Moonshadow had both been orphans, raised by rival spy houses, so they shared that kind of training. But at times his hearing was also unnaturally enhanced. It came and went, a heightening that his brother agent Groundspider called "residue." Which it was. Snowhawk, who had recently joined the Grey Light Order, envied Moonshadow's residual hearing, because its source was a rare *shinobi* skill that she did not possess.

Moonshadow had been trained in the Old Country science called the Eye of the Beast. It enabled him to mentally join with a nearby animal, seeing through its eyes or even taking control of it. An animal-quality sense such as hearing or smell would often linger in Moonshadow after he had joined his mind with that of a bird or beast. It could fade and then return unpredictably. Sometimes these random heightenings were so intense they became overwhelming, even making him feel sick. But not tonight. For now, a manageable audio residue, sharp but not too strong, was serving him well.

Moonshadow inclined his head, opening his mouth to help stretch that enhanced hearing even further. They needed more information, and fast! Whoever approached was high on the roof's hidden face now, about to peep—or plunge—over that bumpy apex. Moonshadow and Snowhawk would be seen at once, then attacked, *shuriken* flying at them or, worse still, the lurking *shinobi* might leap straight onto *their* roof, sword flashing, the commotion blowing their cover!

With stomach muscles tightening, Moonshadow gripped his back-mounted sword.

"Get ready to throw," he whispered to Snowhawk.

With a short, crisp nod, she brought her right hand up, in line with one high cheekbone. The curved blades of a Clan Fuma *shuriken* peeped between her fingers. Moonshadow frowned at it and then looked back up to the next roof's apex.

How strange. Despite being given a pouch of Grey Light Order throwing stars with the classic straight-bladed Iga-Koga design, she was still using her old supply.

Why use a style favored by the very clan she had fled? Was it just familiarity?

They both recoiled as movement broke the next roof's skyline. A head appeared.

Snowhawk's hand dropped. She and Moonshadow sighed heavily, their shoulders relaxing. Above them bobbed a tiny head with pointy ears.

A *cat*. Though not just any passing cat. The temple cat that lived with them.

"What are *you* doing here?" Moonshadow whispered to it. "Have you tailed us all night?"

The temple cat strolled up and down the high roofline, flicking its tail but not making a sound. Moonshadow never ceased to marvel at the animal's oddity. Like any other temple or "kimono" cat, it had been born with rare markings that were considered sacred. They resembled an image of a woman in a kimono, and by tradition, such cats lived on the grounds of temples or shrines. But regular temple cats had stumpy, triangular tails. This one's tail was long, thick, and expressive.

Smiling with relief, Moonshadow looked up at the eccentric creature that had adopted him two months earlier. It had been during the first real mission of his life, when he had also met Snowhawk. The fearless, skillful Snowhawk.

Moonshadow glanced at her with furtive admiration. He still wasn't sure if he'd rescued her, she him, or they each other. Whatever the case, it had been one crazy, dangerous mission. He'd been wounded and made himself a powerful enemy, the rebel warlord Silver Wolf, whose henchman had almost destroyed them both. Narrowly, somehow, it had all ended in success.

Above, the cat turned suddenly on the apex, drawing his eye.

Snowhawk moved noiselessly to his side. "This is getting ridiculous," she whispered. "It's sweet the way she's so crazy about you, but she's going to get us caught."

He nodded, squinting up at the animal. What was the cat's game? Now she was leaning sharply toward Edo Castle, tail swishing around fast. She turned and glared down at Moonshadow, then resumed the same antics. Thankfully, without a single meow.

"Wait," he muttered. "She's signaling something." But what? A warning?

Great timing! Both he and Snowhawk needed to

enter this attic, and now. But perhaps there was good cause to have somebody keep watch. Moonshadow scratched his cheek, reasoning it through. He *could* do both at once: sight join with the cat *and* head into the attic at the same time, but it would cost him precious life force, ki energy, temporarily draining his strength. That always increased the risk factor during a mission. If he failed to rest properly afterward, or sight joined again too quickly, total exhaustion — and disaster — would follow.

Yet what choice did he have? If this *was* a warning and he simply ignored it…

He glanced to one side. Snowhawk was staring at him. She leaned in close. Her large eyes flicked briefly to the cat, then she raised an eyebrow at Moonshadow. Her thoughts were easy to discern: she knew he intended to link with the cat, but wasn't sure it was a good idea.

He gestured down at the square opening she had created in the tiles. "We must get into place *now*," he whispered. "If our information's right, their meeting starts any moment, if it hasn't already."

She nodded reluctantly, then deftly made a series of three signs with her hand in Grey Light Order code. The signals told Moonshadow her plan: while he sight joined with the temple cat, she would sweep the attic for chime traps. He showed his acceptance with a sharp nod and, a moment later, watched Snowhawk carefully enter the attic, sliding in headfirst. As her feet disappeared, he turned away to stare up at the temple cat. Moonshadow concentrated on the animal, and for a few seconds his hands trembled. The cat looked down at him and, as their gazes met, a subtle green hue sheened its eyes. Moonshadow knew the same unnatural color was sparkling around his pupils too. His nostrils flared and twitched as he began to share the cat's powerful sense of smell.

The barrage of new odors threatened to overwhelm him. The smell of old incense from a house below. Freshly caught fish and pork roasting somewhere in the distance. A sandalwood scent from the damp laundry drying on a pole nearby. And another aroma, sweet, almost sickly, coming from so far off he couldn't identify it.

Focusing his will, Moonshadow accessed the second level of the Eye of the Beast craft. Abruptly he saw through both the cat's eyes and his own.

With his human vision, he saw the temple cat standing motionless, leaning once more from the higher roof's peak, a dark Edo skyline behind it.

Superimposed over that sight, he saw what the

cat saw: the opposite skyline, with Edo Castle at its center. The animal vision rippled through what looked like a thin layer of water, a side effect he was used to. Distant movement in the vista caught his attention. A tiny figure, hard for even the cat's eyes to make out, was cautiously hopping roofs, bobbing as if searching, gradually approaching from the direction of the Shogun's castle.

That explained the sweet, near-sickly odor. The cat smelled man sweat from far away.

Moonshadow cursed. It was hard to see the flitting figure at all, let alone make out any features, such as his weaponry. The intruder was most likely wearing a night suit similar to the kind he and Snowhawk wore. Its bluish purple color was harder to distinguish in half-light or shadow than plain black.

Only *shinobi* had such equipment, and this man certainly moved like one. Moonshadow shook his head. An agent then, for sure. A shudder went through him. Akechi wasn't guarding his secret meeting with samurai! It was far worse than that: he'd hired an assassin to watch his back! Or maybe several!

Moonshadow cast quick glances in all directions. Were *more* enemy ninja closing in, unheard, unseen?

Moonshadow's eyes darted back to the hole in the roof. Snowhawk should have reappeared by now to signal the all clear. What was happening in there? He swallowed.

Was this so-called meeting actually a trap?

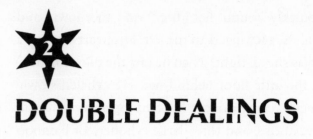

DOUBLE DEALINGS

Moonshadow concentrated hard, taking complete control of the cat. Up on the higher rooftop's summit, it stiffened slightly.

As he settled into the third and highest level of the Eye of the Beast, Moonshadow felt a tug in the pit of his stomach. His ki was already draining fast!

Stay where you are, he ordered the cat. *Watch that man.*

Moving slowly, with the cat's watery vision dancing over the top of his own, Moonshadow dangled his head through the opening Snowhawk had made. His eyes quickly found her, her body facedown and motionless, a few paces to the left. His heart skipped a beat. Was she all right? Then he saw the pile of materials on the attic floor behind her. He exhaled slowly with relief. A tangle of cut, knotted ropes, several small iron eye-hooks, and three large cylinders of bamboo with carved wooden clappers on cords, all of them now severed. He grinned. The attic *had* been armed with chime traps, but their darkened, hidden ropes were no match for a professional like Snowhawk.

Moonshadow crept to her side and she pointed with a special tool, indicating where she had already bored a line of small listening or watching holes in the attic's floorboards. He nodded and carefully stretched out next to her. Moonshadow held his breath, brushing aside the one tiny pile of sawdust Snowhawk's drilling had left, in case a flake or two fell through the holes and gave them away. He turned his head to lower one ear over a hole.

Immediately he heard breathing and smelled men and liquor in the room below. Angling his head, Moonshadow lined up one eye with the peephole, a move made harder by the constant, wobbling view of the Edo skyline he was seeing through the cat.

Through the beast's vision, Moonshadow saw that the man outside was steadily approaching, though his advance had slowed. Now he seemed to be inspecting certain roofs with meticulous care. Why? Was he uncertain of where he was? Was he hunting for them, or did he have some different objective here in Tsukiji? Surely he was a rooftop guard for the conspirators' meeting, arriving a little late after being delayed somehow?

Moonshadow raised one hand, ready to tap Snowhawk's shoulder and warn her about the oncoming ninja. He hesitated. Using hand signals in this near-darkness could lead to confusion! Why were those men in the room below so quiet? Perhaps they were still settling in, but until they grew talkative or noisy, he and Snowhawk had no muffling cloak of sound behind which to whisper safely and so communicate in detail.

Moonshadow blinked at the hole. *Talk down there, will you?*

Beneath his stealth suit, beads of sweat ran down his spine. It was humid, unusually tight in here! And with that intruder approaching, though the man still paused to search roofs here and there, their available time was dwindling fast. If a hostile *shinobi* trapped them in this attic...

A terrible image of licking tongues of fire rushed into his mind. He forced it out again.

The first hint of a headache pulsed in Moon-shadow's temples. Would somebody down there *please* get on with conspiring already? He clenched one fist.

Enough, he had to regain his calm! He tried hard to concentrate on the mission itself.

Moonshadow studied the men below, clustered so tightly around a low eating table that, thanks to the room's high ceiling, he could see all three of them at once. If they, however, looked up, the same ceiling's high band of shadow would hide the spy holes drilled in its thin wooden plates.

The conspirators knelt on the tatami floor, feet folded under them. On the table lay sake cups, chopsticks, small empty rice bowls, and a tall clay beaker. It looked as if they had already shared a snack and then started midnight drinks at the outset of their meeting. Perhaps why they had been quiet so far! That was good in a way: their little feast had probably bought him and Snowhawk some time to get into place. And at least they wouldn't stay quiet much longer: sake generally loosened men's tongues. He peered through a different spy hole and found their weapons. A sword sitting in an elegant rack and, on the reed matting beside it, laid in neat lines, two *tanto*-style daggers. One of them was highly ornate, the kind rich traders wore.

One man covered his mouth and forced a series of coughs as if something tickled in his throat. Snowhawk quickly slid closer. "I sense *shinobi* energy," she whispered. "It's distant, but getting stronger."

He tapped her arm once in acknowledgment. This was one of her strengths that he couldn't match, the ability to feel the presence of another spy. She was very good at it, he quite inconsistent. At least tonight he could rely on her prowess with that skill, should any other uninvited guests turn up.

Below, the man who had been coughing gave a final loud splutter, and his companions started teasing him noisily, joking that he might not live long enough to see their plans fulfilled.

Good, they were getting raucous now! Moonshadow seized the opportunity. "I can see him. One man, very agile," he murmured softly. "Looks big. Bigger than Groundspider. Coming this way, searching roofs hard. *We're running out of time.*"

She nodded back sharply, tension narrowing her big eyes.

As they returned their attention to the conspirators, one cleared his throat imperiously. The others fell silent at once.

With a commanding manner, golden leaf-patterned robes, and a nobleman's hair queue, the man had to be Lord Akechi. He sipped a cup of sake between his sentences. The two facing him—one man was bearded, and the other, clean-shaven and bald—nodded keenly as he talked.

The bearded one wore the thin green indoor kimono of a houseguest, while the bald man had donned the bland grey street robes common to merchants. A silver prosperity charm from the shrine of the money god was stitched to one dark lapel.

"Something big is in the wind," Akechi said confidently. "It grows clearer by the day that not every noble wants this new peace to last. They know that war means opportunities. The chance for those denied power to seize it."

The bearded man in the guest robe raised his cup and spoke in a soft Kyoto accent. "And for those of us consorting with barbarian traders, a chance to make instant fortunes through importing their most wanted commodity... the latest firearms."

Moonshadow grimaced. Within sight of the Shogun's very home, two different worlds now schemed revolt together. The nobles, the old wealth with lands, titles, and mastery over the warrior class. And the merchants, the new rich, a rising caste of money-men who sought illegal foreign allies. No wonder eavesdropping missions were now so common. Something big *was* in the wind.

Akechi's bald guest folded his arms. He spoke fast and firmly, in the manner of many Edo residents. "My lord, a hundred pardons, but I have been wondering how our investment proceeds. Would it be rude for me to humbly ask for an update at this time?"

The bearded one nodded eagerly, as if he'd wanted to raise the same thing.

"Not rude at all." Akechi smiled. "As long as details are fittingly avoided. We must remain...cautious."

The bald one gestured. "But our determined friend to the west is still keen to right the *great wrong*?" Akechi smiled and nodded quickly. The three laughed together.

Snowhawk nudged Moonshadow. "Somebody wants to reverse the outcome of the Battle of Sekigahara that ended the last civil war, crush old enemies, make *himself* Shogun." Though she had only whispered, he'd felt the outrage in her words. Moonshadow scowled. Akechi would know many nobles who lived to the west of Edo, but *he* knew of only one with such lofty ambitions: his mortal enemy, the ruthless Silver Wolf, lord of Fushimi.

He grimly refocused on the figure the cat was

watching. Much closer now, the man appeared to be checking every rooftop in this part of Tsukiji. Heat flushed through Moonshadow's body and he felt his heart rate speed up. Panic tried to snatch at him, but he shoved it away. Below, one of the conspirators, talking affably, refilled his friends' sake cups.

"He's *really close*." Moonshadow breathed quickly. Snowhawk's eyes widened at the stress in his face and she gave a fast nod.

"Our friend," Akechi said below, "is currently organizing specialists to help in our cause. Once they have struck a certain blow, we should reconvene. And then I will ask you to invest even more."

The two merchants grunted supportively. The bearded one half-bowed.

Moonshadow scowled. These three men each owned so much, but because of their greed and opportunism, and the ambition of their "friend to the west," a new civil war might break out within the year, in which tens of thousands could die. As Brother Badger had always said, a little bitterly, the world's history was a centipede of gluttony wars. Moonshadow clenched his teeth. Not this time; he, Snowhawk, and all the Grey Light Order, the Shogun's eyes and ears, would stop them. He stilled himself, etching their words into his mind so he could

later recall them verbatim. As trained, he and Snowhawk would each write a version of what they had
heard, then the two accounts would be used to check
each other's accuracy.

Suddenly Moonshadow's beast sight moved, and
his heart began pounding wildly. The agent outside
was just five roofs away. Snowhawk slid back from
the holes she had made in the attic floor.

Below, with sake cups raised, the conspirators
launched into a series of toasts to their unnamed
friend, to their plan, to its success and victory.

"I know," Snowhawk whispered. "Time to go. I
can feel him. He's almost on us, right?"

Moonshadow nodded and quickly but silently
followed her back out onto the roof. He kept watch
through the cat as Snowhawk carefully replaced the
tiles. The moment the last one had muttered softly
back into place, he gave the cat a final command.

Go home, now. Moonshadow broke the beast link,
and he and Snowhawk turned to run.

Side by side they scuttled low across Lord Akechi's
roof and then jumped to the next frozen tsunami of
tiles that arched in the moonlight. Snowhawk glanced
over her shoulder. She clicked her tongue.

Moonshadow stopped and hung his head knowingly. "The cat's following us, isn't it?"

She nodded with a sigh.

"Then let's outrun them both," he mumbled with irritation.

They tore off, springing up and down over a long series of identical rooftops that formed a dappled, rolling road in the moonlight. As they ran and jumped, quickly choosing sound landing spots and handholds in advance, Moonshadow smelled his own streaming sweat as well as their pursuer's scent.

After traveling the distance a bow shot could cover, they paused on the roof of a temple and looked back. The cat had dropped out of the race, but the unknown spy was still coming, closely following their path. Now there was no doubt. He *was* after them, and his orders were easy to guess.

Kill the Grey Light Order spies before they could report what they'd heard!

INTERCEPTED

O ver there!" Snowhawk pointed at a line of homes. Moonshadow looked. Two among them appeared brand-new. Perhaps they had replaced buildings that had recently burnt down. They were new and different. "See the two flat roofs, one close, one far?" She patted her pack. "They look ideal for traps."

"Let's do it!" he hissed. They began house hopping toward the first roof.

On arrival Moonshadow looked down at it, his eyebrows knitting. So these fashionable new flat roofs weren't truly flat; their angle was just very subtle compared to the steep, sweeping curves of traditional Japanese roofing. He glanced about. Clothes-drying poles. A wooden ladder fixed to the outside of the building. Moonshadow padded across the tiles to take up a sentry point in the darkest corner.

He watched the skyline behind Snowhawk as she quickly pulled two blackened trip wires from her pack. She worked fast, using the bamboo drying poles at each end of the roof, and tied one wire at throat height in a long shadow, the next at ankle height in another dark patch two strides from the edge. Moonshadow nodded approvingly at her cunning; if their pursuer sensed and ducked the first wire, he just might relax enough to trip over the second and plunge from the roof. It was no certainty, but worth a try for sure.

Moonshadow's gaze probed the night. Where was the enemy now?

Suddenly he made out a large silhouette, flitting nimbly between rooftop shadows. Moonshadow flinched. The ninja was moving faster now, really gaining on them, so close that Moonshadow could even see the outline of the man's back-mounted sword. The stranger's scent grew stronger in Moonshadow's nostrils, making them flare. His heart pounded against his ribs as he met Snowhawk's eyes. "Go, go, *quick*," he whispered.

They resumed roof hopping, both panting hard now but increasing their speed until they vaulted, side by side, onto the second flat roof. Moonshadow rubbed his burning thighs as he looked around.

This roof's entire surface was bathed in the shadow of the mansion next door.

The higher rooftop was undergoing alteration. A thick cedar beam, drilled clean through with large holes at regular intervals, was roped along its apex.

His eyes locked on the beam. It was high enough to offer a hiding place from which they could observe both roofs. The big holes made it a ready duck blind.

Snowhawk saw the same potential. "I say we get behind *that*"—she gestured up at the beam—"wait, then ambush him."

Moonshadow nodded agreement, and as he jumped for the next roof, she half turned and scooped something from her pack. Before following Moonshadow, Snowhawk turned back, carefully giving the roof a single, wide wave.

Low skittering sounds told Moonshadow that she had strewn *tetsubishi* across the rooftop. A wise move. *Tetsubishi* were tiny caltrops designed to pierce the sandals—and feet—of anyone following in a *shinobi*'s wake. Some agents used cast metal or twisted-wire *tetsubishi*, but Snowhawk preferred the natural kind: the spiky dried seedpods of a certain water plant. Unlike their man-made relatives, they often broke when stepped on, which actually made them even more effective. Usually at least one of their four rather nasty curved prongs wound up lodged deep beneath a howling victim's skin.

"Where is he?" Moonshadow peered warily through a hole in the beam. "There! He keeps stopping. Must be having trouble tracking us. Hope he doesn't notice your—"

Snowhawk cut him off. "Say he does. Say he dodges all my traps. Do we try to take him alive?" She gripped the sword strapped beside her backpack. "You're the senior on this mission. The decision is yours." She slowly unsheathed her blade, keeping it low, out of the moonlight. "I'm happy to go either way...unless he's a Fuma agent."

Moonshadow frowned. "You mean because they raised you, if he's of Clan Fuma you're reluctant to kill him?"

"No," she said lightly, "the opposite. If he's Fuma..." She gestured, making a cut with her weapon.

He stared at her, his concealed mouth open in surprise. Snowhawk leaned close. Even in the moonlight, he could see that deep anger filled her lovely eyes.

"Raised me?" She gave a low hiss. "They trained me well, but as for how they raised me…" She found another hole and checked on their pursuer before going on. "My mentors were beyond harsh. I saw friends our age put to death or abandoned to the enemy for failing one mission. It's why I defected; why I'd never go back."

"Good. You suit the Grey Light Order," he said quickly.

"I know," she said with a nod. "Look, I told you before: both Fuma and your order train suitable orphans, but the Grey Light treats theirs like human beings." She shrugged. "So don't worry about this guy. Leave him to me. He comes, I'll happily take care of it."

While Moonshadow watched the unknown agent approach the first flat roof, he started weighing his decision at feverish speed. His it was! Young or not, he *was* the senior agent tonight.

Which meant he had to make that hardest choice of all: to kill or not to kill.

What to do? The dignified Heron would suggest caution. Many times while teaching him *naginata* fighting, disguises, and potions, she had warned him not to be impulsive.

Perhaps, since he was now thinking this through, she had succeeded in training him to be cautious. But what if sparing the stranger was overcautious?

"He's poised before the first roof now, looking it over," Snowhawk said quickly, "about to jump for the side where my throat wire is. Don't like how long he's taking."

Moonshadow nodded absently. If those trip wires worked, he might escape this decision. Badger, the Order's irritable archivist, would simply snap, "*Review the mission rules!*"

So he did. No special limits on the use of force had been mentioned. He could therefore slay a skilled pursuer and be neither dishonorable nor disobedient. He could, but *should* he?

"Curse it!" Snowhawk clenched a fist. "He just dodged *both* trip wires. He's on the move again." She shrugged. "Oh, well. Might not do as well against my *tetsubishi*."

Groundspider, Moonshadow decided, would advocate cutting down the pursuer without hesitation. Moonshadow's sparring partner and trainer in throwing knives and smoke bombs had a dark, ferocious side. A true follower of Lord Hachiman, the god of war, Groundspider was the "if in doubt, kill it anyway" type. Moonshadow sighed. He knew *he* wasn't.

"Look," Snowhawk whispered, elbowing him gently. "He's almost here—see, far edge of the second flat roof. Darn it! He's looking around. I think he saw the *tetsubishi*."

Moonshadow's stomach churned and he felt his mouth turn dry. Any moment, he'd have to make this decision. His mind raced. Brother Mantis would take the opposite line to Groundspider. Once a famous duelist, Mantis now stood for mercy and compassion and would say just don't kill, unless you have no choice. As a strategist, he'd also advise gaining a prisoner—and potentially all he knows—rather than simply notching up a kill.

Moonshadow shook his head. Which voice should he listen to? Was *this* leadership? It was confusing!

Even trying to imitate Brother Eagle, the head of their order, wouldn't help right now. Eagle, born and raised samurai but trained in Iga *ninjutsu* and the Eye of the Beast, had lived in two different worlds and thought flexibly: Eagle's counsel to Moonshadow was always to trust his own instincts.

He grumbled a curse. What *were* his instincts saying? He wasn't sure!

Snowhawk gave a soft gasp. "He's balancing on

the edge, sneaking around the *tetsubishi*. This guy is sharp." She patted Moonshadow's arm and raised her sword. "Better not take any chances. I'll just slay him then, huh?"

Moonshadow swallowed hard. Where was the instant wisdom he needed? Then he thought of one of Mantis's obsessions: the real meaning of part of their *furube* sutra, the shrugging-off rite intoned each dawn, each sunset, and before every mission.

Scatter not one grain of life. Since it was the sutra of spies and assassins, it meant, surely, one *unnecessary* grain. At least his instincts about that message were clear. It was, in itself, a code to follow whenever in doubt. A reminder too: where possible, walk the highest path, always winning yet doing no needless harm.

"He's heading for this roof." Snowhawk started to rise.

"Alive," Moonshadow whispered quickly. "That's my decision. We take him al—"

He heard a minute grunt of disappointment from Snowhawk, but there was no time for debate. With a soft *whump* the pursuer landed on their roof and began hurrying up its slope for the apex and the cedar beam. Snowhawk sheathed her sword, irritation in her eyes. Moonshadow turned from her and squinted through one of the beam's holes.

The man was bigger than Groundspider and easily as agile. They were in for a tough, ugly fight. What if it spun out of control? It might be *him* doing the slaying.

The stranger reached the beam and one of his large hands slid across the top of it, fingers probing for a sound grip. Snowhawk launched up, grabbed his wrist, and twisted it quickly into a nerve-stretching lock. From beside her Moonshadow vaulted over the beam, clamping a headlock on their pursuer. The man gave a snarl and then pushed off hard with his feet, somersaulting over the beam, dragging his attackers with him until all three of them were upside down. The bold maneuver broke their grips, and with a muffled clatter the trio tumbled apart down the sloping roof behind the cedar beam. One of the ninja's flailing feet caught Moonshadow in the head, stunning him. Limp and disoriented, he slid quickly for the edge.

As his head cleared, Moonshadow felt the outermost tiles scrape along his ribs. Then his stomach pitched wildly. He scrambled with his feet. There was nothing under them!

Realizing where he was, he clawed desperately for handholds. His fingers ripped through patches of moss between the tiles, tearing the damp clods apart but failing to stop his slide. Moonshadow ground his teeth together, snatching vainly for anything he could hang on to.

It was no good. He was dangling over the edge, and any moment he'd plunge!

MIDNIGHT MELEE

A hand seized Moonshadow's wrist. Snowhawk hovered over him. With a determined
grunt, she hauled him back up onto the
roof then spun away quickly to take on their recovering foe.

As Moonshadow stood up, the stranger gained
his feet with equal speed and rounded on Snowhawk,
hastily grunting something. But before he could complete even a phrase, Moonshadow darted in to swing
a hard back-fist strike into his jaw. The man's head
shuddered, but he recovered fast, hurling Moonshadow
away with a flashing side kick. Impulsively, Snowhawk

reached for her sword. Seeing that, the big man aimed a powerful front kick at her, forcing her to abandon the draw. Snowhawk sidestepped his blurring foot, then snapped a firm hold on his ankle with both hands. The stranger tried to speak once more, but his jaw appeared numbed by Moonshadow's blow, and he succeeded only in stuttering.

Who cares? Moonshadow scowled. *Who wants to hear his threats?* He closed with the man again, clawing for the ninja's back-mounted straight sword, but the large spy volleyed himself into a powerful, one-legged backflip. The sheer force of his fast, high turn propelled Moonshadow clear. The stranger's free foot rose and whipped Snowhawk in the head. She reeled backward and teetered on the roof's edge, arms wide and circling, trying to regain her balance. Moonshadow gasped.

If she dropped, her great agility and many climbing tricks might enable her to cut short the fall, but how would he capture this powerful spy on his own? With a determined forward sway, Snowhawk reclaimed her balance and thrust away from the edge.

Bounding up from the crouch he had landed in, the stranger stood tall, working his jaw painfully at desperate speed but still unable to speak.

Thinking fast, Moonshadow advanced on the man. Time for a calculated risk!

He and Snowhawk couldn't afford to breach the *no overt combat* rule and start a full-scale swordfight on a randomly chosen rooftop. Very bad idea! The noise might attract aggressive samurai who could easily decide to cut first, ask questions later. Knowing that, their pursuer should hesitate before drawing his blade...hesitate just long enough...

Closing with his opponent, Moonshadow smoothly drew his own sword behind his back. In a flash he shoulder-rolled to the man's feet, then rose to one knee and swung his blade on a horizontal plane, the tip swishing straight at his enemy's thigh. The ninja darted to one side, evading the cut. Then, to Moonshadow's horror, he drew his own sword and assumed a warlike dueling stance. Either he didn't care about *shinobi* field rules, or he'd just totally lost his temper!

"No," Snowhawk called in a whisper behind them, "no loud noise, don't break cover—"

Too late! One glance at the man's stance told Moonshadow that both he and the ninja were full of battle rage and tension now. Each was committed to try and cut the other! Yet despite that, neither of them dared to block. Echoing rings of steel on steel would bring chaos and death to encircle them all. They would have to trade cuts that neither of them dared intercept with their sword.

This duel was going to be duck, weave, cut, and hope for the best!

Moonshadow clenched his teeth. He met his opponent's eyes. What if this guy was faster? The man looked furious, determined, but something else flickered in that stare: was it fear, hatred, or confusion? It looked like the last; but what could he be confused about?

The ninja darted forward with surprising speed for such a large man. He dropped easily to one knee and then hacked low, left to right, angling for Moonshadow's kneecap.

Moonshadow saw it coming and leapt over the streaking blade, landing well inside the man's guard. Turning his sword quickly in his hands, he jabbed the ninja hard in the center of his forehead with the sword's pommel. There was a nasty *crunch* as the man's head snapped back. Stunned, he dropped his sword, and with a muffled *clunk* it stuck upright in a moss patch sprouting between two tiles.

Recovering yet again with alarming speed, the ninja lunged and seized Moonshadow's wrists. His tight, controlling grip trapped Moonshadow's flailing sword, rendering it useless.

Snowhawk attacked the *shinobi* from one side with a rising crescent kick, but sensing her, the man stepped clear. He then swung Moonshadow off his feet, into the air, turning him into a human club. Moonshadow's trailing legs whipped Snowhawk's shoulders, and with a deep *whump* she was flung to the edge of the roof.

Struggling hard to break free, Moonshadow lost sight of her, and his skin instantly prickled with worry. Had she hurtled right over the edge or managed to snatch a grip in time? He dared not take his eyes from his opponent to find out!

Moonshadow paddled with his feet until he felt them touch the tiles. Then, instead of resisting the ninja's powerful grip, he forced himself forward, even deeper inside the man's guard, until he managed to plant one foot on his enemy's stomach. Before the ninja could guess his intentions, Moonshadow curled his spine and ran up the man's stomach and chest.

Driving the attacker's elbows apart, he turned his last step into a strong stamping kick to the ninja's face. There was a sickening *crunch*.

Forced to release his iron grip, the big pursuer staggered backward, both hands flying to his nose.

Free at last, Moonshadow fell to the roof, landing on his shoulders, but he quickly back-rolled out of harm's way and rose to his feet. He glanced around and saw Snowhawk, her face creased with effort, struggling back up onto the roof from the edge. His gaze snapped back to his foe. The man was already rushing him! Moonshadow cursed. This guy recovered way too fast!

As he plowed into Moonshadow, the big *shinobi* snatched a hold on the grip of Moonshadow's sword. Driving his opponent backward, he broke Moonshadow's balance, forcing him to stumble. With blurring speed, the ninja brought one elbow up in a half circle to strike at Moonshadow's forearm. The glancing blow was incredibly strong and forced Moonshadow to drop his sword. It fell to the tiles with a low *clank*.

The instant Moonshadow was disarmed, the big ninja stopped shoving and began pulling at him instead, spoiling any chance he had to regain his balance. The *shinobi* glanced over his shoulder and then dropped smoothly onto his back, one foot rising, as he dragged Moonshadow down on top of him.

Moonshadow grimaced as his enemy's foot burrowed into his stomach muscles. Then the man straightened his leg, flinging Moonshadow up, over, and behind him with a powerful one-legged stomach throw.

As he crashed to the tiles, landing on his back, Moonshadow caught a gleam in the corner of his vision. He turned his head quickly, and his eyes went wide.

He'd just missed the ninja's sword, sticking upright from the roof!

Moonshadow began to rise, but the attacker was on him in an instant, firing kicks at his head, maneuvering cleverly, trying to drive him back and into the sharp edge of the sword. Suddenly the big *shinobi* shuddered and let out a wheeze. Moonshadow looked past him. Snowhawk had just hit the guy from behind with one of her strong flying side kicks!

Spinning around, the *shinobi* struck back at her, counterpunching with blinding speed, but Snowhawk ducked under his flurry of punches and scrambled out of range.

Coiling his body tightly, Moonshadow rolled clear of the sword, then tumbled again, wheeling higher up the slanting roof to seize the little battlefield's high ground. He stopped and turned, staying low, glaring down angrily at their pursuer. The man was distracted now, his eyes firmly locked on Snowhawk, who circled him like a hungry wolf. *It was time to end this!*

Moonshadow noted the position of the fallen swords, then slid on his side, his body flowing with the angle of the tiles, right down to the man's feet. He quickly swung a leg to each side of the spy's ankles, trapping both legs. Moonshadow closed his legs tightly, like scissors, then twisted his hips with force. The agent pitched forward, snatching wildly for Moonshadow. He missed and fell. Snowhawk rocketed onto the man from behind, wrenching on a forearm choke. Arching his spine, the agent threw his head back and headbutted her in the face, the force of the blow breaking her hold. He rolled down the roof, flicking Snowhawk from his back, and dragged Moonshadow right to the edge.

Moonshadow and the stranger disentangled speedily as they ran out of roof.

Each slid over the edge but this time managed to claw a good grip. They dangled less than a man's length apart, scrambling to haul themselves up. Snowhawk, shaking her head as if stunned, launched across the tiles and stamped on one of the big agent's hands. He let out a muffled groan. Grinding his teeth, Moonshadow pulled himself up and stood on the roof.

Snowhawk's hand flashed into her jacket. Moonshadow frowned curiously.

She dropped to one knee, her opposite foot still pinning the man's hand as she held a Fuma *shuriken* against the side of his neck. A curved black blade point poked the skin above his vital neck artery.

"Here's poetic justice! A fitting way for one of *you* to die!" Snowhawk growled. "By a *shuriken* of your design, in the hand of one you mistreated!"

Moonshadow gaped in startled horror. Her voice was weirdly deep, thick with rage, her *shuriken* pressing into the helpless man's neck now, starting to break his skin.

Terror streaked through Moonshadow. Would she kill this guy before his very eyes?

"Stop!" he gasped, his chest heaving. "This is vengeance! This is wrong!"

"Hah!" Snowhawk snapped at him. "I need a better reason than *that* to stop!"

Confused thoughts hit Moonshadow at the speed of flashing arrows. He was the mission leader; he couldn't allow this! The harsh rules on dealing with any mutiny in the field were clear. They called for immediate, lethal action, but... *this was Snowhawk!*

He floundered for a moment, then took a deep breath, turned, and snatched up his sword from the tiles. Bounding back to the roof's edge, Moonshadow swung its tip straight to Snowhawk's throat. At once a cannonball's weight clunked in his stomach, and his extended hand began shaking.

"I want him *alive!*" he snarled, trying to sound strong and commanding. Within, his thoughts pleaded, *Please, please, don't make me do this!*

Snowhawk didn't even flinch. She kept the *shuriken* pressed to the man's throat as her head turned in Moonshadow's direction. He faltered at the sight of her eyes.

They were wild, mad, almost unrecognizable.

"No," Snowhawk said with absolute conviction. "He dies."

5

THE DEEPEST GRUDGE

I mean it!" Moonshadow warned her. "I'm…
ordering you…as the mission's senior!"

"You don't understand!" Snowhawk's
voice grew recklessly loud. "He deserves this. They
all do! Each and every Fuma dog—" She began mumbling heinous curses.

Moonshadow was speechless with disbelief.
What to do? Opposite instincts tugged at him.
*Stop her, stop her now, end this rebellion with lethal
force*, as his *shinobi* field training demanded. *No!*
Spare her, cover for her, lie for her if need be, but
just let her kill this man because the Fuma *were* their

enemies and she was his best friend in the whole world!

Keeping the blade at her throat, Moonshadow sagged to his knees. "Please!" He shook his head. "Don't make me slay you!" He drew a deep breath. "Don't do this to me—I'm your *friend*."

Snowhawk glowered at him. "I hate you saying that! Vengeance has no friends!" She nodded at her dangling, helpless prey, who was working his jaw as if struggling to speak. "You and I don't come into this, Moon! It's between this...this *insect* and me! This Fuma scum!"

Moonshadow felt his heart skip several beats. He steadied his hand. She'd saddled him with an impossible dilemma. If he was to remain loyal to the Grey Light Order, there was only one thing to do, one *terrible* thing. Snowhawk had left him no choice!

He tensed his arm, settled his grip on the sword. Could he really do this?

"Free him *now*," Moonshadow said sternly. "Or, on the count of three, I'll do what I must!" Snowhawk shook her head sharply. Moonshadow swallowed hard, then slowly counted, "One...*two*..."

"I'm not Fuma," the dangling agent said hoarsely. "I serve the Grey Light!"

Snowhawk and Moonshadow, both wheezing, traded startled looks.

"Prove it," she demanded. "But if I think you're lying—"

"I can, I can," the man spluttered, trying to get too many words out fast. "I'm a freelance agent, but I run messages for the Order, so I know the trust codes."

"Two butterflies tied by impossible dreams," Moonshadow said quickly.

"Are like the cold water," the spy panted, "that can't brew fragrant tea."

Again Moonshadow and Snowhawk exchanged glances. "Test him again," she snarled.

Moonshadow nodded. "At the festival of the dead, a paper lantern bursts—"

"And goblins and shape-shifters scurry out," the man replied without pause.

"Why didn't you identify yourself a lot earlier?" Moonshadow slowly withdrew his sword from Snowhawk's throat. "See all the trouble you've caused?"

"Forgive me," the *shinobi* said earnestly, "but I couldn't speak for ages.... You almost broke my jaw.... Besides, for a while there I thought you'd gone mad or been *turned* or something, the way you two—" He let out a long, frustrated sigh.

Moonshadow sheathed his blade and hung his head. "Yes, I apologize for both of us, it *was* a strong attack, but we have been expecting trouble any day now from the Fuma."

"And forgive *me*!" Snowhawk pulled the *shuriken* away from the agent's neck, slid her foot off his hand, and stood up. "I—I lost all control," she muttered, looking at Moonshadow. "What has happened to me? I almost murdered one of our own."

Moonshadow offered his hand to the stranger, leaning backward hard to offset the big man's weight as he helped him regain the roof.

"I am just glad that no one was slain." He fired a sideways look at Snowhawk. "We were startled, sir, and overly wary. Your presence was...unexpected."

The large spy retrieved his wedged sword, flicked and sheathed it, then sat down heavily on the tiles to examine his nose. It clicked loudly, making him wince. "I think it's broken, but that's happened a few times, so it breaks easily now. Please consider no harm done." He blew out a long breath. "That kind of reception greets us freelance dispatch runners from time to time. All *shinobi* are wary while on the job." He rubbed his wrist. "Which is as it should be. I should have been quicker with that trust code on my arrival—" He half grinned, nursing his jaw. "I know I will be next time, huh?"

Moonshadow bowed. "I was far too impulsive. Please excuse me."

"Not at all." The freelance agent waved a hand. "Resources are stretched thin, out-of-town faces like me have been brought in to help…it all makes people jumpy." He thumbed over his shoulder at the Edo skyline. "The Grey Light has been steadily forced to deploy so many of its senior agents to distant provinces. And why? To investigate these infernal conspiracies! Rumors of new plots against the Shogun appear with each passing week—"

Snowhawk and Moonshadow looked at each other thoughtfully. Moonshadow shook his head. No wonder they were getting so many eavesdropping missions!

Something very big and very dangerous was in the wind. Was one man behind it all, Akechi's friend from the west? Moonshadow scowled. Fushimi, the lair of the rebel warlord Silver Wolf, lay to the west. Was he the black heart of this plot? So a wide web of conspirators was tying up agents to the point where independent spies for hire had to make up the manpower shortage. Such things had happened before, from time to time, but never on the scale this man spoke of.

Moonshadow sighed. Brother Eagle, wise and diplomatic, had ties to certain Iga ninja masters and was highly respected among most of the Clan Koga families. But if those shadow houses were now sending Eagle hirelings he didn't personally know, could all of them be trusted?

Some could be infiltrators or, worse yet, double agents, perhaps even from the Order's ancient enemy, the House of Fuma.

"I just heard someone walking in the alleyway below," Snowhawk murmured.

"We were pretty noisy," Moonshadow whispered. "Was it overheard?"

The big agent turned his head to the edge, cupped his hands around his mouth, and expertly meowed, sounding just like a real cat. Moonshadow grinned at the clever ploy. Offered an easy explanation for the rooftop scuffling sounds, whoever it was might just go back to bed.

Silently the trio shuffled away from the edge, into the deepest shadows on the rooftop, where they crouched, face-to-face, in a tight circle. The agent studied Moonshadow's troubled expression and seemed to read his thoughts. "These are doubly uncertain times." He shrugged. "But every warrior class has its mercenaries, right? I can be relied upon. I bought my independence from my clan because I wished to marry a non-*shinobi*. But I honor the *furube* sutra daily and live by stringent oaths of service to whoever hires me. Master Eagle can vouch for my character." His black eyes flicked over the pair. "And I know who you are. Master Eagle sent me in all haste. I bring word."

"*Master* Eagle?" Moonshadow grinned. He hadn't called Eagle that for a long time.

"His formal title, bestowed by the Iga as a mark of respect." The agent laughed softly. "But of course, I see you well know how humble he is. He prefers *Brother*."

"Clan Iga trained you?" Snowhawk eyed him. "That's where you met Eagle?"

"Indeed," the man said. "Many years ago." He stared at Moonshadow. "I too am schooled in the Eye of the Beast, though I sense I'm far less gifted than you." He glanced over one shoulder. "As I hunted for Lord Akechi's roof—not easy for a man from out of town, mind you—I saw a strange cat watching my approach. Its markings suggested a kimono cat, yet it had a long tail! I tried to link with it, but it proved impervious to all attempts. Were you already controlling it? At the third level?" Moonshadow nodded and the spy shook his head. "Impressive. You are so young."

"Thank you, sir." Moonshadow dipped his head. "What is your message from Brother Eagle?"

"Master Eagle instructs as follows: since agent Snowhawk has shown herself a particularly skilled and fast rider, you must steal a horse and return to the monastery at once. He needs you debriefed, briefed, and on the road north before dawn."

The messenger watched surprise crease their faces. "Please." He wearily raised a hand. "I brought an urgent dispatch to Edo that came through a chain of country agents, by what path exactly I know not, though I knew the man who handed it to me. Master Eagle took it from my hand, read it, then ordered me to forget my night's sleep and find you quickly." His eyes flicked earnestly between the young spies. "I know nothing beyond that already said. I swear it before Lord Hachiman!"

Moonshadow gave the freelancer an appreciative nod, but as they made ready to leave, he found himself studying the big stranger warily.

A disturbing question nagged at Moonshadow.

Is this man really known to Eagle, or should I have let Snowhawk kill him?

If this *was* a trick, and he an enemy after all, they wouldn't live to see the sun rise!

SUMMONED BY A SAGE

It was just before dawn, that time of the human body's lowest ebb, when assassins preferred to strike. Reactions were slower and minds more easily confused at this hour.

Snowhawk sat in the monastery's shadowy briefing chamber, part of a circle of agents: Brother Eagle, Mantis, Groundspider, and Moonshadow. A map lay in the middle, surrounded by candles that cast long shadows up the paper-screen walls. The silent group stared down at the map.

Despite her sleepless night, Snowhawk's mind was as clear as a high country stream, though not solely due to her exceptional fitness and lifelong training. Fear that Moonshadow would report her shameful rage and breach of discipline had filled her with dread, and that too helped keep her watchful. But throughout their debriefing, he hadn't said a word about it.

She glanced to where he too sat staring. What did he think of her now?

She hoped he'd be as forgiving as the rest of the Grey Light Order seemed to be. At each stage of her induction, Snowhawk had compared her new trainers with the brutal instructors back at Clan Fuma. The contrast was like night and day.

The Grey Light Order encouraged, rewarded, and tried to cultivate the joy of noble service in their young spies. They even joked and laughed!

Such behavior earned beatings among the Fuma. Snowhawk bitterly recalled a saying one of her Fuma coaches had made child agents recite: *A punch for attitude, a kick for laziness.* She closed her eyes. The oldest of the great shadow clans was nothing more than a pack of bullies.

She sensed Moonshadow turn to watch her. Sooner or later, they would have to discuss these nasty, brooding feelings of hers, not to mention their little dispute on the rooftop. It was unavoidable, now that her feelings had started to escape her control. Snowhawk prayed the others would never learn of her fury. These people were strong *and* kind, but she didn't want to test the limits of that kindness.

It was no surprise that Moonshadow had protected her yet again. Young or not, he was unusually noble-hearted and loyal. She was so embarrassed that he had witnessed her rooftop rebellion.

Snowhawk felt his persistent gaze but stubbornly refused to acknowledge it. Before the discomfort could turn to squirming, she opened her eyes and doggedly stared again at the large map on the floor. Snowhawk reviewed its every detail until an instinct made her look up sharply.

Eagle, Mantis, and Groundspider sat mutely on their heels around the map, legs folded in the traditional *seiza* position, with their feet tucked under their bodies, backs straight, and palms flat on their thighs. The three stared at her.

Were they just waiting? She hoped none of them could read minds.

Behind the trio, though uninvited, the temple cat lounged and groomed itself.

"Has everyone now memorized this map?" Brother Eagle flicked his long single plait of hair over one shoulder. The circle nodded. "Good. Moonshadow, Snowhawk, thank you for so quickly reporting what you heard at Lord Akechi's palace and for answering all my questions. You have served the Shogun well. I am proud."

Along with Moonshadow, Snowhawk replied with a deep, seated bow.

"And I am pleased, Snowhawk, that you feel you've also taken this map in properly. I know our way called 'passive recall' is still somewhat new to you, but I am confident of your mastering it quickly."

Snowhawk nodded back. She *was* mastering passive recall, along with many other Grey Light ways. And though Brother Eagle's encouragement was always a delight, pangs of guilt now marred that joy. If only he knew what she had done. How differently he would speak!

Eagle looked around the room, drawing nods from the other teachers. "We have trusted this Old Country technique many times and found it most reliable. To stare at a diagram or scene until the information sinks deep into the mind, making that knowledge the *fly*, your will the *spider*, and your deepest memory the *web*. I'm sure you'll find this method of ours the best way to employ your memory."

Snowhawk smiled humbly. Just after their return journey on horseback, she and Moonshadow had spoken of a web of a different kind, the one the conspirators were weaving, perhaps right across the empire. But who were they about to be sent to eavesdrop on now?

Eagle sighed, running one hand over his shiny bald head. "Now let us speak of the reason you cannot yet rest. A message has been received, in verified code, from the White Nun. She has foreseen an imminent attack on her mountain shrine home."

"Then we must get there in force, now." Groundspider shook his fist. "As many—"

"No," Eagle interrupted. "Her message says that wise spirits whisper on the wind that the Order's two *youngest* agents must be sent to lead her to safety. Only them. It is destined, she says."

Mantis turned his solemn eyes to Snowhawk. "Arriving undetected is every bit as important as arriving fast, for she believes this attack will not be instant. Nonetheless, her instructions are that you start out at once. On foot. No horses or palanquins."

"It's never straightforward with the White Nun, is it?" Groundspider's face creased. Eagle and Mantis each turned to him.

"Do I sense a complaint coming?" Mantis half smiled at the powerfully built spy.

Groundspider held up a hand. "I mean no disrespect. It's just the wording of her order." He gave Snowhawk a glib ghost of a bow. "Now don't take offense, Snowy, but you're still on probation, learning our ways with Moonshadow there."

"None taken." She smiled coolly. "But if you ever call me Snowy again, I'll shove Saru-San through the door next time you're in the bathhouse. Who knows? You might really enjoy sharing a tub with a thieving, irritable monkey."

Mantis quickly dropped his chin and covered the bottom half of his face with one hand. His eyes flicked up at Snowhawk. He liked her feisty spirit.

Groundspider waved his other hand. It was bandaged. "You keep that insane monkey away from me." He turned to Eagle. "What I mean is, technically, since Snowhawk is still in training, Moonshadow and I are actually the Grey Light Order's youngest agents."

"He has a point." Mantis folded his arms quickly, robes swishing. "The White Nun was instrumental in our decision to train Moonshadow, but she has yet to meet Snowhawk and officially approve her." Mantis raised his eyebrows at Brother Eagle. "Having said that, I do think that she and Moonshadow are the ones to send."

"Mmm." Eagle gave a thoughtful frown. "The sage's insight is powerful and accurate, but often hard to fathom. The challenge is always in the details." He caught Snowhawk's eye. "Whenever her wishes appear cryptic, I adopt the same stand: go with the most obvious meaning. If there are no hints by which to judge, then take her literally."

"Fine." Groundspider pouted, gesturing at his bandage. "Leave me here to get ripped apart by Badger's lunatic pet." He stared at Moonshadow. "That monkey wants my head, but Badger protects it!"

Snowhawk watched Moonshadow shrug evasively. Had he been setting the monkey on Groundspider? She stifled a smile.

Groundspider rounded on Eagle. "Maybe she meant the two youngest agents *must* go, but others *could* go with them? Me, for instance?"

"Dear Brother Groundspider," Eagle said gently.
"Shut up." Groundspider hung his big head.

Snowhawk grinned. Though Groundspider often baited her, she liked him. He bragged, told ridiculous lies, and ate like a sumo wrestler. His balance was imperfect, but his sword cuts astounding in their power. His twisted sense of humor was irresistible. She recalled it in action, just days ago, in one of the monastery gardens.

"I've been working on my own Old Country mind powers," Groundspider had announced. "I can read thoughts now. Think of something. I'll tell you what it is."

"Go ahead." Moonshadow had rolled his eyes skeptically. "What am I thinking?"

"Stop. Anything but *that*." Groundspider had wagged a finger. "That's the one thought I can't read." So it had gone on. And on. "Nor that one," he had said at the next try, then, "or *that one*."

He'd stayed so serious. Eventually, she had collapsed into laughter.

Moonshadow's voice broke her reverie.

"Brother Eagle, could you please lock up the cat until we have left? She keeps following me on missions, and I fear she will come to harm."

"So many animals here now," Groundspider mumbled. "Let's import a panda next."

A wicked glow lit Moonshadow's face. "Perhaps while I'm gone, Brother Badger could look after her...."

"Not Badger," Eagle said firmly. "Your cat's already at war with Badger's flea-ridden Saru. If they had to share a room—" A tiny shudder registered in Eagle's shoulders. "And say, when are you going to name this creature? I'm weary of saying 'the cat.'"

Moonshadow bowed humbly. "I'll...come up with something."

"What about a *shinobi*-sounding name for her?" Groundspider enthused. "How about Stink Bomb?" Eagle silenced him with a sidelong glance. Groundspider hung his head again.

The paper-screen door glided open. Heron and Badger entered, bowing to the circle. Eagle and Mantis nodded back. The three younger agents bowed low.

As she raised her head, Snowhawk studied Heron fondly. Born a noblewoman but trained in *shinobi* ways, Heron taught the science of potions, the art of disguises, and *naginata*—bladed pole-fighting. Next, Snowhawk eyed Badger, though with slightly less affection.

A great scholar with no ninja skills whatsoever, Badger was the Order's archivist. He also tutored on military history and battlefield theory and translated foreign books. But despite his obvious brilliance, there was one science he had never mastered: getting along with others.

Brother Badger rubbed one eye, cocking his bald, scratched-up head to one side. Snowhawk saw a neatly folded piece of paper in his hand.

Badger held it up and shook it hard. "I hope this one gets filed in its proper place when everyone's finished arguing over it," he grumbled.

Snowhawk avoided his gaze. Being woken early didn't agree with Badger.

Heron flashed one of her patient, coaxing looks and patted the archivist's shoulder. "I'll see to that—I've already promised. But you speak up now, tell the others what you just told me. What niggled at you, made you get up?" She gestured invitingly.

Everyone watched Badger, the circle of faces now curious. Becoming the center of attention while half asleep seemed to provoke him even more. "Ah!" he snapped. "I can't be certain, so what's the point? I'm going back to bed. You tell them, Heron!"

"My opinion," Heron said softly, lowering her eyes, "carries less authority than yours. Please, in this matter, we need your wisdom above all else...." She bowed respectfully.

"Oh?" Badger blinked, stretching his neck. "Is that so?" He glanced around, then raised his chin with renewed self-importance. "Very well then."

Snowhawk hid her amusement. Heron was a skilled manipulator; those wiles of womancraft were useful for gaining trust and cooperation at home as well as in the field.

"I'm uneasy about this urgent message," Badger admitted. "Its code is current, the wording familiar, but something about it doesn't feel right. I can't say what, however."

"Could it be real yet incomplete?" Mantis speculated. "Was something removed?"

Eagle rubbed his short, greying beard. "Such things have been done. Or perhaps, though a genuine dispatch, its text has been minutely altered in some way."

"I told you, I don't know." Badger yawned. "But if you wish, I'll go on examining it. I warn you though, I *might* be wrong. There! Are we done? Can I go now?"

"Please stay," Heron said warmly. "We may need more of your vast knowledge."

Badger stretched, working his shoulders loose. "Oh, all right, if you put it like that."

"Here's the problem," said Eagle, frowning. "We must act quickly. Even if your fears are later confirmed, we cannot delay sending our juniors. The White Nun is this order's oldest and greatest adviser, trainer, and...secret asset. No risks can be taken with her life."

Mantis looked from Moonshadow to Snowhawk and back. "Expect the unexpected. And *serious* opposition. Whoever dares to go after the White Nun must also expect to face her bodyguards before taking her. So there will be no half measures."

"Does she even have bodyguards?" Groundspider put in. "If not, I could—"

Heron's glance shut him up properly. She sat down opposite Snowhawk. "I once heard, years ago, that, in addition to her many Old Country powers, a giant bear protects her. The ancient shrine in which the White Nun lives is here, on this mountain." She leaned forward, slender fingers brushing the map.

Eagle's face tightened. "Forget the bear. The forest below that mountain has quite a reputation. One that would keep most people away."

Moonshadow tensed. "Why? Is it haunted? What happened there?"

"Shh! Bad luck to speak of it," Badger snapped. "I may be a scholar, but even I heed the old taboos. As everyone civilized should!" He yawned again and sat down.

"Forget about luck," Mantis sighed. "Discussing the place could bring bad karma."

"Let us *not* speak of it," Eagle said somberly, "simply out of respect for the dead."

Snowhawk said nothing but flashed Moonshadow her reliable *tell you later* look. He replied with a hint of a nod.

"A final question, before they leave." Mantis cleared his throat. "Few even know of the White

Nun's existence, much less of her service to the Grey Light Order. Those who do, the other shadow clans, also know the extent of her unearthly powers. Surely none of them would presume to move against her?"

"Mighty or not, she's no warrior," Heron said. "A healer and teacher, not a fighter. She has reminded me of that during our lessons together. No, despite her great powers, the White Nun has no taste for blood. And I think our enemies know that too."

"Please excuse me," Snowhawk said, bowing. "Why is she called the White Nun?"

Heads turned her way, a circle of knowing looks— except for Moonshadow. He had met the sage once, as a young boy, but had no memory of her. Eagle broke into his secretive smile.

"You'll soon find out for yourself," Badger muttered. "Just... be patient!"

"Has Heron not raised the real issue?" Eagle addressed them all grimly. "Who is the enemy? Who would dare try to kill or capture such a saint?"

"Who indeed," Mantis sniffed, "could be this reckless?"

Everyone fell silent. Snowhawk knew who.

Nobody wanted to say his name. Mentioning a traitor was also bad luck.

She stared down at the map as a wave of fear

rolled over her. If enough bad luck—or bad karma—settled on this mission, their journey would end in the worst possible way.

With failure and destruction.

Sensing Eagle's eyes on her, Snowhawk looked up. Brother Eagle gestured at Moonshadow, then her. "You both seem a little uneasy. I understand that. This mission has come as a surprise and it raises many questions. But I need to know that you'll set off in the right frame of mind: clearheaded, relaxed within." He made a solemn face. "So, before you leave, I want you to do what I used to do before each and every mission."

Moonshadow and Snowhawk glanced at each other uncertainly and then bowed to Eagle.

"Recite the *furube* sutra first." Their leader broke into an encouraging smile. "Then choose a quiet part of the garden and...fight! Without weapons. Just a friendly spar; show each other some moves." Eagle's eyes twinkled. "It always helped my field partner and me to...talk things out." He quickly rose. "Meeting dismissed!"

The circle of agents stood and, in time with one another, bowed their respect.

As dawn lit the monastery's grounds, Snowhawk found a quiet corner of a walled garden. Sitting down on a stone bench, she carefully recited the *furube* sutra. It failed to truly calm her. She tried again with the same result. Halfway through her third intonement, Snowhawk sensed a presence behind her.

"So, are you ready?" Despite their overnight clash, the usual hint of playful mischief was still there in Moonshadow's voice. "Ready to show me more second-rate Fuma moves?"

Snowhawk grinned competitively, then gripped the edge of the stone bench, readying her legs. As Moonshadow stepped closer, she pushed off hard with her hands and feet, springing up from the bench into a powerful backward somersault. In a flash she was uncurling above him in the air, her feet descending for his shoulders.

Moonshadow dived clear, nimbly cartwheeling on the garden's tiny lawn. Snowhawk landed on balance with a soft *whump*, and he twisted around to face her, a sneaky light in his eyes.

"Nice try," he baited. "Love that acrobatic Fuma style. But you'll soon learn ours.... It's a bit plainer, but kind of more...practical!" He skipped sideways and then launched into a fast, flying side kick.

Snowhawk hunched to one side, narrowly avoiding his outstretched foot. "Nice try yourself!" she snapped as his feet met the ground. "How 'bout *this*!" With one leg she swept his ankles out from under him, but Moonshadow deftly let himself tumble with the momentum of her attack, folding, rolling quickly into a ball, and escaping along the ground.

Ten paces away he bobbed up fast in a fighting stance.

"Holding back because I'm mission leader again?" Moonshadow smirked. "Don't bother, please! Try properly instead.... You can't hurt me!"

Her face darkened. He was trying to provoke her. This always happened when they sparred. The routine practice of needling your opponent was a good tactic and she often did it too, but this morning, partner baiting might not be a good idea. Though her outburst on the roof had appalled her, Snowhawk still felt rage simmering in her gut like a hidden volcanic pool.

She wrestled with it. This fury had to be staunched; they had a mission to get through, a dangerous-sounding one at that....

Too late!

Spurning her own wise counsel, Snowhawk clenched her fists until the knuckles of both hands turned white and gave off loud *click*s. With a furious hiss she closed on Moonshadow. "Can't hurt you?" Snowhawk snarled. "Let's see!"

She abruptly spun into a reverse roundhouse kick, her long legs and great flexibility combining to hurl her foot—at blurring speed—straight for the side of his head.

Snowhawk's foot slapped Moonshadow's tail of hair to one side as he barely ducked her powerful strike. Completing the turn, she saw his eyes widen at the force of her attack, and before Moonshadow could recover his full balance, Snowhawk launched a devastating front kick at his stomach.

His wrists flashed together like snapping chopsticks. Moonshadow caught her ankle and lifted it fast and hard, ready to tip her over. But Snowhawk flowed with his powerful upward motion and launched into the air instead. Harnessing their combined inertia against him, she spun backward quickly, her trailing foot slap-kicking him under the chin. As he reeled from the blow she somersaulted, landed with perfect balance, and then rushed him hard.

But this time he was ready. As Snowhawk threw a powerful straight punch for his jaw, Moonshadow blocked the attack, seized her wrist with a grip of iron, then turned and dropped into a crouch that quickly flowed into a jujitsu throw. Snowhawk, her arm extended, twisted, and trapped, crashed hard against his back and then went tumbling over his shoulder, the air knocked from her lungs. He cunningly hung on to her wrist as she fell, controlling the plunge until her back struck the ground with a nasty *thud*. Before she could recover from the impact and try to break free, Moonshadow dropped to his knees and snapped on a strong knot-hold, tangling her arms but staying behind her, where kicks from those long, flexible legs couldn't reach him.

"Know why you just lost?" She could hear his frustration. "Your anger! It clouds your reason — makes you do stupid things!" He released her, bounded away, then stood and glared.

With a resigned sigh she clambered to her feet. Brushing herself off, Snowhawk creased her lip at him. "Yeah...well...that's *my* problem, isn't it?"

"*Your* problem?" He put his hands on his hips. "Maybe it is. Or maybe it's *my* problem. Because I'm not sure you'll follow my orders on this next mission! After all, you didn't —"

"Keep your voice down!" She glanced over one shoulder.

"What, in case the rocks hear you acting crazy?" He frowned. "Just tell me the truth: this time, are you going to ignore my orders and try to kill anyone who crowds you?"

"Don't act so perfect!" she sniped back. "You

make mistakes, I've seen them! And don't talk down to me! I've done a lot more field missions than you have, just remember that!"

He rolled his eyes. "Yeah? And did you obey your orders…on *any* of them?"

They glowered at each other. Moonshadow gave an annoyed *hiss* and turned away. Shocked and disappointed in herself again, Snowhawk stood silently, watching him until he vanished indoors. He never looked back, but shook his head just before he strode out of sight.

Her chest heaving with exertion, Snowhawk turned a circle, making sure that nobody had witnessed their exchange. Great! Now Moonshadow had *two* unpleasant secrets to keep for her; *two* losses of control that, if revealed, would definitely see her suspended from field duty. She bit her lip and narrowed her eyes.

Despite his obvious frustration, would Moonshadow go on covering for her?

Snowhawk swallowed hard. Suddenly she wasn't certain anymore. The Grey Light Order were very Buddhist in their ways, very self-controlled and… *merciful*, especially for *shinobi*. How much of her dark Fuma style would they tolerate? What if she couldn't change?

As she walked slowly to the equipment room, worse questions began plaguing her.

Assuming they did encounter the Fuma on this mission, could she trust herself? Would she obey Moonshadow as mission leader or, just as he feared, again lose control and try to kill without authority? Snowhawk hung her head and folded her arms as she walked, crushing handfuls of loose sleeve in her fists. How about the big question?

If she rebelled again, would he do it? Could Moonshadow actually slay her?

Snowhawk reached the sliding door to the equipment room. She stopped before it, hand outstretched, picturing the look in her best friend's eyes, the tension that had racked his body just before he'd turned his back on her and walked away. Her arm fell limply to her side.

Yes, she nodded. He *could*, and next time, he would.

HEART OF ICE

Silver Wolf heard the birdsong stop, the trees behind the roadside inn grow silent.

Good, he nodded, they were here, and on time. Silver Wolf breathed in the cool air. The overnight rain had eased, the sun had now risen on a fresh, dripping green land, and once this final meeting was over, he could go home. Sitting alone at one end of the inn's largest room, he drummed his fingers on the tatami mat beside his generous cushion.

As always these days, his sword lay within easy reach. His hand brushed it and he sighed, impatient to get back on the road. There was much to do on his return to Momoyama Castle in his fiefdom's capital, Fushimi. As long as the weapon makers did their part, he could look forward to a busy few days. He eyed his lacquered scabbard.

They wouldn't fail him. He'd made it clear: if they did, he'd execute them.

Silver Wolf stared down at his family's crest on the sleeve of his opulent silk jacket. One day soon, it would adorn public buildings everywhere.

He traced the long scar on his left cheek. It reminded him to keep his resolve. His face had been slashed by an enemy's spear tip during the cavalry charge he had led in the Battle of Sekigahara five years earlier. A daring charge into a narrow, misty valley that had turned the tide of a seemingly hopeless battle, ending the civil war, handing the Shogun his throne.

A throne the Shogun had proved he no longer deserved.

The warlord scowled. Three things were required to free a nation. Noble blood. Sharp steel. And a heart of ice that knew no flinching.

He heard the horses outside shift and whinny. Horses often reacted to *shinobi*, sensing their hidden power more acutely than humans did. Silver Wolf dragged his sword closer. His visitors had better be the right *shinobi*.

This inn, on the great road called the Tokaido, lay near the turnoff to Fushimi. He had just traveled under full escort in an armored palanquin to the Hakone Barrier, the northeastern edge of his domain, and back again. Officially for a routine inspection of his lands, a duty every lord fulfilled regularly.

In reality, a trip to a series of secret meetings. This morning's was the last.

Outside, his entire retinue had fallen silent: spearmen, archers, and his elite, proven cavalry unit. Today, in tight formation around his convoy, they would march him home. Anyone the procession passed would kneel in humble salute.

A sound made his eyes flick to the wooden sliding door. It was decorated with a landscape of mountains rising from mist. As he studied it, the door slid open. Out in the corridor stood the stooped, lined innkeeper, looking as frightened as he had the night before. Two of Silver Wolf's twitchy samurai bodyguards hovered on either side of him, watching his every move.

"Great lord." The little man dropped to his knees and touched his forehead to the cherry planks in the corridor. They shone, smooth from years of daily buffing with damp rags. The innkeeper nervously looked up. "I trust your breakfast was satisfactory?"

"Mmm." Silver Wolf gestured vaguely for him to rise. "Adequate. The rice porridge could have been warmer. The sliced and pickled vegetables, fine. Good variety."

"I treasure my lord's kind words. Our poor establishment is so far beneath you."

"Yes." Silver Wolf yawned. "But you did your best. Now, are they here?"

The innkeeper cringed as he answered. "Yes, great lord. And as you instructed, from dawn onward, I confined my family and staff to the kitchens." He winced fearfully. "Other than your men, only I have seen your visitors. As you ordered, all other guests were made to leave last night, for my lord's privacy."

Silver Wolf fixed him with a cool stare. "Then send them in, and remember: if you ever speak of this, or record it in any way, I will not fail to return for your head."

With terrified glances at the swords flanking him, the innkeeper bowed and fled.

The warlord's new personal bodyguards entered the room first, taking up positions on either side of the door. Their hands never left the grips of their swords.

The older guard, the chief samurai, was middle-aged, scarred through the lips, with darting, shrewd eyes. He had fought beside Silver Wolf at Sekigahara. His loyalty, horsemanship, and speed with a blade were all beyond question.

The junior guard serving with him was his son, a strapping, bull-shouldered youngster—smart, eager to please, and full of potential. Silver Wolf had appointed the pair for two reasons. Talent ran in their family, and he was confident they'd both die to protect him without hesitation. His face darkened as he remembered the injuries his last two personal guards had suffered in a skirmish with a young Grey Light Order spy.

A big-boned man in town robes appeared in the corridor. The two guards bristled until he bowed low to Silver Wolf and the warlord showed recognition, motioning the man into the room. The robed one carefully laid his long hardwood staff on the matting just inside the door, his eyes steadily moving between the ever-watchful bodyguards.

"My master." He gave the warlord a second bow. "I trust we're on time."

"Of course you are," Silver Wolf chuckled. "Why would you be late, Katsu? You have no desire to annoy me and die for it, do you?" He slapped his thigh, enjoying Katsu's startled expression. "Relax, my loyal hound, I jest! Again you have pleased me!"

Katsu's face lit up. He dared a half grin, relief swamping his eyes. "My lord."

"So." Silver Wolf raised an eyebrow. "Where is he? Where is this legendary Chikuma?"

A useful man, this Katsu, the warlord thought to himself. *Versatile.* Once a sumo wrestler and now officially a private investigator, the diplomatic Katsu had proved himself a reliable all-purpose hireling. He dug up information, delivered sensitive messages, even secretly escorted people others feared.

Such as shadow assassins of the ancient House of Fuma.

"Great lord Silver Wolf." Katsu gestured formally to the door. "It is my honor to introduce Chikuma-San. *The* Chikuma of Fuma." Katsu forced a polite smile, but beads of nervous sweat made his wide forehead shine.

The youngest bodyguard stifled a grin. Silver Wolf knew why. *Chikuma of Fuma,* it sounded cute, almost funny. But the man behind the name, himself not much older than the young guard, was no joke.

Only last year Chikuma had served a certain minor lord, Lord Akechi, in Edo. The Shogun had planted infiltrators in a Tsukiji trading house that

Akechi dealt with. Gradually, all the Shogun's spies vanished. Not so much as a single drop of blood was ever found.

A lanky young man entered, bowing in the doorway with a slow, unruffled elegance. He straightened up and stepped softly into the room. He eyed Silver Wolf, almost too boldly, then his face broke into a charming, meek smile. Chikuma bowed again, this time lower.

"Great lord," he said quietly. His deep voice was as soft as his step.

The warlord looked him up and down, openly intrigued. What kind of warrior was this? Like all true samurai, when meeting anyone, Silver Wolf carefully noted the newcomer's weaponry first. Assessing every stranger's arsenal was a samurai survival habit, drummed in throughout childhood.

This Chikuma wore only one small dagger, of a type popular among highborn ladies. And there were other surprises.

Chikuma of Fuma wore his hair long in one of those untied, girlish styles growing fashionable in the cities. He was a handsome youth, with an intelligent face, high cheekbones, and a smooth, strong jawline. Silver Wolf noticed Chikuma's eyes: he wore dark makeup to emphasize them. Like his brightly colored kimono, makeup on men was all the rage these days in Osaka. Silver Wolf had already banned his samurai from wearing it.

Ironic, the warlord decided. Here stood a man, himself drenched in the silly trends of this age, who would help Japan return to its warrior heritage. Silver Wolf motioned for his special guest to sit. Chikuma fastidiously stretched his kimono under his legs with quick little twitches as he sank to the reed mat. Straightening his back, he tossed his hair and gave an excited nasal snigger.

"I stand ready to head north at my lord's order." Chikuma flashed an eccentric, remote smile. Silver Wolf studied his manner. Despite the fashionable hair and clothing, *peculiar* and *otherworldly* were the words that came to mind. He'd seen hired killers before, but this pretty youngster was the most disconcerting he had met. He just didn't *look right*. But there was more to it than that. The warlord smiled. A simple test might be enlightening.

"A mutual friend," Silver Wolf gently baited him, "says you are quite deadly."

A lick of wild excitement tainted Chikuma's eyes. Then he appeared to swiftly take control of himself. *Interesting*, Silver Wolf thought, and frowned. The man was a mix of outlandishness and tight discipline.

So how *did* he kill? Perhaps he was the kind that put you to sleep with a gaze, then cut your throat. It was said that *shinobi* women in particular excelled at that dark art, and this young guy certainly had a feminine style.

"Would my lord enjoy a demonstration?" Chikuma asked amiably.

Seasoned instincts told Silver Wolf to be careful. "Perhaps just before we go our ways." The warlord grinned, creasing his scar. "Using the little innkeeper, maybe?"

A tiny hint of that crazed anticipation lit Chikuma's eyes again. He nodded.

A demonstration of dark *shinobi* arts that Silver Wolf had once watched in his castle came back to him in vivid detail. He glanced at the corridor. Forget the mousy innkeeper. A more entertaining idea was forming.

But there were other matters to deal with first if the mission was to be launched on time.

"Katsu!" the warlord demanded. "I also charged you with organizing support for this man. Before we move forward, brief me on your progress!"

Katsu bowed. "On his way north, Chikuma-San will be met by Wada, an old sumo training partner of mine who now works as a very successful bounty hunter. Put simply, the guy is special. He feels virtually no pain. No one knows why."

"No pain at all? Is that a good thing?" Chikuma narrowed his eyes.

Katsu gestured expansively. "It is if you're a fearless human battering ram."

"Good." Silver Wolf folded his arms. "Inventive, I like it. But, detective, what of my requested candidate? Did you find *her*?"

"Yes, indeed, great lord. As you bade, I sought out the lady...Kagero."

The two samurai guards tensed at the mention of her name.

"As a freelance assassin and bounty hunter," Katsu said, "her reputation is second to none."

"True!" Chikuma volunteered. "Though she's an 'independent' these days, the lady Kagero is well regarded by the House of Fuma. Originally she *was* a Fuma agent. But after arranging a lucrative ongoing contract for our masters, she successfully negotiated...leaving us. Such outcomes are rare, and offered only to the best."

Silver Wolf nodded. He had learned something new: elite shadow clan members could buy their freedom! Deserters and failures, of course, shared the opposite fate; they were slain by the very people who had trained and often raised them.

Katsu blinked delicately. "She…was expensive, lord."

Silver Wolf nodded, staring mildly back at Katsu. He had expected that.

At their last meeting, Lord Akechi had told Silver Wolf of her. "Kagero is some kind of sorceress," Akechi had said. "And middle-aged or not, she slew the great Kaiho Shundai of Edo. Without a sword. She never uses one."

"How then?" Silver Wolf had asked, lowering his sake cup. "Kaiho was strong."

"No one knows," Akechi had answered. "The swordsman's wounds—and there were many—were unique."

"Well, Katsu, we shall speak of the price of Kagero's help later." The warlord gave his hireling a shallow nod. "For now at least, everything else seems to be in place. I am particularly pleased with how you handled our grand opportunity—the one that brought us such pivotal, rare information."

"It was nothing I did, lord." Katsu averted his eyes. "He was an old traveling monk, in the process of losing his mind to age. Plying him with sake and tricking him into revealing such a vital secret was no feat of skill on my part. Verifying his information was actually more taxing! In all truth, my master, we were simply lucky!"

"Perhaps so." Silver Wolf smiled malevolently. "But what you chanced upon through him now helps me strike down the dogs who guard my enemy's gate!" He drew in a deep breath. Katsu's chance encounter with an ancient, half-mad pilgrim up north had proved no idle twist of fate. It all confirmed that Silver Wolf's path was, in the end, a glorious destiny. He thrust out his full chest. Yes, he had been born to save Japan, to purge her, wash her clean—in blood. "Now, a final matter." He looked around commandingly. "I have funded one more specialist to support this mission. This one I included for several reasons. He is disposable. He is not samurai and therefore brings no house into disrepute if captured. And he petitioned me to reemploy him—at very low rates—owing to his personal vendetta with an agent of the Grey Light Order. With which, of course"—he grinned—"I heartily sympathize. And don't mention the limp."

Silver Wolf gestured to his younger bodyguard. The samurai gave a sharp whistle.

From down the corridor came the innkeeper's voice. "Sir, they call for you!"

Uneven footsteps approached the doorway. The warlord smiled with anticipation.

The hireling about to enter was a ruthless, black-hearted rogue, but he had a redeeming quality: he lived for a single purpose.

To kill the young *shinobi* named Moonshadow.

RULED BY REVENGE

A familiar scruffy man limped into view in the doorway. Silver Wolf took in the guy's wily eyes and long, unkempt hair. Jiro, gangster and throwing-knife expert. He hadn't changed much. Still that same thick, untidy beard and loud patterned jacket denoting an urban gang member. The warlord squinted. Something *was* different. Jiro's neck and forearms had always been covered in red and green tattoos of textured dragons and carps. Now the artwork had spread to his face. Calligraphy ran down one cheek.

"Great lord." Jiro bowed, a little awkwardly. "An honor to serve you again."

"Welcome." Silver Wolf eyed him. "What is that writing on your face?"

Jiro straightened up. A wince implied his bad knee was bothering him today. "It reads, *Pledged to avenge*." Fire filled his eyes as he added, "It's a lifelong commitment."

Silver Wolf smiled. Perfect! Jiro *had* changed, and not just in appearance either.

When first in the warlord's service, Jiro had been injured during an encounter with Moonshadow. The gangster now held this young *shinobi* responsible for his ruined leg. It seemed he'd been stewing on it throughout his recovery. There was a new sense of steel to Jiro now, a single-minded determination. Had the urge to get even driven him to develop as a killer?

Maybe. The lord nodded. He'd seen that process before in men, many times. Hate was a powerful poison. It helped drive him too.

His eyes flicked left and right and Silver Wolf caught his bodyguards scowling. That was to be expected. Samurai despised gangsters, took offense at sharing the same air with them.

Chikuma turned and examined Jiro, then caught Silver Wolf's attention.

"Yes?" The warlord inclined his head. "What is it? You may speak freely."

"Great lord, a gangster with a lame leg? In a small strike force, the potency of every member is crucial. I seek no trouble here, but...what can *he* contribute?"

Silver Wolf glanced at Jiro. So much for *don't mention the limp*. Chikuma obviously cared little for diplomacy, and already the gambler was simmering with anger. This could prove *very* entertaining. He just needed to keep a rein on things. Hirelings were expensive; it was frivolous to waste their peculiar talents by making them fight to the death like dogs on some whim. Silver Wolf's eyes lit up. Tempting, though.

"Call the innkeeper!" he ordered his samurai.

The strapping youngster bowed neatly and, as before, whistled.

The small man quickly appeared, hunching in the doorway with eyebrows raised.

"Bring me two plain, cheap fans. Run out and buy them if you must. Hurry!"

"My lord," the innkeeper swooped into a low bow, "I think I have just what you need." He turned and scuttled away down the corridor's cherrywood floorboards.

"Jiro," Silver Wolf said. "When he returns with the fans, I want a demonstration. Chikuma-San here will open each fan, then throw them into the air without warning. Bring them down, without leaving a mark anywhere in this room."

Chikuma's face contorted with surprise. "Is he really that good?"

"You'll see, pretty boy," Jiro mumbled.

With his gaze locked on Silver Wolf, the gangster gave a half nod, half bow. "Yes, lord." His wrists crossed, and both hands disappeared between the lapels of his bright, loose jacket. Along with the bodyguards, Silver Wolf flinched involuntarily. The oldest samurai took a short step toward Jiro. The gambler drew out a *bo-shuriken* in each hand, apparently from twin concealed holsters. The warlord stared at the uncommon straight throwing knives. Each was black, cast from iron, about the length of a man's hand, fingertip to wrist. A tapering grip lay between the double-edged spearlike blade at one end and the small ring at the other.

Silver Wolf scratched his jaw thoughtfully. Jiro had formerly used circular, star-shaped *shuriken*. Converting to this very different design was no small accomplishment.

Bo-shuriken were the hardest kind to use; they were bladed at one end only, so if the spinning throw was mistimed, the ring end hit the target, and the knife merely bounced off it. Their advantages? *Bo-shuriken* had a proper grip, so, if used deftly, were ideal for stabbing in a close-range fight. The ring on the end could be used as a tiny club. It was also a tying point when securing the black knives in spring-loaded or rope traps.

The innkeeper slid into view in the corridor, a plain folding fan open in each hand. Silver Wolf stared at them: oiled, unmarked white paper and dark wooden spokes. Simple and light. *Ideal.* Holding the fans up, the innkeeper smiled warily.

"Well done!" Silver Wolf nodded. "Now, close the fans and give them to him." He gestured at Chikuma.

The innkeeper shut the fans and bowed low, then approached Chikuma like a crab, shuffling in a series of little sidesteps, avoiding eye contact with the *shinobi*. Keeping his face turned away, the innkeeper leaned, his outstretched hand trembling as he passed Chikuma the fans. The agent took them with a wry, knowing smile. After shuffling back to the door, the little man bowed hurriedly and made his escape.

Remarkable, the warlord observed. Even a lowly, untrained peasant sensed something fearful in Chikuma of Fuma. He couldn't wait to find out what it was. *Soon!*

"Are you both ready?" Silver Wolf looked from Jiro to Chikuma and back. Each man nodded. "Good. One fan at a time, I think. Begin!"

Chikuma flashed Jiro a skeptical glance, then opened the first fan and threw it up.

It wheeled and fluttered unevenly into the center of the room at about head height. There was a sharp *hiss*, startling Katsu, Silver Wolf, and his guards as a dark blur streaked across the room from Jiro's hand into the white, tumbling triangle. The *bo-shuriken*'s impact swept the fan across the room. It flailed to the matting like a wounded bird. The warlord stared down at it. That black iron throwing knife had pierced paper and wood, buckling the fan while bringing it down. So these *bo-shuriken* had another advantage: they were heavier than the circular kind, striking harder, cutting deeper.

Most impressive!

The guards blinked at Jiro, their faces betraying a new, reluctant respect. Katsu stared at the fan, his nose creasing. Even Chikuma of Fuma nodded admiringly.

Jiro's eyes gleamed. He turned and stared at the *shinobi*. It wasn't a friendly look. "Oi, pretty boy! I'm warmed up now, see? Throw the second one up—*closed*."

Silver Wolf inclined his head. Now the gangster was getting carried away. Hit a closed fan tumbling in midair with a *bo-shuriken*? Surely an impossible challenge.

Chikuma held up the second fan, closed, patiently watching Silver Wolf's face.

"Do it," the warlord said. The instant he spoke, Chikuma threw the fan.

Jiro's hand whip-cracked the air. This time the *hiss* was closely followed by a dull impact sound. The merged fan and knife streaked across the room, a spinning black-and-white flash that ended with a *whump* on the tatami near the door. Again, it left no mark.

Silver Wolf craned forward, examining the fan. Everyone else in the room did the same. Everyone but Jiro. He folded his arms with a superior smile, looking away, refusing to check the result.

Taking it in, the warlord's mouth fell open. The *bo-shuriken* had skewered the fan at a perfect ninety-degree angle, going through both its outer wooden spokes and every paper fold in between. He shook his head. A good thing he had seen it with his own eyes.

"If my lord liked *that*"—Jiro half bowed, then glanced sideways at Silver Wolf's personal guards—"I have an even better trick, for use against *armed* targets." He raised a challenging eyebrow.

Silver Wolf was too fascinated to decline. "Very well…but spill no blood," he warned.

"Understood, great one." Jiro covered his heart and nodded earnestly.

The warlord gestured to his bodyguards. They hurried to their master, bowing as one. "Don't make it easy for him," he whispered to them. "Go to opposite ends of the room, then draw and advance on him as you like. Let's see his 'even better trick' work under pressure."

The father-and-son duo bowed again, exchanged steely glances, then hurried to opposite ends of the room.

Jiro went to the center of the chamber, where he held up a *bo-shuriken* in each hand.

"Begin!" Silver Wolf's eyes darted between the three men. What would the gangster do?

The stocky young bodyguard immediately drew his sword. Jiro stood with his back to the samurai, but on hearing the *snick* of an emerging blade, he whirled around quickly. Before the guard could take his first step, Jiro hurled a throwing knife.

As the *bo-shuriken* hissed through the air, straight for the warrior's head, the samurai's father gasped.

In a heartbeat the young bodyguard's sword flashed up into a strong block, meeting the incoming missile with a loud *shiiinnng*!

A blue spark flew from the sword's blunt edge, and the *bo-shuriken* spun up to the ceiling and then tumbled to the floor. Before it landed, Jiro launched a second missile and, as that flashed across the room, he drew and then hurled a third *bo-shuriken* with equally freakish speed.

There was a sharp *clack-clack* and the young samurai guard found himself pinned to the wall, a dark *bo-shuriken* puckering each of his generous sleeves. He looked down, surprise twisting his face. Silver Wolf leaned forward, squinting, shaking his head. *Unbelievable!*

The stocky youth leaned out from the wall, trying vainly to free himself. Silver Wolf marveled. The boy's sword was already drawn, but with his arms now so restricted, he couldn't hope to control it. Before he could fight he would have to break free, but while he did—

As if reading Silver Wolf's mind, Jiro drew another *bo-shuriken* and held it high.

"Normally, I'd finish him off while he's busy trying to tear loose." The gambler wagged his head self-importantly. "But since we're just playing this time"—Jiro's eyes glided to one side as the older samurai began a slow, quiet draw behind him—"instead I'll do...*this!*"

Despite his bad leg, Jiro spun around with superb control and launched his *bo-shuriken* at the senior bodyguard. All eyes followed its frenzied streak across the room.

With a sharp *thwack!* the throwing knife bit into the wall right beside the samurai's neck. His sword only half drawn, the older warrior shuddered. He blinked, then turned his head and ogled the *bo-shuriken*. Its horizontal shaft was just a finger's width from his neck vein!

"Wonderful accuracy, Jiro." Silver Wolf folded his arms. "But *this* opponent could still rush you now. What would you do then?"

Jiro smiled, showing crooked yellow teeth as he pulled out another *bo-shuriken* and tapped it in the palm of his hand. "With all due respect, my lord, he couldn't. He is glued where he stands, and with *this*"—he waved his throwing knife—"I can pin him *properly*, anytime I like."

Instantly challenging Jiro's claim, the older guard forced himself forward, only to be jerked back by the fabric of his own collar—which *was* pinned to the wall. He grunted with frustration, then stared coldly at Jiro. A lick of hard-won respect flickered in his eyes.

Silver Wolf laughed heartily. Had Jiro been allowed to go on throwing at his usual pace, he would have killed both guards. Pinning foes like arranged flowers—how ingenious!

The warlord signaled his men to sheath their swords, and Katsu to free the guards.

A hush fell over the chamber as everyone studied Jiro afresh, still loathing his nature but now forced to admire his skill. Silver Wolf voiced the question on everybody's lips.

"How?" The warlord inclined his head. "How did you become *this* good?"

"Two months of constant, all-day practice, my lord, under a brilliant tutor," Jiro said bitterly. "The only way to spend one's...rehabilitation." His eyes, bright with the flame of his all-consuming vendetta, flicked down at his ruined knee. Then he rounded on Chikuma. "Anyway, so much for me. Now *I* want to know what *you* can contribute."

Silver Wolf hid a smile behind one hand. Jiro had trained fanatically to reach a whole new skill level, but he was still a reckless hothead and about to step on a tiger's tail. This would be fun, if it stayed within limits.

"How about it then, Chikuma?" Jiro put his hands on his hips.

"Chikuma-*San*." The *shinobi*'s voice was soft but firm. His eyes grew dark as they moved to Silver Wolf. The look in them was easy to interpret: let me destroy him now.

Jiro went on, taking a step toward Chikuma. "You're kind of...pretty, I guess, but you're wearing only a short *tanto* dagger. I guess we'll just hope that whoever you fight is happy to come that close. While they admire your nice new clothes, maybe? Better pray they don't carry anything long, like a sword! Might mess up your hair!"

Chikuma of Fuma let out a long, weary sigh. "Lord?" He waited.

"As long as nobody dies or is made useless," Silver Wolf said, "you may forget the innkeeper and show me...on *him*." He pointed at Jiro. Full of bravado, Jiro shrugged.

Chikuma bowed and broke into a grateful smile. He rose to his feet, twitching and primping his clothes and hair. Then he turned and glared at Jiro. Black, silent fury built in his eyes, but his face, curiously, became expressionless.

"What art is this?" Jiro gave a mocking cackle. "What? You stare them to death?"

Silver Wolf held his breath. So which strange killing science had this *shinobi* mastered? Might it be some form of paralysis? Did Chikuma induce weakness, strip the strength from a man's limbs, before knifing him? Whatever it was, he would soon unleash it on Moonshadow and the Grey Light Order.

The *shinobi* closed his eyes, body motionless, hands dangling at his sides.

Silver Wolf watched Jiro's face intently. No sign of sleepiness or paralysis yet.

"No." The gambler laughed. "Whatever it is you do, it's just not working today—"

But suddenly Jiro's head jerked up, eyes darting to a spot in the air as high as a horse's bridle. With a frown, Silver Wolf tracked along his stare. What did he look at? There was nothing there! The warlord's gaze returned to Jiro just in time to see the color drain from the gangster's features. He gasped, took a step back. His hands rose, shaking.

"Run, r-run," he stammered, eyes wide with terror. "Run! Lord Amida save us all!"

Everyone in the room but Chikuma looked back and forth between Jiro and the empty space that now terrified him.

Silver Wolf felt a rush of exhilaration tinged with fear. He gripped his sword.

Looking up as if something tall was slowly advancing on him, Jiro stumbled backward. He gave a high-pitched scream and collapsed to his knees, covering his face.

"Make it go away," he whimpered. "I...I... apologize."

Jiro fell onto his side and curled into a trembling ball.

Chikuma blinked and raised his eyebrows slightly. He smiled secretively.

Jiro snarled a curse and sat up, blinking quickly, looking around as if searching.

"Wasn't really there," he mumbled. He checked the room again. "Wasn't...there."

The warlord gaped in astonishment. Alarmed and confused, his guards had half drawn their swords, but Jiro, the actual subject of the attack, had been so disturbed he hadn't managed to pull one *shuriken*. Against such dark wizardry, who could stand?

"Magnificent!" Silver Wolf raised his hands and clapped enthusiastically.

The father-and-son samurai sheathed their blades and joined in, smiling with relief that whatever had just happened was now over. Katsu shook his head and clapped slowly.

Chikuma bowed, gave a nasal giggle, and flicked

his hair. The warlord nodded back at him thought-fully. What manner of man was this? His entire appearance was camouflage; his powers were incredible. Silver Wolf beamed. This team could not fail.

"Great lord Silver Wolf." Chikuma glanced at Jiro, who immediately cringed. "Since my…*team-mate* here has been allowed to show off one of *his* best tricks, might I also thrill my lord with something…a little unexpected?" He made a sly expression, pointing through the doorway. "I offer a further display, showing the range of my powers. Let me distress an unseen target, a victim not even in the room." He grinned wickedly. "Our little innkeeper, perhaps?"

Silver Wolf frowned. "You can do that? Without knowing exactly where he is?"

"He's close by." Chikuma licked his lips. "Since I've already laid eyes on him and marked him, that's all I need."

Marked him? Again fascinated, Silver Wolf half smiled. Had the innkeeper *felt* Chikuma doing that while handing over the fans? No wonder he had looked so frightened!

The warlord nodded his consent. Chikuma immediately closed his eyes and concentrated.

Jiro edged away, glancing furtively in all directions. Katsu and the two samurai exchanged uneasy looks. A heavy silence descended on the room. Silver Wolf felt a growing sense of dread. Was Chikuma indirectly causing it? To retain his calm, he began a silent count.

Outside, several horses neighed sharply. Silver Wolf swallowed, then kept counting.

As he reached *ten*, a long, terrified scream came from somewhere in the inn. It made Jiro jump and the two samurai clutch their swords. The voice was familiar, but the scream so fearful that even Silver Wolf's blood ran cold.

An image flashed through the warlord's mind: a sparrow in the talons of a great hawk.

As the awful, stricken wail finally subsided, there was a loud *thud* and then a swell of other voices from the same location—men and women, babbling with alarm, speculating about what had just happened. Silver Wolf stared in their direction, picturing them: the innkeeper's family and staff, shocked and mystified by his sudden terror and collapse...apparently over *nothing*.

"You didn't actually...*kill* the little man?" The warlord watched Chikuma open his eyes and stretch lazily.

"No, my lord." The *shinobi* played with a handful of his shiny hair. "Shall I, for fun?"

Silver Wolf broke into a morbid grin, hesitated, then slowly shook his head.

"Any other questions," Chikuma softly asked Jiro, "about what I can contribute?"

Jiro snatched a deep, trembling breath. "Never, Chikuma-*San*."

The warlord glanced back and forth between his hirelings. A pecking order was now clearly established with this pair, but anything could happen when they met the rest of the team on the road north. Jiro's baiting mouth or Chikuma's cool arrogance might provoke Wada or Kagero. Silver Wolf had seen assassins squabble before, and this plan had to succeed. The warlord frowned. Though it meant yet more expense, he needed to take out some insurance! *Shinobi* relied on ancient ways; he would guarantee success by employing modern science too.

He motioned Katsu to his side. Sharp samurai eyes tracked the big man's steps.

His every move measured and careful, Katsu bowed low. "Great lord?"

"Before you leave," Silver Wolf murmured, "I'll arrange more money. I want you to hire the best sniper you can find, one with the latest foreign musket and a fast horse. Station him low on the White Nun's mountain. I'll give you detailed orders for him." The warlord's eyes flicked at Chikuma and Jiro. "I want a cool head, you see, lurking in reserve, independent of Kagero, Wada, and this pair. Independent of wizardry too." As Katsu nodded astutely, Silver Wolf thought of Moonshadow and his Grey Light cronies. Dark hatred roiled in the veteran warrior's eyes. "Get our forces on their way, then! There are things to do, people to kill!"

A QUIET DAY
AT THE MARKET

On their fourth day on the road, the weather turned humid. High, thin clouds formed a prism that trapped the sun in a silk curtain of white glare.

A predawn conversation on the day they left Edo came back to Moonshadow as he pounded along a dusty hill road beside Snowhawk.

Perhaps feeling the need for a bold gesture, Brother Eagle had recommended what he called "fitting disguises" for Moonshadow and Snowhawk's journey to the White Nun.

As a result, they now wore identical rough hemp

jackets, dark blue and wadded, with matching loose pants. Under their backpacks, flattened sleeping rolls hid their swords. He felt a little self-conscious about the bold white characters running down his sleeves.

"Edo Golden Future Traders," each column read, "a highly sincere Company."

"Would it not be poetic," Eagle had suggested after their briefing, "for the two of you to travel as merchants' laborers? Brother Badger tells me that he happens to have two uniforms of about the right size among his stores. Heron's skills would make short work of adjusting them for you."

After accepting, Moonshadow had spoken solemnly. "I've been thinking. Merchants and their companies, men who are *not* warriors, men with no code but profit, now number among our mortal enemies. That's strange. I would never have expected—"

Eagle had cut him off. "The White Nun once told me that she had seen the distant future. One day, merchants will rule the world, their companies, like the warlords of today: a few doing good, but many... unspeakable evil. The empire, we *shinobi*, even the samurai... the White Nun told me that all would be gone by then, echoes lost in time."

Moonshadow had shaken his head. Life in the future sounded really confusing! At least here, in the present, their cover-story lives were simple: they were orphans, brother and sister, experienced in managing storerooms, seeking jobs in the country after a year in hectic Edo.

The road north had been lonely and dull, just the odd group of farmers passing by, with much of the terrain—oceans of rice paddies and islands of trees— almost identical. So they had talked themselves hoarse all through the farmlands and into these foothills, covering a surprisingly wide range of topics.

Their favorite things. Earliest memories. Theories about who their parents might have been. Since their first meeting in Fushimi two months earlier, the pair had shared hours of hard training, several eavesdropping missions, and more conversations than Moonshadow could count. Snowhawk understood his uniquely powerful, lonely life because she had lived the same way. And she told great travel stories! Having specialized in daylight infiltration missions, she'd seen more of the regular world than he had, visited far-off cities, met a wider variety of people. Yet even during their most enjoyable talks, he had sensed the buried darkness lurking in his friend.

Last night, it had finally broken the surface. Now, though they still talked and joked almost as usual, he felt an unseen barrier between them. Perhaps this mess was all his fault! He was the team leader, her senior in the Order, and supposedly a good example of Grey Light ways. But before they had even set out, he had compromised his standards and broken the rules, by keeping her dangerous outburst a secret instead of reporting it. Some example. Some leader!

So why *was* he covering for her? Moonshadow shook his head. Was it just fear of losing the best friend he'd ever had? Or were his instincts actually sound? Did he *rightfully* trust her to come through this and prove herself in the end? Moonshadow sighed. Currently, he couldn't tell.

The road grew steeper as it approached the first hill town. A breeze brought the aromas of pine needles and late spring flowers. Peasants trickled from gullies beside the road, forming a swell that moved toward the distant buildings. Many carried vegetables or fruit in back-mounted woven baskets. Some hauled rice sacks or lugged strings of dried mushrooms.

"Look at this." Snowhawk gestured at a man shouldering chickens in a bamboo cage. "It must be market day in this town. That'll make a nice change, things to look at. If the place is quiet, we should rest there, enjoy the market, and take rooms overnight." Her face brightened. "It's been a long time since I was let loose in a marketplace!"

Moonshadow felt a tinge of envy. For the most part, his life outside the monastery had been one of night missions. He had *never* freely explored a market! "As long as it *is* quiet and stays that way." He studied the people around them suspiciously. He saw nothing to alert him, and Snowhawk obviously sensed no energy. But all that could change in a moment. "Remember, if it doesn't work out here, the second town is not that far away."

She gave a faint sigh, flashing him a look that said *stop worrying so much*.

They neared the little town, and Moonshadow smiled at the beauty of the way ahead. Distant snow-capped mountains peeped over green hills framing the settlement. Cherry trees lined the road, their petals wafting in the breeze like white and pink snow.

"It's all so lovely, isn't it?" Snowhawk stopped walking. She clicked her tongue. "Except for some of the local brats."

"What do you mean?" He followed her stare. Ahead, a group of boys stood in a half circle around one boy. He was smaller than the rest, softer-faced too.

Snowhawk had sensed their aggression first. Now Moonshadow could feel it. But though he was willing to simply keep walking, he sensed instantly that she was not. As they approached, the oldest-looking boy in the group shoved the small lad in the chest. He staggered backward.

"Everyone in *our* town can fight," the older boy snarled from under a mop of tangled hair. "You want to live here, prove you can too. Get it? Or are you stupid?"

Snowhawk's hands became fists and she muttered under her breath. Moonshadow saw her face harden, eyes glaze over. *Not again.* He winced. Stirred by hurtful memories, her rage was surfacing once more! He glanced about quickly. What could he do? Dragging her away might draw more attention than letting her intervene. But what if she went too far?

"This," Snowhawk glowered, "*this* is what I grew up with…every darn day!" She stepped forward. "And I swore if I ever escaped it, I'd never stand by and let it happen to anyone else."

"Look, I agree, it's rotten. But we shouldn't get involved," Moonshadow warned. "No overt combat, remember? We can't risk blowing our cover."

"I won't blow it." Snowhawk strode ahead of him. "But I *have to* do this!"

"No!" Moonshadow caught up and grabbed her arm. "You're too angry!"

Snowhawk's granite face and fixed stare almost made him shudder. Once *this* incensed, she would rather die than back down. Moonshadow weighed the options desperately.

Could he let her do it? No! Anything might happen. Try to order her away...*no*. She'd resist, maybe go berserk at him. It was hopeless! He groaned, feeling trapped. No matter what he chose, she was about to cause quite a scene. Only this time, they weren't on a rooftop at night.

His heart sank. Was this it? Was her rage about to get them both killed?

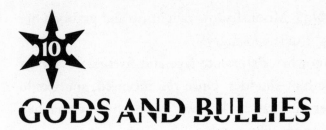

GODS AND BULLIES

An idea came to him: risky, but the best option so far. "If—if it has to be done…*I'll* do it." Moonshadow narrowed his gaze at her sternly. "That way, people are less likely to die."

She sneered as she yanked her arm free. "Mantis has ruined you as a warrior." Snowhawk stepped aside and gestured disdainfully. "Go on then, fix it, O Wise One. Or I swear *I will*!" He glared at her, then walked up to the biggest boy and pushed past him. Putting his back to the group's intended victim, Moonshadow faced the half circle of his persecutors. His eyes glided left to right. Unworthy foes! The oldest lad and two others were tall, brawny country kids. None appeared armed or moved as if trained. The rest were the typical cowardly runts that followed bullies around like a string of goldfish dung.

"Get on your way and stop picking on my friend." Moonshadow scowled.

The three hefty boys read his jacket sleeves and then exchanged frowns.

"You're from Edo," the leader sneered. "He is *not* your friend!"

Moonshadow looked over his shoulder at the boy and winked. The gang's target, realizing that he was being rescued, half smiled. Moonshadow turned back to face the leader.

"He is today." He raised one eyebrow. "So if you want him, you fight me first."

"This'll teach you to mind your own business!" With that, the leader attacked.

To Moonshadow, the boy's angry punch for his jaw appeared to approach in slow motion. He dodged it lazily, sidestepped, then thrust one leg out. Off balance, the lunging bully tripped over Moonshadow's ankle and plunged to the dusty road, landing hard and winding himself. His two biggest friends darted at Moonshadow, the first remarkably hefty for his age, the other more long-legged and gangly. The more solid boy swung a crazed, open backhand strike, aiming for Moonshadow's face. Moonshadow swayed backward and felt the close rush of air as it missed him. With a *thwack* the wild blow met the face of the skinny lad, who let out a howl and crumpled, cupping his nose. The stocky boy turned back, growled, then shot his best punch at Moonshadow's stomach, throwing his shoulders behind it. Again, from Moonshadow's point of view, the fist approached slowly, giving him time to consider his next move. He needed to end this fast, so why not startle them all into quitting? Yes...a little bluff to frighten them.

An instant before impact, Moonshadow locked up his stomach muscles, rock hard from a special diet and a lifetime of hard training. The bully's fist struck home.

Along with the *thump* of impact came a nasty clicking sound. Squealing with pain, the boy sagged to the road, nursing his hand. Moonshadow gave a detached sigh. It served him right. Bad technique and broken fingers went together like rice and fish.

The former group of pack hunters stared at Moonshadow, each frozen to the spot with awe and fear. Moonshadow grabbed their leader and dragged him to his feet.

"The gods secretly roam the land in many forms, watching for cruelty!" The bully's eyes grew large. He looked at Moonshadow in a whole new way. "This is your chance to change. All of you!" Moonshadow looked around the group. "Now go, live good lives, *or else!*"

The terrified gang ran. It was over. Moonshadow quickly glanced in all directions. Had the scuffle drawn attention? He peered ahead, toward the center of the town. At the edge of the marketplace, only one man stood watching, a slothful-looking giant. He was built like a wrestler, so he couldn't be a *shinobi*. The big guy stared idly for a while, then turned and plodded away.

Moonshadow grinned with relief. The *real* gods were with him. He'd gotten away with it!

He turned and bowed to the boy the gang had picked on. The child gave him a humble bow back. He was speechless, wonder sparkling in his eyes. Moonshadow could read his thoughts: *why have the gods been so kind to me?* He fished inside his jacket and handed the boy a few copper coins.

"Run home now, share this with your family. Live life to the fullest, but keep the law, honor the old and all the gods."

"Thank you, I will, sir." The boy backed away,

bowing again, glancing between Moonshadow and the coins in his own hand. "I promise!" He turned and ran, his face glowing.

Snowhawk cupped one hand above her eyes and watched the last of the children disappear from sight. "Nicely done. But should you *really* be impersonating a justice *kami*, or any other god for that matter? What if a real god curses us both for the insult? Did you ever stop to think about that?"

He rounded on her in frustration. "I'm not the one who needs to stop and think!"

They stared at each other coldly. He saw guilt flicker in her eyes, then watched her anger swallow it. Snowhawk shrugged irritably and then turned away. Gesturing once for Moonshadow to follow, she paced off quickly into the town.

He trailed her, shaking his head. He had just saved her from wrecking their mission and who knows what else, and all she could do was *criticize*?

Was it just Snowhawk, or were all girls this impossible?

As he caught up to her, a droning temple bell from the far end of town announced that it was midday, halfway through the Hour of the Horse.

Buildings lined the main street. In the heart of town the road flared into a central square around a circular stone well. Rows of booths and stalls edged the square. Strings of colored flags above each counter and table bore large characters that described the goods for sale.

Between the stalls and the well, banks of trestle tables and rugs covered the square's packed gravel floor. Neat lines of products adorned them all.

Local farmers and townsfolk poured into the square now, some selling, most just shopping. Hearing an Edo accent, Moonshadow's head turned sharply.

He followed the voice to a table selling winter quilts. A one-eyed man haggled energetically with a woman carrying a baby in a sling. Moonshadow studied his movements. No, harmless. Not everybody up here from Edo was a spy. He smiled. Just them.

A set of flags read "Doctor Fish can make you young." Moonshadow and Snowhawk exchanged curious grins, then approached the stall. Below the flags, it contained only a skinny peasant behind his counter, a large iron pot filled with water, and a hanging abacus for calculating payment rates. While they looked on, an elderly lady approached the stall. She bowed and paid Doctor Fish. He smiled and gestured. She plunged her hands into the pot. Moonshadow shuffled closer, watching intently.

Something teemed in the cloudy water in a frenzy of tiny bubbles.

The lady flinched twice, then, urged by the vendor, withdrew her hands. They gleamed in places, pink and shiny. Doctor Fish can make you young? It was sort of true; the woman's hands no longer matched the rest of her skin. They looked...younger.

"I've seen this in Osaka. Thousands of tiny fish." Snowhawk shook her head. "They eat the dead skin off."

Moonshadow nodded and grinned in fascination. What a wondrous place! Snowhawk had seen so much of life. This market was like a chance for him to catch up! He eagerly moved to the stall next door, where two soft-eyed women, a mother and daughter perhaps, were selling handmade water containers fashioned from cells of giant bamboo. A dense little crowd surrounded their table. Moonshadow stood at the edge of it, sampling the intriguing food smells of the marketplace, its bright colors, strange sounds, and unfamiliar faces.

A twinge of guilt abruptly made him check himself. This amazing place was drawing them both in. It felt great, like borrowing an hour from someone else's life, a *normal* life. But could they afford to relax, even a little, in any public place? He scanned the interesting, happy faces around him and decided that maybe Snowhawk was right: he *did* worry too much.

Somebody pushed Moonshadow from behind, quite a hard shove. Moonshadow hung his head and hissed with irritation. Were those stupid bullies trying for a rematch? Or was Snowhawk playing a prank on him? He turned around, his eyes lining up with the biggest chest he had ever seen in his life. Moonshadow gasped. After blinking with astonishment, he took in its owner.

A mighty giant, obviously a sumo wrestler, loomed over him. It was the same big man he had seen watching as the bullies made their escape! His great arms looked impossible, thicker than any human limbs should be. His massive body had the girth of a young cedar tree. The giant wore a sky-blue jacket and matching pants that were tied at the knees. Moonshadow stared up at the man's face. Clean-shaven and dull-eyed, his features were as meek as his form was powerful. Moonshadow glanced down at the giant's sandals. They held enormous, ogrelike feet the size of water barrels. Like his forearms, the man's ankles and shins were covered in bruises and scars. Some looked to be very recent.

He seemed to have no weapons. But why would he need one? He *was* one.

The wrestler shoved Moonshadow again, his massive fingers digging into one shoulder. Moonshadow stepped back and found himself trapped against the stall's table. He gripped the instant throbbing in his shoulder, glowering up at the sumo.

"Hey, big guy," he called out. "That hurt! You can't keep pushing me when there's nowhere to go. What's the matter? Did I cut in front of you?" Moonshadow gave a wary bow, keeping his eyes on the man. "If so, forgive me."

"No. No forgiving," the wrestler said slowly. "You are my enemy." He brought his hands together in front of Moonshadow's face and loudly cracked his enormous knuckles.

The crowd around Moonshadow and the sumo quickly broke up. Whispers filled the air.

"Do you give up?" the wrestler asked patiently. "You *should* give up."

Moonshadow couldn't stop his mouth falling open. This was too bizarre. He was being threatened, challenged in fact, in the mildest, flattest, least angry voice he'd ever heard.

"Give up now," the sumo persisted nonchalantly. "You will be my prisoner."

The man's entire manner was ridiculously calm, almost lethargic, which provoked Moonshadow to laugh. His eyes flitted from the sumo to hunt for Snowhawk. Where was she? Before that first shove she'd been right—

As he glanced back at the wrestler, a high-pitched scream broke through the even gaggle of marketplace voices. Moonshadow's head snapped in its direction. Between jagged ranks of fleeing peasants, he saw Snowhawk ducking low. Then he saw a man with his arm extended. He'd just thrown something at her!

A scruffy man...who he recognized at once.

"Jiro," Moonshadow breathed. "The *shuriken* gangster." So he *was* still alive. Moonshadow's stomach knotted. Alive, and part of an ambush!

He let out a startled cry as huge hands clamped his ribs, and his feet left the ground. The sumo wrestler yanked his victim up to his own eye level, holding Moonshadow out at arm's length as if he were unclean. It appeared to be absolutely no effort for the giant.

"Will you give up then?" he asked placidly. Moonshadow snarled and shook his head. The sumo wrestler sighed. "Very well, then. It's your fault."

Moonshadow opened his mouth to retort, but the wrestler, moving with blinding speed, hoisted him overhead.

"Stop! Wait!" Moonshadow roared, looking down at the top of his attacker's head.

He felt a nauseating rush, and suddenly he was flying, tumbling head over heels.

Startled people flashed below as he whirled out of control. Moonshadow gritted his teeth, bracing himself for the first Jiro *shuriken*. Would he die before he hit the ground?

ENEMIES OLD AND NEW

Moonshadow landed on a fleeing group of farmers, banging heads with a man in a conical straw hat before dropping to the ground, stunned.

Despite his insulating bedroll, the hand guard of his hidden sword ground into his spine. Moonshadow groaned, sat up, shook himself hard. People rushed away in all directions. Vendors unwilling to leave their stock behind were cowering inside their stalls. One man, desperate to protect his exquisite white pottery, was stubbornly kneeling in front of his rug of wares.

With a wince Moonshadow realized that his ribs were badly bruised from the giant's grip. He clambered to his feet, looking about for Snowhawk. He could neither see her nor sense her presence nearby. Gravel crunched. Sharp, closing strides made him turn.

Side by side, they came toward him: the slight, limping Jiro and, dwarfing him, the bull-necked, towering wrestler. Frightened locals dodged past them, then ran. Moonshadow blinked. What an impossible situation! A bold attack in public, and in broad daylight—using mercenaries! These two foes weren't ninja, but no doubt they knew that he and Snowhawk couldn't just shed their disguises and let fly with *shuriken* of their own. If they did, their identities and mission would be hopelessly compromised. Not only that, but more innocent people would get hurt!

Despite his racing thoughts, Moonshadow's head was still light from being used as a human cannonball. He couldn't let that happen again. He stared at the approaching sumo's enormous hands. Nor fall into *those* bone grinders once more.

If he was grabbed, nothing less than his sword would stop the giant tearing him apart. In a place *this* public, drawing any blade was out of the question. Moonshadow cursed under his breath. *Even if his enemies did.* He tracked Jiro, watching the gambler's hands.

The wrestler and Jiro stopped, about ten paces away. They glanced at each other. The huge sumo motioned for Jiro to do the talking.

Jiro greeted Moonshadow with a cackle. "I love reunions! Remember me, kid? We have unfinished business, you and me. Don't bother looking for your little girlfriend. Sweet that she stuck with you." He gave a cruel sneer. "But I just stuck her with one of *these*!"

His hand flashed in and out of his jacket. He held up something black. A *bo-shuriken*. What a nasty surprise. So since their last encounter, Jiro had upgraded to this oldest style of *shuriken*, the classical straight design with a grip.

They were the hardest of all to throw. But they did the most damage.

The crook was lying about Snowhawk, Moonshadow decided. She was no easy kill. She'd tricked him, given him the slip, that's all. He swallowed—hopefully.

Jiro waved his new weapon. "Oh, don't look so amazed." The gangster sniffed. "Think it's just you cockroaches of the shadows who train to better your crafts?" He thumped his chest so hard the wrestler flinched and looked at him. "Well, even the likes of me can want that!"

Moonshadow felt daunted. Jiro had changed. A darker fire drove him now. "Congratulations," he told the gangster, concealing his reaction. "So what do you want? Not a dice game, I hope. Because I don't gamble!"

"Very funny. Your kind's entire lives are one long gamble! *What do I want?* Can't you guess, kid?" Jiro's mouth quirked to one side. He limped a step, pointing down. "I'm not blaming you for this, not anymore. People say I do, but I'm over it."

"No blade of mine did that to you," Moonshadow replied coolly. "It was another of Silver Wolf's henchmen, as well you know." He looked Jiro up and down with open disdain. "I even left money for them to get you fixed."

"Sweet of you, kid, but it must have been spent on someone more valuable. Anyway, forget my bad knee. Know why I'm still riled at you? You ruined my record. You and the girl were the only targets ever to escape me! Let's fix that, shall we?"

With alarming speed, Jiro drew a second *bo-shuriken* from his jacket.

Raising a throwing knife in each hand, he took careful aim at Moonshadow's head.

MARKETPLACE MAYHEM

The sumo patted Jiro's shoulder with one finger. "Who is he again?" he asked.

Lowering his *bo-shuriken*, Jiro made an irritated sound. "Moonshadow, they call him, just like the sword move." He rolled his eyes. "You see, kid, my large friend here, for some reason, is a stickler for manners. So he wants *introductions* before he crushes you into the dust."

"You should just give up," the giant said slowly, "be my prisoner. Then you won't get hurt, just tied with rope. I am Wada. Once sumo, now bounty hunter. Just, uh..."

"Just give up," Moonshadow prompted impatiently. Wada returned a slow, earnest nod.

With one hand on his hip, Jiro eyed the giant. "Happy now? Good. Then *get him!*"

At once Wada leaned forward, lowered his head, and broke into a fast, accelerating charge. Moonshadow felt each impact of the wrestler's feet through the small stretch of ground that separated them. In two or three seconds Wada closed the gap.

Moonshadow bent his knees and swung his arms hard at his sides, pushing off into a leap, straight up. Once airborne, he curled his spine and raised both knees to his chest.

Wada's scalp of closely cropped hair brushed the soles of his sandals. The sumo thundered below him, moving too fast now for a controlled stop. As Moonshadow's feet hit the ground, there was a commotion behind him: a terrified scream, the shouts of bystanders, splintering wood and tearing fabric. Wada was plowing into a stall like a runaway bull.

Moonshadow looked over one shoulder. What had been a little folding shop front, trading in charms for safety and good luck, was now a tangle of broken planks, torn flags, and snapped cords. Tiny charm packets were scattered far and wide. An ashen-faced middle-aged lady was being hauled from the rubble by the back of her pink kimono. By Wada.

With one hand, he set the shocked woman down next to her destroyed stall.

"Uh. Sorry," Wada said sluggishly. Moonshadow squinted. Wada's shoulder bled, but he appeared not to know it. He thumbed in Moonshadow's direction. "His fault," Wada murmured.

Moonshadow was turning back to face the gangster when he heard the sound. A sharper *hiss* than typical Grey Light Order *shuriken* made, growing ever louder. He twisted, evading quickly. The whirling *bo-shuriken* passed so close to his eyes that its wake stung them. Moonshadow cursed. That was a *good* throw! An accident, or had Jiro markedly improved?

A warning tremor shook the ground behind him. Moonshadow cartwheeled to one side and Wada tore past, head and shoulders down, grunting, flicking up grit and stones. Jiro had to scramble out of his way. The wrestler changed course just in time to avoid trampling the terrified man relentlessly guarding his fine clay cups and jugs with his own body.

All of a sudden Jiro let out a shriek and grabbed the back of his own head. A small rock danced across the ground behind the gangster's feet. Snowhawk, another rock in her palm, stalked up behind him. Moonshadow noticed that she held something behind her back. But what?

"Hey! Jiro! See what happens when you throw things?" Her tone and eyes were icy.

The gangster turned around, blurting a startled curse. "So I missed you!" He chuckled. "Never mind. Let's try again!"

He drew a pair of *bo-shuriken* from his jacket with impressive speed. The remaining onlookers and vendors cringed at the sight of the twin throwing knives. A young girl started screaming. Taking a short step forward, Jiro let a *shuriken* fly at Snowhawk.

A blurring circle of death hissed sharply across the marketplace. Moonshadow opened his mouth to shout a warning, but out of the corner of one eye he saw Wada charging at him. This time there was a little more distance between them and, thus, more time to think.

Wada the bounty hunter was extraordinarily tough, but once he hit full speed, controlled stops seemed hard for him. That was something to work with.

Moonshadow turned and ran, a town watchman and a pair of woodcutters scattering out of his way. The giant followed, pounding up behind him, gaining at a scary pace. Moonshadow glanced to his side to check on Snowhawk. She was running in a zigzag near the well, a tin-lined tea-serving tray in one hand. Snowhawk had acquired a shield! The tray was pierced through the center with Jiro's knife, and now he was lining up for another throw. Moonshadow changed course and led Wada, right behind him now, straight between Jiro and his flitting target.

"Madness!" shouted an old man with a stick as Moonshadow tore past him. "Lunatics! You wreck our town!"

Jiro swore as Wada's thunderous passing blocked his field of fire. Moonshadow heard heavy breathing at his back and knew that the giant had closed the distance between them. He changed direction sharply and vaulted for the center of a wide stall table.

It was strewn with farming implements such as hand sickles and rice-bale chains, the kind *shinobi* clans often converted into weapons. No license to grab one today, however.

Moonshadow plunged for the tabletop. As soon as his feet struck it, he launched himself again, aiming for the roof of the tent stall next door. He landed on his side against its angled fabric, rolled off before his weight could tear it, and dropped to the ground in a crouch as the stall next door was noisily destroyed.

Wada's headlong impact snapped the table in half,

flinging tools into the air. Moonshadow glanced up. A scattered shower of blades and hooks was about to fall. He skipped instinctively to one side. A spinning sickle dug into the earth beside his foot. A young farmer let out a strangled croak on the other side of the wrecked stall. Moonshadow saw him struggling to free a chain that had been flung, whirling, and wrapped around his neck.

The sumo wrestler picked himself up out of the debris, mangled planks and a narrow digging tool sliding off his vast back. Blood ran down one of his cheeks, and there was a nasty tear in his left ear. As before, he didn't seem aware that he'd been injured.

Wada shook his head several times as if waking, then mumbled, "Sorry...sorry."

Moonshadow looked about. Snowhawk was backing up to the well, brandishing the tea tray's flat tin base between her hands. Jiro faced her. *Two* throwing knives now stuck from the tray. No wonder she disappeared earlier, Moonshadow thought. She'd quickly hunted down the right counterdevice for the job, one offering protection without disclosing *shinobi* skills. Good thinking! He ran to her side. Jiro drew two more *bo-shuriken* from his clothes. *Jiro!* He'd forgotten that this gangster always brought so much ammunition.

The four faced off. Moonshadow locked his gaze on Wada, who stood hunched, panting as he stared back, blood dripping from his chin. He was not going to quit.

Snowhawk's eyes were bright with challenge as she held up the tray, baiting Jiro with a teasing smile. He loosened his wrists and squeezed the *bo-shuriken*'s grips.

Moonshadow tensed. What if Jiro could throw two at once with the same accuracy?

Jiro lunged forward and hurled the first knife. Simultaneously, Wada dropped his huge head and accelerated at Moonshadow.

Moonshadow cursed the timing. What if Snowhawk took a hit? He glanced sideways fast. She snapped the tray up in front of her face just as the *bo-shuriken* slammed into it with a *thunk*. His eyes flicked back. Already, Wada was only a breath away, his huge body low to the ground, coming at Moonshadow with amazing speed.

With a growl of effort, Moonshadow somersaulted backward up onto the lip of the well, his sandals narrowly missing Wada's head. As Moonshadow landed, a tremor shook the stones under his feet. He caught his balance and looked down.

The stones were cut and fitted but not mortared,

and the well wall had come apart. Wada's head and shoulders were wedged between two sections that had held. Moonshadow heard loose stones tumble into the inky funnel, clicking off the walls until loud splashes echoed from far below. The pinned sumo let out a strange groan. Surely he had felt *that*?

Moonshadow looked up quickly at Jiro. Someone was approaching behind him. Another attacker? A woman, one of the locals, so probably not. She was middle-aged and wore a pink kimono. Just as Snowhawk had, she was hiding something behind her back.

Jiro cackled, tapping his second *bo-shuriken* on the palm of one hand. "Aw…Moonshadow." He grinned, displaying yellowed teeth. "*You* have no shield!"

The gambler drew back his arm. At the same time, the lady behind him heaved something long and black around her body. Moonshadow glanced at it. With white knuckles the woman raised a heavy, cone-shaped iron saucepan and swung it hard. A sickening, nearly hollow *clunk* quickly followed. Jiro's head lolled on his shoulders. His arm sagged, and his eyes became slits.

"Who did that?" Jiro asked, dazed. He sank to his knees. With a moan he fell forward, his face hitting the ground hard. Moonshadow scanned him care-fully. Unconscious.

"Here's *my* good luck charm for you!" The lady dropped her weapon, leaned over Jiro, and spat. "Swine! Filthy gangster beast! Ten curses on every part of your painted corpse!" She kicked one of Jiro's legs. He twitched. "Monster! Get gut worms and die! Mind-less wrecker! May the next dice you roll...poke out your eyes!"

Moonshadow jumped down from the lip of the well. He elbowed Snowhawk. "Aw, I'm glad she's on our side."

"That lady is pretty mad," Snowhawk panted, "and she won't be the only one. Let's get out of here before people turn on *us*. That *next* town's looking better and better."

They crept around the well, stepping over the motionless giant, whose head and shoulders were fused into the stony wall. Moonshadow leaned over Wada, checking him. Semiconscious, but somehow alive. Badly hurt, whether he felt it or not. *How* did he feel no pain? Surely it wasn't a *shinobi* science? Whatever the reason, it hadn't helped him win the day. Snowhawk passed a knowing look over Wada. Moonshadow knew what she was thinking.

Pain was good, important. It alerted you that you

weren't winning. Warned that your tactics had failed. Told you to quit so you could live to fight again later. Operating without it had not helped this mountain of a man defeat a slender opponent like Moonshadow.

He shook his head at Wada. Here lay a lesson worth discussing with Mantis and Eagle. A weird truth: pain was a warrior's valuable friend.

All around them, the locals were slowly starting to move, glancing blankly at each other and the devastated stalls. Their drawn expressions implied mass shock. Perhaps this town didn't see much trouble. Good! Then maybe they didn't even have—

Snowhawk grabbed his wrist and pointed. Moonshadow looked along her arm to the incoming road. He groaned. He'd hoped in vain. They *did* have a policeman.

A purposeful-looking inspector in official robes, flanked by two burly samurai, approached along the road. His eyes were already locked on the chaos in the marketplace.

Moonshadow and Snowhawk darted away from Wada and into a tight little crowd huddling in the least damaged corner of the square. Stunned faces turned to look at them as they pushed past, heading for a narrow lane between two buildings.

One person in the crowd stood out. Snowhawk

paced right by him, but he caught Moonshadow's attention with his stare. It was constant, bold almost to the point of arrogance. He was young, perhaps just a few years older than Snowhawk or Moonshadow. He wore a dagger, eye-catching clothes, and an unusual hairstyle, long but untied. Makeup too. His whole appearance suggested a big-city dweller.

The youth was so remote and confident, he might have been a *shinobi* but for one factor. Snowhawk hadn't reacted to him, and Moonshadow himself sensed no *shinobi* presence. So that was that. *Or was it?*

Oddly, when he'd first seen the youth staring, Moonshadow *had* felt a strange chill. It had lasted only seconds, a weird sensation like an icy wave breaking over him. Probably just a moment of panic, coincidentally timed to spook him. He frowned hard. Maybe, but he should take no chances. Snowhawk was better at detecting hostile ninja than anyone he knew.

Best to double-check with her!

He caught up with Snowhawk in the lane. "Wait! You feel any *shinobi* energy?"

She grinned widely. "None, just a vague sense of being unpopular around here."

He laughed with relief. It made her giggle as she turned to move on.

"They went down that lane!" a man's deep voice called from the square.

"You know what?" Moonshadow started to run. "You're right. Let's *not* stay in this town."

THE KINDNESS
OF STRANGERS

The middle-aged innkeeper smiled back at Snowhawk as she led her to the room.

It was at the end of a long corridor on the river side of the inn. Snowhawk counted the doors they passed on the way there. Ten, which meant that every room in this place was as tiny as that booth Moonshadow had just been given. She shrugged to herself. It didn't matter. They were both exhausted, he covered in bruises and nursing aching ribs. If her room was big enough for a bedroll, it would do. She sighed wearily. Besides, though it looked oddly deserted tonight, this was the only inn in town.

After traveling across country from the market town, moving parallel to the north road, they'd crept into this place just after sunset. Built on a teeming river, it was a pretty, serene-looking town, smaller than its neighbor. White-blossomed cherry trees ran along the entire main street, and a great wooden mill wheel turned beyond the last building.

While hiding between narrow thatch-roofed cottages, they'd overheard the locals excitedly trading gossip. The market town's inspector and his men had paid them a visit, searching for a gang of deranged vandals responsible for disrupting market day. Finding no unfamiliar faces or new information in this town, they had given up and returned south. Moonshadow and Snowhawk had waited until the snoopers were long gone before approaching the inn.

Patting the bun of grey-streaked hair on the crown of her head, the lady stopped outside the last door. She turned to Snowhawk and bowed, sliding it open with one hand. The creases around her soft eyes multiplied as she smiled warmly.

"There you are, dear. The quietest end of the inn. You'll get a good night's sleep here." She covered her mouth and gave an eccentric little titter. "Your poor brother looked like he would sleep anywhere, on a peak under thunderclouds, maybe?" The innkeeper tittered again. "So young to be tramping so far, but I envy you both. What freedom!"

Snowhawk bowed and stepped into the room. It *was* tiny, lit by a single wall-mounted lamp, but she was surprised to see that it wasn't empty. A thick duck-down quilt lay folded in one corner. Snowhawk's mouth twisted. She hadn't paid an extra copper to add a quilt to the room rental. But the spring nights were cold in these hills, especially in places near water. That quilt would be a welcome extra. She grinned at the thought of it, deep and soft, above and below her.

The lady's eyes batted as they moved from the quilt to Snowhawk.

"A little gift, no extra charge," the woman sighed. "I'm a sentimental old thing."

"Good lady, you are far from old." Snowhawk gave a grateful bow. "Thank you for this wonderful kindness, but why me? How do *I* make you feel sentimental?"

The innkeeper looked wistful as she stepped inside the room and closed the door.

"You look just like *me* when I was your age. That's all." She dropped her eyes humbly. "Though I never went traveling, looking for work at my brother's side, like you. I've never left this village. I was born here, and here I will die. No doubt, in this inn."

A lump rose in Snowhawk's throat. This poor woman was lonely. She probably had been all her life. Snowhawk looked about, avoiding the lady's eyes while she weighed a decision. *Why not?* What harm could come from repaying a kindness?

"Would you like to stay awhile?" Snowhawk offered gently. "Talk with me?"

The lady's face lit up. "You're very sweet, child. But are you not also weary?"

"Yes, but I'd love some company. Just for a while." Snowhawk sank into the *seiza* position, gesturing for the woman to also sit.

The innkeeper studied her with probing maternal eyes. "May I be very forward, miss?" Snowhawk frowned at the question but nodded slowly. "You and the lad...you don't look at all alike, you know." She tittered. "Forgive me. He's not really your brother, is he?"

"Why do you ask?" Snowhawk felt a twinge of irritation. This was too personal!

Staring down at the reed mat in front of her knees, the lady shrugged. "It's none of my business, I know. But if the two of you happened to be in some sort of trouble, on the run even"—she looked up, tears in her eyes—"I would let you both hide here."

Snowhawk met the lady's gaze, and her own chin

began to tremble. She was both surprised and overwhelmed by the woman's remarkable offer. This lady, a total stranger, was reliving her unhappy life—or at least trying to—through Snowhawk. How generous—and how sad. At once Snowhawk felt that she could guess the woman's history intuitively. The lady had probably never had children of her own, but her heart always yearned for a daughter to care for. In a way, she was a lot like Snowhawk, who had never known a mother. Snowhawk's eyes grew hot. Loneliness could be its own lifelong prison, as dark and cold as any castle's dungeon.

No wonder the woman had said so vehemently, "What freedom!" She had never escaped her miserable, empty life. Instead she'd been stuck here, alone, running this remote inn.

It was time to take a little chance. Snowhawk wiped her eyes and nodded. Since joining the Grey Light Order, she'd had two very satisfying girl-talks with Heron. But they had left her hungry for more. This gracious lady, perhaps a stand-in parent the *kami* had sent her way, might also give great motherly advice. Snowhawk sniffed. Yes, though in seeking it, she would have to be careful what she revealed. No details.

"You are so very kind." Snowhawk touched her

forehead to the matting. As she straightened up she saw the lady blush at the deep bow, normally given only to warlords or highly respected teachers. "In fact, we need no haven, but I would still be grateful to talk." She waved vaguely at the door. "About him, I suppose. Him and me and things."

"And I would be honored to listen." The lady wiped her eyes. "Perhaps even to offer advice." She looked demurely through her wet lashes. "If only an old fool's advice."

Snowhawk hung her head with shyness as she began. "It's true, he's not my brother, but we did…we do…work together." The innkeeper nodded patiently. "When we first met, he really helped me out. There was…anyway, I was in danger, and he came to my aid when I needed it. Since then we've worked closely…" She looked away, suddenly too self-conscious to go on.

"Let me guess," the innkeeper said astutely. "There's a problem between you now, isn't there?"

Snowhawk nodded. "He's become the best, the truest, friend I've ever had, but lately, well, I've failed him, failed our friendship. Now I'm afraid that I'll lose it! I even failed the"—she caught herself—"the people we've been working for." Her stare fell into her lap. "I've been angry, you see. Over things done to me."

The woman folded her arms slowly. "So either the boy or those you both worked for saw your anger." She watched Snowhawk nod. "Did you lose control?"

"To my shame, yes. But only *he* saw it." Snowhawk looked up quickly, her voice breaking. "And he covered for me. Kept it a secret. He remains loyal, even though I've now broken the rules twice! But I know I've disappointed him. In a way, betrayed him!"

The first tear rolled down her cheek. She forced herself to sit stiffly, breathe more slowly, regain control. Suddenly it all felt crazy. Why was she turning to a total stranger?

"Poor girl." The innkeeper shook her head. "This will make you feel better...a little truth, a little straight talk between women, huh?" Her expression grew firm. "If he's said nothing to your masters, he's still watching out for you, caring for you. Nobody continues to do that when someone has *really* let them down. They back off. No, for now at least, I wouldn't worry about things with him. What you *do* have to work on is this anger you speak of."

"You're so right," Snowhawk said. "I know it in my heart, even as you say it."

"Good, then listen to this and remember it." The lady thumbed over her shoulder. "Hear the river?

It flows, fed by springs and snow melting up in the mountains, no matter what the season. No matter what the weather. It's like ki, the life force itself, yeah?"

"True," Snowhawk murmured, wiping a cheek. Since she spoke of ki, the lady had to be a healer. That would fit. No wonder she was skilled at helping others to open up.

"The river also teaches us something of how to live life too. It always flows on. It accepts the rocks it was born in, the ones it was thrown against, then moves on." The innkeeper pointed directly at the spot between Snowhawk's eyes. "It's natural to get angry if you are wronged. But not to trap black energy in there. So don't. Forgive who you need to: yourself, them, the dog that bit you, the gods themselves. And be like the river. Find a way to just flow on."

Snowhawk filled her chest and slowly blew out a long breath. "I will try. That's the wisest advice I've ever heard. Thank you so much. For everything. Forgive me if now, I'm—"

"Trying not to yawn?" The lady gave her gentle titter. "Come, come, I can see you need to sleep now." She hesitated. "May I ask you a small favor, sweet child?"

"I'm hardly sweet." Snowhawk beamed at her. "But ask. What can I do for you?"

The innkeeper squirmed. "May I...tuck you in? As if you were my daughter?"

After forcing a new lump back down her throat, Snowhawk nodded warmly.

The lady lovingly prepared her bed. She positioned, folded, and then fluffed the quilt into a big puffy envelope that almost reached to the edges of the little room. Snowhawk smiled with anticipation. This just might be her best night's sleep in years.

Traveling as lightly as possible, she had brought no sleeping clothes. Snowhawk took off her pack and roll, keeping the sword hidden, and turned in, wearing her uniform to bed for extra warmth. Once she was snuggled inside the quilt, the kindly innkeeper literally tucked her in, smoothing its top edge into a perfect line that ran under her chin. Snowhawk grinned up at her. This was like being a child again. No, not again. Childhood had never been like this. Her face grew solemn. It was like being a child for the first time.

"One last thing," the woman said earnestly. "And I want you to remember this too, for as long as you live." Snowhawk nodded keenly. The lady smiled. "Despite what I do for a living, you should really listen to my advice. Take it on its own merits, okay?"

"Yes, of course. I promise I always will," Snowhawk pledged.

"Good." The innkeeper stood up and looked down at her. "That's settled then."

Without warning she bounded nimbly onto the quilt. As her feet landed, each perfectly on target, they stretched the quilt's top edge tight across Snowhawk's throat!

Wide-eyed with shock, heart pounding in terror, Snowhawk thrashed around and tried to kick upward through the quilt. It was impossible to raise her knees anywhere near enough. She tried to raise her arms. Immediately they became tangled. In seconds she realized that the quilt had been folded ingeniously. It was a restful-looking trap!

Looming above her, the woman maintained balance effortlessly, riding the tiny waves of each struggle with ease. Abruptly she thrust both hands into her kimono.

As Snowhawk spluttered and bucked, already gasping for air, the innkeeper's face changed. All traces of kindliness left it and every soft line became harsh. The streaks of grey vanished from the lady's hair and her eyes grew larger.

A completely different woman stood over her now, still middle-aged but aglow with a frightening vigor. Her appearance was more youthful, her stare bright...and filled with ruthless aggression. Snowhawk stopped struggling. She had to save her strength.

Think! And do it fast. Brute force was not going to get her out of this.

She always kept a tiny flat blade in a sheath deep inside her belly wrap. It was an old habit, instilled by her former clan. If cornered and disarmed, Fuma agents were expected to take their own life, the unwavering penalty for failing a mission.

If she could only get to it now, it might serve the opposite purpose. She could cut her way out of this quilt. Then, once free, she'd stand a very good chance because whoever this mystery *shinobi* attacker was, the scheming hag appeared not to be armed.

Hah! Snowhawk summoned up her resolve. No weapon, eh? This agent didn't know whom she was dealing with! That insulting underestimation was going to cost her.

The hovering woman raised one eyebrow. "Look what I have for you."

After sliding her feet out to stretch the fabric tighter across Snowhawk's throat, the stranger carefully drew twin war fans from her kimono. They instantly popped open, bright green with black iron spokes. Each spoke tapered into a sharp point.

Fixing her victim with a superior smile, the attacker flexed her fans.

"Don't resist me, child. Cuts from these fan spikes are very fine, very shallow. They won't kill you...just make you sleep for your journey home to Fuma... with Kagero."

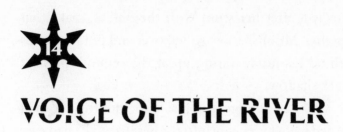

VOICE OF THE RIVER

Moonshadow yawned again and turned over on his bedroll. His room was tiny, its cool air still, the light dim now that most of the corridor lamps were also out. He stretched. Why, despite feeling wrung out, couldn't he sleep?

Was Snowhawk asleep yet?

It felt like an hour since the innkeeper had led her away to her room. He sighed. Snowhawk! It was probably just as well they hadn't been roomed next door to each other. Exhausted or not, they might have ended up talking for half the night. No, he scowled, after her stunt with the bullies, make that *arguing*. Moonshadow rolled over and put his hands behind his head, staring up at the ceiling's pool of black shadow.

Life was strange. In just two months she had turned from his enemy into the best friend he had ever had. But her transition from Fuma assassin to Grey Light Order agent wasn't exactly going smoothly. Was he right to cover for her, to keep giving her chances?

Surely Brother Eagle, if not all his trainers, had sensed Snowhawk's hidden problem? But if so, why was she out here in the field? Was it a kind of test? He narrowed his eyes. Maybe they were both being tested! She for ultimate loyalty, he for leadership instincts.

His doubts became a long sigh. *Moonshadow the mission leader.* So far, was he making the grade, or just making things worse with hasty decisions? He simply couldn't tell.

Another nagging concern made him frown. What would happen when the White Nun met her? Would the great seer heal Snowhawk's hurt and rage, then validate her as the latest member of the Grey Light Order? That would be wonderful! But what if instead—

His hearing picked up a distant, muffled sound.

What was that? Moonshadow rose up on one

elbow, opening his mouth wide to stretch his hearing even farther. A sound of impact came over the background mutter of the river. Moonshadow flinched. It came from the direction Snowhawk and the innkeeper had gone!

He vaulted from his bedroll to his feet.

So that was why they had been roomed so far apart in an empty inn. His eyes flashed.

Another ambush!

Quickly he slid open the door. Louder sounds now, again from the river side of the inn, pierced the thin walls and paper screens. Multiple strong crashes, the unmistakable signs of a violent struggle in progress.

Moonshadow ran down the corridor, ever louder *thud*s and *whack*s leading him.

At the end of the passage lay two sliding doors, one to the right, one to the left.

The right-hand door was made up of strips of cedar, framing opaque waxed paper. Through it came the diffused glow of a wall lamp, and across its squares ran wild, shifting shadows. His heart began pounding. Snowhawk *was* under attack.

Opposite her room, the left-hand door—made of solid, dark wood—led outside.

It led to the river. With that thought, an intense wave

of light-headedness rolled over him. Moonshadow's legs turned weak and he sank to one knee in the corridor, just paces from Snowhawk's room.

Go outside, a voice in his head echoed. It was his own voice, but not his thoughts.

Moonshadow grunted and shook his head hard, trying to make it disappear.

See what's outside, the voice said firmly. *You know you want to.*

"No, I don't," he said aloud through gritted teeth. "Snowhawk—"

Suddenly he *did* want to go outside. Leaning on the corridor wall, Moonshadow struggled back to his feet. With each breath, the irrational urge to use the door on the *left* expanded like a smoke bomb's cloud, attacking his reason, willing him to obey.

No! Moonshadow argued with the compulsion. *I will not.* He cursed, hanging his head. He would *force himself* to stride, one grinding step at a time, to *her* door.

Moonshadow looked up at the end of the corridor. His face creased with horror.

Now there was only one door: the door that led outside. Opposite it, where Snowhawk's paper-squared door had been, stood a solid wall of heavy-looking dark timber reinforced with vertical beams.

Moonshadow blinked, reeling with confusion. What was happening? The door had vanished!

Go outside now, the voice urged. *To the river. Then you will understand.*

His feet began to move of their own accord. Moonshadow looked down at them, his mouth twisting. Another wave of light-headedness struck him, stronger than the last.

He staggered forward and fell against the door leading outside, to the river.

"Snowhawk," Moonshadow murmured. His hands gripped the solid sliding door. He had no say in it; he was going outside, though with all his heart and mind he didn't want to.

A dreadful awareness dawned on him. Where it came from, he had no idea.

He was going down to the river. It was simply meant to be. It was his fate.

There, something ancient, inhuman, and nasty would be waiting for him.

Moonshadow tried to say her name again, but instead, he opened the door and walked toward his doom.

CRAMPED COMBAT

A sound like a whistle pierced the air.

Kagero's eyes flared with surprise. The tip of a small, flat blade flashed along a perfectly straight line toward her feet, the quilt peeling open behind it. Kagero hunched closer and peered.

Grunting, sweaty, and red-cheeked, Snowhawk drove the knife up in line with her own shoulder, cutting the taut band of fabric pinning her throat.

Its last bundle of threads gave way with a *snap*. Snowhawk hissed and glared up at Kagero, anticipation glazing her eyes. The bounty hunter hesitated, as if in disbelief, as her prey dropped the knife.

Snowhawk arched her back, brought her knees to her chest, and planted her palms at her sides. With a roar she swung her feet up and then thrust backward, rolling into a handstand that quickly became a double back-kick.

One foot glanced off Kagero's wrist, ramming her fans together and off to one side. The other foot connected hard directly under her chin. Kagero stumbled backward, snatched at her upper throat, and coughed. Her eyes narrowed furiously.

"I hope that hurt!" Snowhawk landed on both feet, snatched up the knife, and skipped sideways to her pack and unused bedroll. Watching Kagero warily, she sank to one knee and thrust a hand into the mouth of the rolled-up reed traveler's mat.

"Stop! You *are* full of surprises, child." The bounty hunter grimaced hard and raised her fans, blocking the door in a warlike stance. "But don't you dare try drawing that sword." Deftly snagging the edge of her lapel with one fan, Kagero pulled her kimono top open a finger's length.

Snowhawk saw a pouch inside, bristling with curve-bladed Fuma *shuriken*.

"Let's not escalate the weapons." Kagero winked. "You're worth more alive."

"Slimy old dragon," Snowhawk shouted. "I trusted you! I let you give me advice!"

"Aw, so *now* I'm old, you insincere little squirrel!" Kagero curled her lip. "And don't disrespect my advice. On the road home to the Fuma's mountain fortress, I'll give you some more if you like. What? Don't make that face! Even people I've later killed have said I give excellent advice. I once helped one of my employers with his marriage!"

"And later slew his wife, I bet!" Snowhawk felt herself erupt with fury. It was beyond her control, *again*. "May death find all the Fuma! Don't you ever call those rat-hole caves *home*! You want to go home? I'll send you!" She heard her own voice arc into an explosive, nerve-stretching shriek. Its intensity disturbed her, yet the rage plumed on. "I'll send you on your final journey! Across the River Sai to the land of the dead!"

Kagero's face again betrayed surprise as Snowhawk leapt at her, flying fast and high, slashing wildly with her tiny knife. The bounty hunter closed the fans and ducked, turning sideways and rolling along the reed mat into the heap of slashed quilting.

Snowhawk hurtled over her, crashing into the door of cedar planks and paper.

It tore and splintered apart, debris whirling around Snowhawk as she burst through it and landed in the corridor. She cartwheeled down the passageway, flicking small broken sticks of wood into the air. Using only one arm as she wheeled, Snowhawk slashed behind her with the knife in case Kagero was pursuing closely. She landed and turned. Her attacker had not followed. Why?

Panting, eyes on the doorway, Snowhawk waited for her nemesis to appear. Still nothing. Instinctively, she backed away down the corridor, knees bent, feet gliding slowly without making a sound.

Her heart had already skipped several beats. Now the full realization of her plight made it pound like a distant war drum. Unless her attacker was telling a pointless lie, she was facing *the* infamous Kagero. Long ago, among the Fuma, she'd heard of this veteran *shinobi*, raised and trained by her former clan, now a man catcher and killer for hire. Kagero had been one of only a handful of agents to attain elite status, so respected by their masters, it was said, that they were permitted—for an almost impossible sum— to buy their own independence from the clan. On hearing such tales, Snowhawk had wondered whether agents that powerful were truly allowed to buy their freedom out of respect. Or was it that even their masters came to fear them? This Kagero was certainly a frightening opponent, and one with a unique approach to the art of ambush!

Why had she not sensed the presence of *shinobi* energy when her disguised attacker first appeared? Why wasn't she feeling it now? Snowhawk ground her teeth together. And what in all the heavens made Kagero think she could be a stalking predator *and* a roving wisewoman at the same time?

Give your prey *advice*? That was as insulting as it was crazy!

What was that? Snowhawk's head inclined quickly. Her eyes flicked up.

The white wooden ceiling panel directly above her rose. It flashed to one side, vanishing. For an instant blackness replaced it, then she saw the soles of white cotton *tabi* boots and the ripple of a silk kimono's hem. Out of the dark ceiling Kagero plunged, feet aimed for Snowhawk's shoulders.

Diving into a forward roll, Snowhawk just avoided the attack. As she regained her feet, Kagero landed heavily in the passageway behind her. The bounty hunter straightened her knees and bounded forward with uncanny speed, snapping one of her fans downward, eyes narrowing at her target. Snowhawk howled as the closed war fan struck from behind, rapping her knuckles so hard that she was forced to release her knife.

It twirled to the passageway floor, sticking in the wood with a dull *thok*.

Snowhawk twisted around, tensing her hands into blades, fingers locked together. She launched a flurry of jabs at nerve points on the bounty hunter's neck, but Kagero parried them effortlessly with the closed fans. Snowhawk winced as hard iron spokes slapped each blow off course, bruising her wrists and forearms. Kagero swung a fan at her face, making her lean back. With a gasp Snowhawk realized she'd been cunningly driven off balance.

Kagero didn't waste the chance she had created. Dropping into a crouch, she spun on the ball of one foot, locking her other leg out to snag Snowhawk's ankles.

Her legs swept from beneath her with tremendous force, Snowhawk almost flipped upside down. Shoulders first, she slammed into the floorboards with a yelp of pain.

Darting forward nimbly, Kagero stamped for her enemy's throat but, with a determined grunt, Snowhawk rolled out from under the attack. Scrambling to her feet, she backed away.

Scheming desperately, Snowhawk eyed the

corridor, noting the height of its ceiling, the width between its walls. Kagero cleverly blocked the center, but there had to be a way to squeeze past her and get to Moonshadow. Together, they'd stand a far better chance!

The bounty hunter glanced to her left and right, then smiled and raised an eyebrow.

Cursing her careless signals, Snowhawk retreated faster. Her enemy knew her plan!

Kagero started to whirl, arms extended, twin fans flashing as she turned. Like a human top she advanced on Snowhawk, the revolving iron fan tips just missing the walls. Snowhawk scrambled back, crouched low, and scuttled at Kagero. Building up speed, she threw herself onto her side and slid along the floorboards feetfirst. With a determined roar, Snowhawk crashed into Kagero's turning ankles, knocking her off balance.

The bounty hunter's spin broke and slowed into a turning stumble. Snowhawk leapt up and made for the tiny knife. But Kagero regained her footing with astonishing speed and ran backward, cutting her opponent off.

Gasping for each breath, Snowhawk took her eyes from Kagero to glance at the embedded blade. Was it dug in deep? Could it be snatched out?

The glance lasted a second too long.

Kagero took a quick, nimble stride and then jumped high into the air. A mighty double-footed kick broke Snowhawk's half-formed block, slamming into her chest.

Snowhawk's head snapped forward as she was flung along the corridor. She skidded on her back, through broken sticks and torn paper, up to her room's doorway.

Her neck throbbed; her head went light. Snowhawk knew at once that she was badly stunned. She opened her eyes, groaning loudly as Kagero landed on her chest, settling down heavily, weight spread to pin her to the floor. The iron-spoked fans hovered at her throat. Kagero smiled down at her, as if daring her to move, even to flinch.

Snowhawk's face ran with sweat. Despite the terror of the moment, she found herself marveling at her strange opponent. The infamous Kagero was no kid, yet she was astoundingly fast and able to mete out powerful blows. Her incredible disguise and fan tricks were unique.

With eyes locked on those menacing fans, Snowhawk swallowed. At least Kagero wanted her alive. What a lucky break! That agenda restricted the veteran *shinobi* to nonlethal techniques, which probably cut her bag of tricks by half. Without such a handicap, Snowhawk was certain that Kagero would have killed her by now.

She rallied her courage. Every warrior had at least one weakness. Even Kagero would have chinks in her armor. Snowhawk just needed time to find them. She *had to* stay conscious! If Kagero succeeded in putting her to sleep with those fans, it was over. Where was Moonshadow? He would have easily heard the noise of this fight. Since he hadn't come to her aid, did that mean he was already dead? A pang of distress clawed at her. She fought it off; Moonshadow might just be drugged or otherwise delayed. Might someone else come to investigate the din and break this up?

"Did you kill the real innkeeper?" Snowhawk scowled up at her attacker.

The bounty hunter panted heavily. "She's sleeping off the tea I gave her." Kagero huffed and tossed her head with mock indignation. "You think I'd kill *anybody* for free?"

Kagero's eyes were momentarily off her. Snowhawk saw her chance and took it. Her hands flashed up, each grabbing a wrist and pushing hard, forcing the fans and their drug-coated tips back, away from her throat. Kagero grunted, leaning forward, trying to return them to Snowhawk's neck.

As the two pushed and shoved, each grunting and

sucking in air, Kagero's eyes, filled with black menace and determination, lingered on Snowhawk's.

Your biggest mistake so far. Snowhawk smiled as she forced her next breath steady. Her stomach turned hot. Her heart was already pounding, but now it thrummed even more intensely as she activated her most specialized skill. Either Kagero had forgotten whom she was dealing with, or the Fuma, perhaps overawed by Kagero's reputation, had stupidly failed to warn her!

Snowhawk was one of a tiny handful of ninja women who had learned to forcibly hypnotize attackers. Even rarer than the gift itself were those who proved naturally immune to it. As Snowhawk felt familiar invisible energy surge from her eyes to Kagero's, she prayed her enemy wasn't one of them.

"*Kunoichi* hypnosis, eh? Pah!" Kagero leered. "Don't you try that kids' stuff on me!" Her face was full of confidence, but abruptly one eyelid twitched and then sagged.

Snowhawk felt herself losing physical strength fast. Unleashing her special power always had that effect. The fans, trembling now in Kagero's hands, moved closer.

She doggedly fired a second bolt of energy into her foe's eyes.

"It won't work!" Kagero snorted, forcing one fan right up to her throat. Iron spoke-tips danced a fingernail's width from Snowhawk's skin.

Gulping in a desperate breath, her mind frenzied and heart racing, Snowhawk loosed a third bolt. At once she felt her stomach cool. That was all she had.

Her wide eyes flicked desperately between the fan spokes and Kagero. It wasn't going to work! She was about to be cut, drugged, and then dragged back to her old life in hell.

BEWARE OF THE KAPPA

Moonshadow stood on the riverbank, rushing water at his feet. Green-tinged starlight lit the nightscape around him, drenching everything with its peculiar color.

The river flickered constantly with splashes of emerald-silver as if a vast school of fish teemed in it. Beyond its banks, a thickly wooded hillside climbed away from the town, tiger-striped with the shadows of tall trees. Moonshadow's eyes hunted for movement.

No, not there. The voice was back in his head. *Down here, look down.*

As he did, the water at his feet erupted in all directions and a manlike form hurtled up from the river at him. He caught a glimpse of mottled skin, tangled hair, claws.

Moonshadow tried evading to his left, but the unknown creature moved too quickly. For a split second his view of the riverbank was upside down, then, in a flash of bubbles, he was underwater. It had him by one leg and was dragging him to the bottom.

Looking down, Moonshadow flinched as he saw what gripped him: a Kappa!

The most infamous of legendary water spirits, Kappas were known for mischief and murder. At times they were content just to startle those crossing rivers or wading as they fished. But, quite randomly, they also attacked and drowned people. Though even Brother Badger said they were just a myth, there had been many sightings, all with similar descriptions — but none quite as terrifying as *this* beast.

He watched it swim strenuously, towing him down into the river's black depths. The Kappa had a shell on its back very much like a turtle's, and long, seaweed-like hair streamed behind its head as it powered downward.

The crown of its head was hollow, a transparent bowl. It trapped iridescent white bubbles that bobbed in a sea of black brain fluid. The deeper they went, the more the bubbles roiled and multiplied, as if the increasing pressure of the depth stimulated them. The Kappa's sinewy grey-green arms and legs were spotted with patches of what looked like algae, and its fingers and toes, tipped with long pale claws, were heavily webbed.

Moonshadow raised his free foot and stamped down at the creature's wrist. Would it have the same wrist release nerve as humans? Thwarted by the drag of the water, he missed it, striking instead the clawed hand that gripped his ankle. The Kappa slowed its descent and looked up at him. Moonshadow gaped at his first clear glimpse of the water monster's face. It had a turtlelike beak, a tiny two-holed stump of a nose, and large eyes similar to a frog's. Each eye was divided by a silvery slit for a pupil. As he stared, its turtle beak peeled open, and between the gummy folds of its mouth Moonshadow saw a flash of rows of concealed teeth. Every tiny, dagger-sharp tooth slanted backward.

He stamped at the Kappa's wrist again. This time his foot found its mark. The Kappa's grip broke and Moonshadow kicked wildly for the surface. Rising fast, he sensed the creature close behind him. He drove himself on, faster, up for the green light.

Moonshadow burst from the water in a spray of foam and scrambled up the riverbank, sliding and snatching at the muddy grass. Why was he not gasping for air? He touched his clothing, then his head. He was completely dry. How? And where was his attacker?

As he looked around warily, the surface of the river erupted again. The Kappa soared from the water, and Moonshadow stumbled backward as it landed right in front of him with a soggy *flop*.

The creature loomed, its silvery pupils dilating as they focused on Moonshadow's face.

"Cucumbers," the Kappa said, its voice low, wet, and sludgy. "Do you have any?"

"What?" Such a crazy question! Moonshadow shook his head. "No, why would I?"

The Kappa's head swayed to one side as if conceding his point. "Then you die."

It lunged at him, beak splaying open impossibly wide, each row of teeth snapping. Moonshadow hurtled back, but the Kappa darted after him and seized him by the shoulders. With overwhelming strength it pinned him to the riverbank. Its head angled, lank hair swishing as the Kappa prepared to bite into his neck. The beak stretched, rows of teeth inside it working busily, gleaming as they came closer.

Strangely weak and struggling vainly, Moonshadow closed his eyes. There was no escape. It had him; *this was it!*

He threw back his head and gave in to panic, shrieking long and loud.

STRANGE NEW WARFARE

The green-tinged starlight and everything under it was swallowed by black curtains that fluttered in from all directions. Moonshadow felt as though he was tumbling inside one of them, wrapped in its dark folds. With a bump, something solid met his back.

Warily he forced an eye open. For a few seconds, he could make no sense of what he saw. Then suddenly he knew it was real. Moonshadow let out a moan of intense relief.

The Kappa attack had been a nightmare, that was all. He was lying safely on the floor of his own room.

Snowhawk was hunched over him, shaking his shoulders. Her face was red, clothes dark with sweat, but she appeared unharmed. Moonshadow turned his head, chest still heaving with emotion. Snowhawk had relit the lamp in his room. Had she been here for some time? He peered around. Her pack and bedroll lay on the matting.

She released Moonshadow's shoulders and he sat up. Pain stabbed his temples.

"Thank the gods." She sighed with relief. "I thought I might have been too late."

"What…what just happened?" Moonshadow rubbed his eyes.

"We were both attacked, in very different ways. As soon as you can walk, we must get out of here." Snowhawk wiped sweat from her brow with the back of her hand. "While the woman who attacked me is still asleep in the corridor outside my room."

He stared at her. "That sweet old innkeeper attacked you?"

Snowhawk's face darkened. "What you saw was an Old Country disguise…a trick. Underneath it was the *shinobi* who attacked me. She called herself…*Kagero*."

"*The* Kagero?" Moonshadow frowned. "Not the infamous freelance *shinobi* who—"

"I don't know." Snowhawk began dragging him to his feet. "I still can't believe she was the *real* Kagero, the same agent I used to hear Fuma trainers brag about."

"Why not?" He looked around vaguely, massaging his temples.

"Because I'm still breathing," Snowhawk said. "Come on, get your stuff."

They fled the inn, and Snowhawk led him north out of town, keeping to the shadows of the roadside trees. She looked and sounded a little haggard, but still moved with her usual flitting agility. Moonshadow struggled to keep up with her and felt that now *he* moved clumsily, making as much noise as an ordinary man. When Snowhawk finally slowed her pace, a good bow shot from town, he told her how he felt.

"That feeling will pass." She pointed to his forehead. "It's called 'the haze.' It's a side effect of the attack." Snowhawk gave a marveling sigh. "When you let out that cry, I realized what was going on. It looked close. If I had tried waking you a moment later…"

He grabbed her arm. "What *was* going on? What just happened to me?"

Snowhawk hung her head as if choosing her next words carefully. "Have you ever heard of the Fuma

Death Dream skill?" He shook his head. "I'll bet your Grey Light Order trainers have. It's a very rare Old Country science. I only know about it because Clan Fuma once tried to teach it to me."

"Tried?" Moonshadow glanced back along the road, checking for signs of pursuit.

"Yes. Tried, and failed. Or rather *I* did." She shrugged. "They said my temperament made me unsuitable. So they switched me to learning *shinobi* hypnosis, which I picked up easily." Snowhawk's mouth twitched into a half smile. "Strong natures usually do."

"The Fuma Death Dream—how does it work?"

"It's a mind attack that comes at you in the form of a dream. Actually, it's a certain kind of trance your attacker forces upon you and then guides. It can be used in daylight on a conscious subject as well as on a sleeper. The rules are simple: if you cannot defeat the nightmare creature sent to attack you and nobody wakes you in time, your heart stops beating while you're in the trance dream."

"What?" Remembering the fury of the Kappa's attack, Moonshadow wrapped his arms around himself. "You mean it can *kill*? It's not just to frighten or distract?"

Snowhawk shook her head. "No, but to master it, you need a high degree of deep-mind stillness...

great control over your thoughts. Perhaps that's why I wasn't a good candidate." She gave a low, hollow laugh. "After proving unsuitable for that science, many of the Fuma told me I was useless, only good for running errands to the nearest villages. But that kind of talk stopped smartly when I tried out my *kunoichi* hypnosis for the first time...on one of my trainers." She glowered. "That shut them up."

"Yes, well." Moonshadow nodded wearily. "I myself know just how good at it you are." They exchanged knowing glances and Snowhawk grinned. Moonshadow rolled his eyes. "First time you and I were alone in daylight," he grumbled, "do you realize how long I slept?"

"We weren't on the same side back then, that morning in the stable." She took his arm, and even in the scant light he could see her face tense with worry. "I'm afraid there's one other piece of bad news about the Fuma Death Dream skill."

"Oh, great." Moonshadow checked the road again, then stared at her. "Now what? Even if you do get woken up in time, your head eventually explodes?"

"Worse," she replied humorlessly. "You know how I can sense the presence of other *shinobi* better than you can?"

He nodded. "Much better than I can."

"Well, those trained as dream assassins also learn a related skill. A very difficult but useful one. Again, only the still of mind can develop it." Snowhawk took a deep breath. "They neutralize the sensing powers of all nearby *shinobi* before they attack."

"Are you serious?" A deep shudder went through him. "That's actually possible?"

"As tonight proves. A dream assassin went after you and in the process stopped *me* sensing that the innkeeper was really a *shinobi* in disguise."

"A dream assassin? Don't you mean Kagero?"

"No, because your nightmare continued even after I had left her unconscious. That means somebody else, someone we didn't even see, used the Death Dream skill on you."

"If that's the case...if we've an unknown enemy who can stop your sensing power..." Moonshadow shook his head slowly. "We might as well be deaf."

"We *are* deaf now. And we'll *stay* deaf on this mission." Snowhawk raised a fist. "Unless we find that dream killer first!"

Moonshadow gave a bitter chuckle as they turned to go on. "Why work so hard? Isn't it obvious? No matter what we do, he or she is going to find *us*."

A rooster crowed three times in the distance, then the first bird warbled sweetly.

Brother Badger's eyes opened wide. He sat up sharply on his bedroll. It was still dark, but the cold air held that tang of promise; a fresh morning would soon be born.

Saru-San jumped from his basket at the foot of Badger's bed, snorting, looking in all directions. Scratching one armpit, its face screwed up, the monkey turned a circle.

Badger grunted. "Calm down, there's nothing. It was just me."

The monkey stared at him, head sagging to one side. Saru-San lifted his tail and passed gas with a long wheezing sound that ended with a dull *futt*. Then he lowered his tail, sighed very much the way Badger did, and fell sideways back into his basket.

Badger clambered to his feet with his nose pinched, his mind clearing fast.

He hated these moments. He would go to bed while working on some problem, be it tactical, historical, or a matter of translation. Falling asleep, the riddle still unsolved, he'd look forward to an unbroken night of deep, dreamless slumber.

Instead, *this* phenomenon would occur. And here it was again. He had woken up because some other layer of his mind had been working on the problem while he slept. Its solution had now reached the conscious Badger. He wasn't sure how it worked. Had he borne the answer from some already forgotten dream? He grunted again. No matter. Wherever this idea came from, it was going to be tested.

Badger released his nostrils, tightened the light sleeping kimono around him, and prepared a paper lantern on a stick. He lit its candle with a flint kit and hoisted the lantern high. Muttering absently, Badger crossed the corridor from his room into the archives.

There was not a stir from the rest of the Grey Light Order's Edo monastery. That won't keep for long, Badger told himself. He knew that when living among those who were *shinobi*-trained, even stone and wooden walls might as well be paper. Someone, or all of them, would hear him. At least they knew his step and they weren't the *throw* shuriken *first, ask questions later* types. Though Japan had its share of them, for sure.

He glided past the door to the map-drying room and between tall rows of shelves, the glow of his lantern stroking the banks of scrolls and wooden trays of flip books.

A gleam caught Badger's attention. He stopped and reached for its source. Filling his chest, he held the prized possession up to one eye. His brand-new foreign magnifying glass, a personal gift from the Shogun. Gripping it possessively, he paced quickly into a different aisle of the archives, lamp high again, eyes hunting.

He found the month's incoming dispatches, locked the lantern into a holder set between the shelves, then raised a stitched packet of handmade papers to his eyes. Badger swept the magnifying glass over the topmost paper. The message's characters leapt forward, instantly vivid.

Badger pressed the magnifying glass to his chest. "These modern days," he murmured. "Another wondrous device. Doubtful it could ever be improved upon."

The wondrous device would enable close scrutiny of the stack's uppermost message. He examined it, the last dispatch they had received, the one that had sent the junior agents on their way. Then Badger held the stack of papers and his eyeglass up to the lamp, carefully examining the top message's paper itself. He flipped to the next message, then more quickly to the one after it. Badger looked up, muttering a scholarly curse. His hunch was right. If only he'd seen this earlier! Before Moonshadow and Snowhawk had departed. But now—

He grabbed the lantern and left. Pacing quickly through a doorway and out into a long corridor, Badger came face-to-face with Eagle and Heron. Heron shielded her sensitive eyes from the lantern's light.

"Aw, despite the heavy footsteps, it's not an invading panda after all," Eagle said coolly, squinting at him. "How can a brain that can speak and read so many languages simply not comprehend *stealth*?"

Badger bowed, his papers and glass under one arm, lantern stick under the other. "I'm sorry I alarmed you. However, the matter is serious. I was coming to call a meeting."

Eagle dismissed his apology with a wave. "We're all half asleep and grumpy...."

"Speak for yourself," Heron said softly. "Brother Badger. What's happened?"

"It's our controversial last message." Badger raised the stitched packet of papers. "I examined the document yet again, this time comparing the paper itself with that of the earlier dispatches. It's different." Heron and Eagle exchanged looks.

"That paper," Heron said thoughtfully, "is handmade...."

Badger thrust his magnifying glass and the messages forward.

"Handmade, high quality, and quite distinctive, with tiny white pulp threads in it," he said excitedly. He saw Heron cringe at his escalating volume. Badger winced and inwardly vowed to restrain himself, then continued, keeping his voice low. "Our last incoming wasn't written on the paper I supplied our network with. Whoever wrote it used a similar type of paper, but look for yourself, through this device: they *are* different."

Eagle turned his head a quarter. "Brother Mantis approaches." He smiled.

Badger could hear nothing, but he was used to that. He sighed impatiently.

"Groundspider is right behind him." Heron grinned, her eyes narrow.

"Huh." Badger clicked his tongue. "Even *I* can hear *him*." Of course, he couldn't.

Mantis and Groundspider materialized out of the gloom behind Eagle.

As always, Brother Mantis appeared focused, alert. Groundspider was the opposite. His eyes were red and watery, his hair a small mountain of knots. He stared listlessly.

Eagle quickly outlined Badger's discovery while Badger nodded proudly. His leader's next words, however, proved a little deflating. Badger scowled at them.

"Unfortunately," Eagle yawned, "this is all still somewhat inconclusive." Disagreement flooded Heron's face. Evidently sensing it, Eagle looked around at the whole group. "Come now, consider: its explanation *may* prove quite innocent."

"Or tactical." Mantis folded his arms. "I say a cunning enemy—I think we can safely guess which one—has found a weak point in one of our lines of communication. Somehow, somewhere, they have replaced one of our messages with this...substitute."

Heron nodded quickly. "And so deftly that our chain of runners didn't know it."

Mantis tapered his stare. "Strategically, it makes great sense. If I were going to assail a shadow force like the Grey Light Order, I would start by isolating and slaying the least experienced. After that, work my way up. Wouldn't you, Brother Eagle?"

"Yes, of course I would, but...ah!" Eagle threw up his hands. "What you say *does* make great sense, but before I can act on it decisively, I need more. *Anything* more!"

Groundspider was finally waking up. "You mean nobody's really after the White Nun?" He scratched his head. "They're after us?"

Heron gestured at Badger's papers. "Separate the latest one." She turned to Eagle. "I'm not the White Nun, but it's she who has been teaching me this technique. Just as you and Moonshadow can experience animal residues after a joining, so can the White Nun read residues left on paper, garments, even weapons, by the hands of men. Residues that betray much about the owner, or at least the strongest one to *touch* that thing. It's a science that will take me years to master, even with the great sage's guidance."

"So I don't know all your secrets." Eagle beamed. Badger frowned uncomfortably.

"And since I am a woman," said Heron with the hint of a smile, "you never will."

Mantis looked away with a knowing grin. Badger rolled his eyes. He had never grown accustomed to Heron and Eagle's relationship. It was all too revoltingly...*sweet*.

Heron took the paper from Badger, folded it into a starlike pattern, then pressed it to her forehead. "If

184

only the White Nun were here! I am not skilled yet, and really shouldn't be attempting this so early in my training. I may sense nothing, or read the message wrongly, adding to our confusion. I wouldn't even have offered to try, but for the grave situation...." She went quiet, closing her eyes. Everyone waited, watching intently. Her hand dropped. The folded message fell and she caught it. "I can discern but one thing." Heron looked around with a shrug. "It's not much. A feeling. An emotion."

"Which emotion?" Mantis asked quickly.

Heron scowled. *"Gloating."*

"Gloating?" Eagle repeated, a tiny glow of anger in his eyes.

"I can tell you no more," she said. "I know only that this feeling was left in the paper, a residue so strong it probably came from the very hand that brushed the message."

"It is enough for a start." Eagle thatched his fingers. "Enough for me to act on."

Badger joined in the collective sigh of relief.

"Who was gloating?" Groundspider murmured, rubbing his eyes. He was ignored.

Eagle held up a hand. "But I want more, mind you! I must confirm our course of action even as we take it. Heron, please seek one of your prescient dreams. Is your training not more advanced in *that* Old Country science?"

She nodded. "A little. I am still far from mature in the art, but I will do my best."

A flash of great uncertainty crossed her dignified face. "You know the problem. At this stage of my development, I foresee *true nonsense*: facts and lies, haphazardly mixed. It's of limited value, as are the riddle phrases that pass through my mind on waking."

"Muddled and weird or not," Badger pointed out, "they've already served us well."

"Indeed," Mantis said. "So do go after them too! We'll unravel the meanings later."

"Brother Groundspider," Eagle whispered, "I need your very best. And now."

Badger marveled at Eagle's power to motivate as Groundspider snapped to attention and bowed, his eyes quickly brightening. So the junior oaf *could* sharpen up fast when he really needed to. Badger sighed. Astounding, given the nature of young people.

"Muster reinforcements," Eagle told Groundspider, "every available, experienced agent currently in Edo. Even reliable freelancers if you must. Then hurry north."

"If we go after them," Groundspider said slowly, "moving so as not to be noticed, will we get there in time to do any good?"

"Find a way," Eagle said firmly. Groundspider bowed and turned to go.

Heron intercepted him, snatching his arm. "Don't let the task daunt you," she whispered in Groundspider's ear. "Just use everybody's *greatest* untapped gift." He frowned back at her. "Imagination," Heron added.

Groundspider hurried away. Mantis followed. Badger took in the worry lining Heron's face, the tension in Eagle's eyes.

No one was going to say it, but the horrible truth was on everybody's mind.

If the mission was a trap, their most promising young agents were as good as dead.

MOUNTAIN OF THE WHITE NUN

Snowhawk and Moonshadow stood side by side, studying the small forest in their path.

A steep green incline rose behind it, sprouting rocky outcrops and scattered stands of trees as it climbed into a ceiling of patchy white cloud.

They had followed the winding road north from the river town until an hour after dawn. Then, exhausted, they had crawled behind a natural hedge of bamboo covering the mouth of a nearby gully. Snowhawk had slept deeply, but Moonshadow had been fitful and restless. Twice he had woken after dreaming of being drawn to the riverbank beneath green-tinged stars. In each dream, though he had seen no terrifying Kappa, he'd sensed its sinister, lurking presence just before waking with a gasp.

When Snowhawk finally roused him at noon, two things amazed Moonshadow: that he'd eventually gone to sleep at all and that he had slept for so long in daylight.

Now, after another two hours of tramping, they had finally reached the end of the road. It petered out at the base of the very mountain on which the White Nun lived.

"This is a strange place," Snowhawk said, looking up the slope behind the trees. "Have you ever seen morning mist hang around until midafternoon?" She squinted. "Or is it actually a low cloud bank? Weird! At least it's breaking up."

"Whichever it is, it's odd," he agreed. "Something else is too. When I was learning all about poisons and sleeping drugs from Heron, she also taught me about trees." Moonshadow pointed at the forest ahead. "Look, see how rocky the ground is? And the soil looks poor too, all leached out. So tree and shrub growth should be poor."

He waved his hand toward the closest band of forest. There stood strong oaks, beeches, firs, and spruces. Scattered between them, red and black pines. Hinoki cypress too. And even a mighty red cedar, pushing lesser trees aside in the forest's center.

"So many varieties." Moonshadow frowned. "And each so healthy. If there's a lot of rock in the ground and the soil's bad, then why does this forest grow so well?"

A wary look crossed Snowhawk's face. "Let's just move away from the road, get the haunted forest behind us, and push up this mountain a bit. Then we can breathe easier; take a break and talk about it."

Moonshadow recalled the briefing in Edo and the *tell you later* look that she had given him. He stared at the trees and swallowed. This forest was supposed to be haunted, yet Snowhawk wanted the place behind them before she would speak of it. Why? He licked dry lips. It was not a good sign, but since she knew the forest, he would do things her way. Besides, if he demanded information now, it'd probably start an angry argument!

A natural corridor broke the green wall. Peering into it, Moonshadow could see there was a chain of clearings from the lip of the forest to the rise of the slope.

"That way, then. We should run until we clear it," he said quickly, "in case of another ambush. The path through there is good, but that dense cover on the left and right could be hiding anything."

Snowhawk nodded. "Yes, let's make it quick. Wise precaution."

Walking behind her toward the cleft in the wall of trees, Moonshadow sighed gratefully. He was glad *that one* had been settled quickly, and without debate.

He stepped up beside her. Snowhawk shoved his arm, creasing her nose. "You ready to run?" He nodded and her face snapped into a grim, wary mask. "Then be ready for anything!" She pointed ahead and sprinted for the opening in the forest. "Last one there washes Saru for a month!"

"Hey, that's unfair!" Moonshadow broke into a run and quickly fell in a few strides behind her. Snowhawk zigzagged between tree stumps and high banks of ferns, vaulted over rocks and pits in the ground, even ducked low branches to come up running. Moonshadow closed the gap between them, glancing uneasily left and right whenever he could. Snowhawk dodged a branch, thick with folds of bright red fungus. Moonshadow looked up as he cleared it. That overhead cloud was breaking up quickly now, wisps sinking into the forest to drift on tiny eddies through the trees.

His nostrils flared at strong odors, the must of plant decay, the spike of pine. Snowhawk suddenly glanced back at him. "Am I going too fast?" she panted. "I keep forgetting you're only a boy!"

He grunted and drove himself forward, overtaking her. "Only a *what*?" Moonshadow quipped back. "Can't hear you...from out front here!"

An instant later Snowhawk appeared at his side, her red face steely and competitive. "Weak ears *and* legs, hey?" She flashed a wicked smile. "Shall I carry you? No? Later, then!" With little apparent effort, Snowhawk streaked ahead to reclaim the lead.

"Cheat!" Moonshadow forced himself to run faster. "It's not fair...those long legs!"

They passed the great red cedar and one by one hurdled a jagged tangle of fallen trees and hollow logs. As Moonshadow landed just behind Snowhawk, something brittle imploded under his foot in a puff of white powder. He grunted, making her turn.

Moonshadow froze on the spot. "What am I on? Is it a trap?" he whispered.

She glanced down. "No. It's a skull, that's all. Let's go!"

Thinking she meant a wolf or bear skull, he looked down. The shattered remains of a human skull splayed from under his sandal. He looked up. Bones everywhere, poking from the forest's carpet of damp pine needles and rotting leaves. He made out ribs, a smaller skull, a complete spine. His stomach began knotting. What horrors had taken place here?

A sudden impulse made him peer to his left.

Between clumps of soaring trees, a narrow natural corridor stretched into the distance. It vanished into a sliver of drifting cloud. A figure stood out against the white curtain. Moonshadow blinked and hunched forward, staring compulsively. Not one figure. *Two.*

The distant pair slowly came into focus. A very old woman in a mud-stained white burial kimono leaned on a stick, beckoning to him slowly with one hand. Beside her stood a small girl in dark rags, waving him closer. Neither of them smiled, but their gestures were definitely an earnest summons. He should go! He blithely took a step.

"Moonshadow!" Snowhawk's hands on his shoulders made him jump. "Moonshadow!" she shouted, "look at me! No, don't look there, at *me*!" She shook him.

He fixed his eyes on hers. Was she angry again? No, not this time, just determined.

"Let's go!" Snowhawk said. "Look at nothing but the back of my head, do you hear me?"

"No, wait!" He stared at her anxiously, his mind teeming. "What's happening to me *now*?"

Had the Kappa nightmare damaged him more than he knew? Had it made him crazy? He was supposed to be the leader, but so far it was Snowhawk keeping them both alive on this mission!

A strong desire to look back into the forest nagged at him. It felt like that uncontrollable urge to go to the river in his nightmare.

Moonshadow clenched a fist. "This *must* be the dream assassin's work!"

"No, it isn't—*hey, don't do that*—keep your eyes on me!" Snowhawk grabbed his sleeve and dragged him closer. "It's the ghosts of this forest! The Fuma said they try to drag everybody in. The more aware of them a victim becomes, the stronger the call of the ghosts."

He frowned. "That's why you didn't want me knowing the forest's history yet—"

"Exactly! I didn't want your mind on the ghosts, feeding their power!"

Moonshadow eyed her uncomfortably. "Why aren't they calling you?"

"They are." She shrugged. "But the Fuma made a chance discovery years ago. People trained in breath control and deep-mind concentration, like samurai snipers and *shinobi* who can hypnotize...such folk can block out this kind of influence." She winced. "Well, *mostly* block it!"

He gave a thankful nod. He wasn't so pathetic after all! Then the urge to turn and stare into the forest returned. Now its lure was overwhelming. His head involuntarily twitched to one side. The ghosts were getting to him!

"We need to go *now*!" Snowhawk leaned backward, tugging his arm until he started moving. She wheeled around and broke into a sprint, faster than before. He tore after her, setting his jaw, fighting a grasping compulsion to glance to his right. A pale figure flashed by, barely registering in the corner of his eye. He clenched his teeth and kept his gaze straight ahead.

They cleared the forest without further incident. After pressing on hard at Snowhawk's insistence, they finally collapsed at the foot of a gnarled pine tree a hundred paces up the mountainside. Moonshadow scanned uphill as he gulped in lungfuls of air.

"I think there's a small plateau jutting out of the slope up there."

Snowhawk nodded, her chest heaving. "Once we're above that, if the map's contours were right, it's not too steep a climb, remember? Through sparse forest, up to the old shrine." She clicked her tongue sharply. "Hey? What's up? Are you listening to me?"

He stared downhill. "I saw them clearly, you know. I saw two people."

"Very old, or very young?" Snowhawk eyed him earnestly.

Moonshadow scrambled closer to her. "One of each. How did you know that?"

Snowhawk's eyes filmed with sorrow. "Those two towns we passed through. During the last great famine, their very old and very young were brought here."

"Why?" Moonshadow felt a chill enter his bones.

"They were abandoned, left to die, to help the rest survive on the meager food that remained. The forest we just crossed is said to be filled with angry, bitter ghosts." Snowhawk saw his questioning look. "I first learned of this when the Fuma lost an agent in there."

"Lost?" He gestured expansively. "What do you mean, *lost*?"

"When I was a little girl," Snowhawk said, "it was the talk of the Fuma base. An agent chased in there by mounted samurai simply vanished. Never heard from again." She cast a hard glance downhill. "He'd be one of the ghosts now. *Good!*"

"I wish you wouldn't talk that way," Moonshadow said quietly. "Hatred is a poison."

Snowhawk rounded on him. "Well, I'm sorry, *Little Mantis*, but how I talk is like how I think! It's *my business*, and you're not going to control either! So don't even try!" Eyes glowing fiercely, she shook her head. "That would be right: the wonderful Grey Light Order turns out to be just like the Fuma— desperate to *control* my every thought!" Snowhawk wagged an accusing finger in his face. "You should be grateful to me, not critical all the time! I saved you back at the inn *and* just stopped the dead from making off with your little *boy brain*!" She huffed, then covered her face with her hands. Hanging her head, Snowhawk muttered through her fingers.

Moonshadow felt a white-hot surge of his own anger. She could say anything she liked about him, but not the Order. They were his family! Her nasty little jab at them had left him burning to give her a piece of *his* mind back, but good leaders broke up fights, they didn't start them! He took a deep breath and turned away, rejecting his rage, seizing control with a massive act of willpower.

A long, uneasy silence hung between them. He waited, hoping for an apology. None came. Snowhawk made no sound.

Finally he glanced at the forest below and stretched. "I think that's enough rest, fun, and laughter for now. Would you like to kick me in the head next, or shall we just be on our way?" Hearing no answer, Moonshadow spun around. Snowhawk's eyes were closed. He waited until she opened them and rose. Had she also been forcing herself to calm down? If so, that was a good start! He studied the look on her face. Her eyes were watery. She didn't look angry now, more upset. Moonshadow sighed heavily. What weird girl stuff was he in for now?

"What were you doing? The *furube* sutra? We forgot it this morning."

"I was praying"—her eyes flicked at the trees downhill—"for them to find peace."

"It won't happen while they stay angry," Moonshadow muttered.

They started uphill once more, and though he tried to concentrate on the mission, Moonshadow kept wondering how long it would be before Snowhawk's next fit of rage. Was she becoming a liability the mission could not afford? If so, he had made a terrible mistake by not reporting her mutiny up on that Edo roof. He glanced sideways at her, then sighed. On the other hand, her unique knowledge had already proved an enormous asset—twice! And how could he stay angry at someone who kept saving his life?

The map's contours proved accurate. After making a low ridge that cut across the mountainside to flare into a plateau at one end, they reached easier ground. The forest became sparser, the uphill slope gentler. Most of the scattered trees they passed through now were young maples. At intervals, badly stunted pines appeared, some charred as if recently struck by lightning. A gentle breeze swept the slope.

Moonshadow looked back over his shoulder, marveling that the White Nun, said to be so old, could somehow still climb that first and hardest stretch of her own mountain.

"Did you see the ruins on that plateau we pushed past?" He pointed downhill.

"Yeah, I did—just!" Snowhawk was looking in all directions. "You have good eyes! The stands of black-green bamboo down there just about hid them." She took a deep breath. "It's time I told you what else I know about this mountain. There was a small castle on that plateau. It was surrounded and burnt down during the long civil war. I think everybody in it was massacred—or jumped."

Moonshadow threw up his hands. "This must be the happiest place in the world! It—"

His nose twitched sharply, then he dived at Snowhawk and pinned her to the ground.

"What are you doing?" She glared at him. "I sense no danger! Have you gone crazy?"

199

His eyes flicked uphill. "I smelled a gun fuse! *A musket!* It's somewhere above us!"

She tried to rise and grunted when he held her in place. "I can't smell it! You're imagin—"

There was an echoing *booom,* and a small stone beside her leg exploded in a puff of dust.

"Okay, you're right," Snowhawk said quickly, "and *we're* dead!"

19

SNIPER!

His lips silently forming numbers, Moon-shadow scrambled along the ground on his belly, with Snowhawk close behind.

He led her into the cover of a large white rock, then leaned out from behind it, squinting uphill into the forest.

"What are you doing?" Snowhawk tilted her head. "Counting?"

He held a finger to his lips and went on with his soundless count. *Boom!* The gunshot echoed as a lead ball zinged off the nearby edge of the rock. Flecks of grit peppered Moonshadow and Snowhawk. He hunched low and caught her eye.

"Badger made me study a scroll about modern sniper craft. You count the span between shots; that's how long it takes the sniper to reload. The longer that delay, the older his equipment, and the more time you've got to vanish."

Snowhawk looked around and then scowled. "It's daylight! Where do we vanish to?"

"Well, wherever it is, it has to be close. This guy is good! He probably packs a long-range musket, the kind built for just what he does! And he's disciplined. Even with a good weapon, few gunners can reload at *that* rate. He just added gunpowder, a shot wad, and a lead ball, ramrodded it all into place, then fanned the twine fuse, aimed, and fired…in just twenty seconds!"

"Perfect concentration. Explains how he made it past the ghosts," Snowhawk said darkly. "But it won't save him from me! I'll run in a zigzag, that way, outflank him, cut him down!"

Moonshadow peeped over the rock. "Forget that! You have to find him first. A sniper relocates after every shot to avoid being countersniped. But to remain combat ready, he *must* keep his gun's twine fuse alight. You won't find him by sight, only by smell, so why don't we—" Movement drew his eye and he turned.

She was crouched at the edge of the rock, straining forward, about to bolt.

He inched toward her. "Snowhawk, no!"

"Think this is my first sniper? You go the other way, distract him. This dog of Fuma is mine to destroy!" He lunged at her, fingers snatching, but Snowhawk threw herself forward and dashed away. Moonshadow watched her zigzag nimbly up the slope, leaping logs, furrows, and rocks without once slowing. She was agile, skillful, and fearless. And so insanely *difficult*!

Moonshadow cursed her rage and bravado. What a stunt! Had Snowhawk tossed *her* brain to the dead? Her plan was reckless and left him with no choice! He had to support her strategy, or huddle here and watch her fall.

He charged out from behind the rock and started a nerve-stretching sprint uphill. Almost at once, his eyes found her, still climbing fast, weaving between trees, sword already in her hand.

Boom! He flinched and leapt to one side. The gunshot echoed three times. Moonshadow began a silent countdown as he looked up the hill. He saw Snowhawk finish a shoulder roll, rise, and instantly resume running. Leaves fluttered down behind her. The sniper had hit a tree branch right near her head! An amazing effort, given the speed of his target. *And way too close!*

In what was now fifteen seconds, the shooter would be ready to fire again, but who would be the target?

He locked his eyes on the gunshot's point of origin: a short hedge of tangled shrubs, about waist high, perhaps fifty paces uphill. Snowhawk changed direction sharply to close on it. With a grunt, Moonshadow forced himself to run even faster. Ignoring the burning in his thighs, he tore for the hedge.

Nine seconds to go. Moonshadow started running in a zigzag, eyes flicking down, wary of obstacles. If he was going to die, this guy would have to earn the kill!

Five seconds. He looked up at the hedge, and his mouth fell open.

Dressed in a green farmer's jacket, the sniper stood behind the low hedge, musket cupped in his left hand, its stock jammed against his right shoulder. The weapon was trained on Moonshadow, and its muzzle swung smoothly left to right, tracking his path. At the same time, the sniper's right hand guided a loop of smoking twine fuse up to the weapon's breech.

Time's up!

Evading at a sharp angle, Moonshadow dived into a forward roll. He clenched his teeth together and tightened his stomach muscles, bracing himself for the lead ball's impact.

Boom! The roar itself was enormous. This time, strangely, there was no echo.

Moonshadow flinched reflexively, but there was no impact.

He finished the roll, gained his feet, and closed on the hedge, patting his torso as he ran, checking himself for shrapnel wounds. Ahead, the sniper had vanished from sight again. Moonshadow exhaled hard with relief: he felt no hint of pain anywhere; his clothing was dry.

The guy had missed!

Moonshadow dropped into a crouch, using the hedge for cover. As he crept to one end of it, listening hard for his enemy's breathing, a cough came from beyond the hedge. He rolled soundlessly to a different spot and came up in a combat stance, facing the low wall of green. Snowhawk rose from behind it.

"Stand down, it's me," she panted. "It's all over." He relaxed his stance but frowned at her. "And no, I didn't kill him...worse luck!" She shrugged. "Didn't get the chance." Snowhawk motioned downward with her head. Moonshadow skirted the hedge and looked.

The sniper's musket was a distorted, steaming mass of black iron and dark wood. It hadn't fired — it had blown up while trying to! Badger had also told Moonshadow about *this* side of sniping: these latest weapons were powerful, but still far from perfected. It was not unusual for a musket to malfunction and explode, killing its owner or the soldier beside him.

Moonshadow studied the sniper, stone dead beside his weapon. All his clothes were green, the exact green of the surrounding forest's trees. There was a nasty, gunpowder-charred hole in the side of his neck. The man had a strong face. Yes, he had been trying to kill them, but he still deserved respect as a daring, skillful opponent, a professional like themselves. Moonshadow gave his fallen enemy a polite bow. Snowhawk clicked her tongue.

"He took serious damage, hey?" she said provocatively. "The gods did that to him, or the ghosts, maybe. It was his time! In any case, it wasn't *me*." Her eyes narrowed. "But I promise you, if this fate hadn't befallen him, it would have been!"

Moonshadow eyed her wearily. "Then the bad karma would also have been yours. Let the gods,

ghosts, or some shoddy foreign gun maker have it."
He stepped toward her so abruptly that Snowhawk
flinched. "And you know something?" Moonshadow
said forcefully. "I'm grateful that Mantis taught me
to heed my karma! So go ahead, call me *Little Mantis*
again, whenever you like, because when you do, you
honor me!"

Snowhawk rolled her eyes, tossed her hair, then
turned and stormed off uphill. As he started after
her, she looked back over one shoulder. "Yeah, well,
none of that matters anymore," she called miserably,
"because my gut says that neither of us will leave this
mountain alive!"

He glowered as he followed her through the trees.
Thanks a lot! Now what kind of talk was *that*? Had
this creepy place influenced her more than she
admitted?

He hated her doomsaying, but Snowhawk had a
point. Fate had been kind enough to rid them of the
sniper, but this place was still as menacing as it was
remote. It bristled with all kinds of unexpected haz-
ards! What would come at them next, a mountain ogre?
And strong enemies—including an alarmingly powerful one—were on their tail, eager to slay them for
money, revenge, or both! A wave of discouragement

rolled over Moonshadow. Each attack so far had been surprising but also frighteningly potent. What if the next one proved even stronger?

Yes, Snowhawk was right. It *was* starting to look like their last mission.

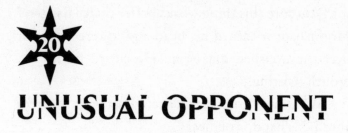

20

UNUSUAL OPPONENT

Finally walking side by side again, they entered a grove of young maple trees.

"Quiet." Snowhawk sank into a crouch and slowly turned a circle. "Hear that?"

Moonshadow bobbed low, listening with his mouth open. "Footfall? Coming from uphill?"

"Better read it properly." She turned, offering her pack to him. Moonshadow fished deep inside it and carefully drew out a tapering brass rod with a tiny polished cup at one end. He dropped to his knees, pushing the rod's thin tip into the soil. He felt it stop, meeting rock beneath the surface.

"You sure this thing works better than a dagger?" Moonshadow turned his head and lowered one ear over the polished brass cup. He closed both eyes, mouth twisting.

"What is it?" Snowhawk peered between the trees ahead. "What do you hear?"

He sprang up and yanked the listening device from the ground. "Four legs!" he hissed. "Striking ground hard. How could anybody get a horse up here?"

She stared uphill, her mouth open. "It's not a horse." He turned sharply.

Galloping downhill toward them, weaving in and out of trees, was a long-haired animal that appeared to be half dog, half wolf. Its head and back were broad, its chest deep.

"Akita Matagi!" Moonshadow shuddered. "A bear-hunting dog!"

He stared in awe at the impressive creature closing on them. Before now he had seen only one other, caged during transport along the Tokaido. They were bred by the Satake Clan in the Akita region, just northwest of this mountain range. The one he had seen in a cage had been brindle striped, but this animal had a pale, uniform coat. Moonshadow and Snowhawk exchanged alarmed looks. What hurtled at them now, already growling, was as formidable as the warriors who had bred it. Worse still, this beast was clearly afraid of nothing.

"Into the trees!" Snowhawk shouted. "They're young, but they should hold us!"

She ran for one. Moonshadow hunted desperately for another that could take his weight. They couldn't risk a midair collision while jumping for the same haven.

His eyes found a young maple with high enough branches. Moonshadow managed three strides toward it before teeth snapped a hand span from his backside. He grunted and leapt. Would he make that solid branch? It loomed closer; he clawed for it.

Securing a hold, Moonshadow swung himself up and into the maple. The young tree swayed. He turned, bracing his legs in a slim fork, eyes sweeping to the base of the trunk. His pursuer gazed keenly back up at him. "Snowhawk...?" he called without looking.

"I'm clear," she shouted from her tree. "But we're not going anywhere, are we?"

"This is crazy. It's...just a dog," Moonshadow said. Who was he kidding? It was no ordinary dog. The Akita Matagi circled the tree, panting but determined. It looked up at him with icy blue eyes as it skipped sideways into a hunch, as if expecting him to leap down that way and make a run for it. Its unblinking stare was cold, ferocious, yet shone with intelligence. The animal's thick coat failed to hide its great muscularity.

Moonshadow licked dry lips. This beast had big, thickly clawed feet but narrow hips. It was built for speed, power, and agility.

He muttered a curse. They couldn't hope to outrun the creature, and it would give them no chance to reach a hiding place, if there even was one nearby.

"Snowhawk," he called. "You're right, we *are* trapped." He looked at her gingerly.

"Well, Wise One!" Her face twisted into a furious scowl. "Get us *untrapped*!"

"How?" Moonshadow snapped. He looked down at the circling dog and sighed. *"How?"*

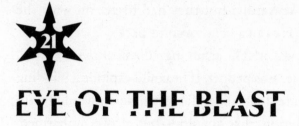

21

EYE OF THE BEAST

Moonshadow inclined his head, studying their new nemesis.

It was unnerving the way Akita Matagi, unlike most animals, looked you straight in the eyes with hardly a blink. Very samurai!

He had heard that these dogs wrestled bears to the ground on command. His eyes flicked uphill. Were there more of them? Or was somebody watching, ready to give this animal orders? Such possibilities meant that wounding the dog might be a bad idea. He grimaced. Besides, how could he hurl *shuriken* at such a magnificent creature? The very idea felt cowardly. But they had to get on with the mission. He ran a hand over his pack.

That was it! The main ingredient of *shinobi* blinding powder was pepper. If he could explode a blinding bomb under that Akita Matagi's snout, it would flee in wild irritation—like any dog—but recover unharmed. *Preferably elsewhere*, he thought with a grin.

Moonshadow unshouldered the pack and dug out his tiny box of pepper bombs.

"That's…a good idea," Snowhawk called, a little begrudgingly, from her tree. "Just don't get its eyes."

"Don't worry." He raised a small bird's egg in one hand. It had been emptied and then filled with *shinobi* blinding powder. "I want it to be able to see its way home as it runs off—sneezing!"

The bear-hunting dog stared up at the black-painted sphere in Moonshadow's grasp. Without a sound, it peeled back its lips and showed him a gleaming set of fangs. Moonshadow faked a throw to see if the dog would flinch. It didn't move. Moonshadow prepared to hurl the blinding bomb for the spot between its big front paws. But once the loaded egg left his hand, the Akita Matagi scuttled backward, turned fast, and ran to the foot of Snowhawk's tree.

The egg tore and crumpled on the forest floor. A small puff of red dust escaped it. The big animal watched Moonshadow impassively, avoiding the bombed area as it trotted back to the foot of his tree. It glanced at the ruined egg, then up at him attentively.

"You're pretty smart," Moonshadow told his canine adversary. "I'd better make you run before you pull out an ax and really surprise me." With a fast whip-cracking motion he threw a second pepper bomb. This time the dog bolted forward with astounding acceleration. The bomb puffed at nothing two paces behind its flicking tail. The Akita Matagi trotted to the base of Snowhawk's tree, waiting for the pepper cloud to disperse.

"I have only one more," Moonshadow grumbled. "What happens if I miss?"

"Don't know," Snowhawk said irritably. "We slowly starve to death? No, wait, I've got it! I know the answer!" She flashed him a cold, sarcastic smile. "Don't miss!"

He lurched forward in the fork, made a misleading feint with his hand, then tossed the last bomb hard, aiming where he thought the dog would go as it took evasive action. But the animal simply held its ground, turning its large head mildly to watch the pepper bomb fly past. Once the egg struck the ground, the dog calmly padded the opposite way.

"Blast you!" Moonshadow pointed at it. "At least you can't get us up here!"

The Akita Matagi tilted its head, eyes moving between its two perched targets. It spun on the spot and then broke into a charge, straight for Snowhawk's tree. As it closed with the trunk, it reared up on its hind legs and planted both paws hard against the bark.

With an unsettling creak, the young tree lurched. Snowhawk scrambled and braced herself in its branches. The dog dropped back onto all fours, then turned and galloped for Moonshadow's tree. It reared up and struck in exactly the same way, shaking the branches hard. Then, taking a few steps backward, the beast turned its great head left and right, eerie blue eyes flicking between the occupied trees. It grinned and panted, wagged its long tail, then ran at Snowhawk's tree again. It *liked* this game.

"Now what?" Snowhawk huffed as her perch was shaken. "We just dangle here? Until our teeth come loose and our enemies catch up?"

"No," Moonshadow said decisively. "There is another way." He caught his breath as he wondered at his own stupidity. He could link his mind to that of any complex animal. Thrown off balance by the Akita Matagi's abrupt and sustained attack, the most obvious solution had escaped him. Link with it, control it, then—his eyes lit up as a plan came to him—send the creature downhill with orders to attack any *shinobi* it found.

He filled his chest proudly. A masterful strategy. Using one problem to fix another. Eagle and Mantis were going to be impressed. They'd call it clever, *elegant*.

"Watch this." Moonshadow signaled Snowhawk. "It will roll on its back at any moment...."

He locked gazes with the dog. It narrowed its eyes back at him. Moonshadow concentrated, waiting for the tremors in his hands that told him a link was being forged.

The dog's head flew back, muzzle creasing, eyes rolling upward. Its nose twitched violently. Moonshadow peered with knitted eyebrows. An unusually strong reaction!

"There," Moonshadow said, but he knew at once that something was wrong.

With a splutter the beast threw its huge head forward. It hunched, muscles in spasm, sneezing hard. A clod of green mucus landed between its paws. Snorting, the dog shook its ears, saliva flicking from its jowls. It sneezed again.

"And *that's* the legendary Eye of the Beast." Snowhawk clapped. "What an amazing science. The power to make an animal catch a cold. Aw, will you teach *me*?"

"Shut up," he snapped. "How can it be immune? Something's not right here."

"*Something*? We're being held hostage in trees by a magical dog, and all kinds of murderous foes are trailing us. Oh, and it looks like we're going to fail our mission too"—Snowhawk's voice rose into a growl as she shook her tree angrily—"and die for it!"

Moonshadow scrambled around on his perch to face her. "We will if you keep reacting that way! I feel discouraged too, but we both have to fight those feelings, push on ahead, get the job done! Besides, we're of the Grey Light Order, remember? If we do mess up, we get retrained. You're not Fuma anymore. You can fail *and* live. And people are supposed to do both."

"I hate being stuck!" She hung her head and thumped the nearest branch in frustration. Moonshadow nodded. He knew the real problem: she hated her own anger.

A shadow crossed his face. Moonshadow looked up. A small falcon spiraled between the canopies, a dead mouse in its claws. It dropped the rodent into the crook of a nearby tree, then perched beside it, hunching low, closely eyeing its intended meal.

"Let's try that again," Moonshadow muttered, staring at the falcon.

His hands trembled immediately. The bird snapped around to gaze back at him.

As if sensing trouble, the Akita Matagi slowly looked from Moonshadow to the falcon.

Pushing straight to sight control, the third level of the Eye of the Beast, Moonshadow willed the falcon to swoop the dog.

He closed his eyes and relaxed in the tree perch, taking in only what the bird saw. Through the usual shimmering waterlike lens, he watched the dog stiffen warily on the forest floor. Its image lurched to one side, then another, quickly drawing closer as the falcon descended on it. He saw the dog skip backward a few steps. It was intimidated.

Moonshadow opened one eye to check the Akita Matagi with his human sight.

It ducked and cowered, belly in the leaves, as the streak of feathered fury narrowly missed its head. *Pursue and harrow*, Moonshadow mentally urged the falcon.

Snowhawk's relieved laughter raised his spirits. They exchanged encouraging looks and she sat back to enjoy the show. The great dog broke into a run between the trees, weaving and tacking, glancing up every few strides to see where the falcon was. Moonshadow closed his eyes again, concentrating hard, his mind one with the bird of prey as he directed its ongoing attack.

Moonshadow sent the falcon into a fast, low glide after the dog, and the bird's strong hunting instincts backwashed into his feelings, inciting him to revel in the thrill of the chase. His breathing grew heavy and he found himself chuckling with exhilaration.

The Akita Matagi led the falcon straight for the base of a tree, then, at the last possible moment, it turned sharply and accelerated away across open ground. The cunning beast!

Mottled bark suddenly filled the bird's entire field of vision. Moonshadow gasped as he narrowly steered the falcon around the tree, the flight feathers of one outstretched wing clipping the edge of the trunk with a sharp *hiss*. He guided his airborne hunter into a tight turn and then lined it up quickly with the retreating dog.

"I'm really getting the hang of this!" Moonshadow called to Snowhawk.

"We'll see!" he heard her shout back. He frowned. *Thanks for the vote of confidence!*

The bird of prey whooshed past the dog's head, making it cringe, then soared into a tight vertical back-roll before descending in a power glide behind its fleeing target. The dog looked back and accelerated, cleverly ducking under low tree branches to shield its back and tail as it made its escape. It charged into a round thicket of bamboo and, through the falcon, Moonshadow saw the Akita throw itself down in the center of the ring of high green-black stalks.

Very clever. He nodded. *Go ahead, dog, lie low and put walls round yourself, then! They won't save you!* He willed the falcon into a steep climb directly above the Akita's bamboo shelter. The bird rocketed skyward, shrinking quickly into a dark speck. *Walls are useless*—Moonshadow smiled menacingly—*if you don't have a roof!*

He made the bird slow, turn, then drop. The falcon plunged, wings folded at its sides, speed building quickly. Moonshadow opened his eyes. *This* was worth watching with his own sight! The bird hurtled from the sky, flashing between surrounding tree canopies, streaking for the middle of the bamboo ring.

Now really scare our prey, Moonshadow told the falcon firmly, *whatever it takes.*

The bird plunged into the center of the dog's haven. There was a loud *thump*, and a split second later an even louder *"Yike!"* echoed across the hillside. Moonshadow watched as the nearest wall of bamboo shook violently. Then it splayed open and the Akita bolted out, head swinging left and right, eyes wild as they tried to lock onto the falcon on its back!

Moonshadow heard Snowhawk laugh again and he marveled at how the falcon had interpreted *whatever it takes*. It had sunk its talons into the great dog's back and now, determined to hang on, it hunched low as its hapless victim ran in panic...carrying it along for the ride!

The falcon beat its wings to sustain its balance, leaning forward as the dog's huge strides over uneven ground jolted and shook its furry perch. The Akita slowed its run and twisted around hard, trying to snap at the falcon, but the bird had placed itself too well: it was out of jaw reach.

The dog took off again abruptly, no doubt hoping its sudden acceleration might fling the bird from its back, but the falcon bobbed low and hung on with a grim, patient determination that Moonshadow could literally feel.

So *that* was how falcons really operated. He nodded. He could tell how intensely the bird was enjoying itself, but despite that, its mind, not its strong, wild emotions, ran the show.

Snowhawk, he decided, could learn a fine lesson

from *this* bird of prey. Even while flushed with the thrill of combat, its mind remained in charge: crystal clear, free of distractions, unswayed by strong feelings. A patient, skilled hunter, focused only on its next move.

He craned forward as the Akita suddenly changed course, the falcon flapping harder than ever to hang on. So the clever dog wasn't out of tricks yet! What was it up to? He watched it head for a dry fallen tree that lay horizontally at waist height above the ground, the ends resting on rocks. The dog accelerated hard. Moonshadow's eyes widened.

It intended to bolt under that dried branch and smash his falcon off!

Let go, hover, harass! he urged the bird. The falcon pushed itself off hard, magnificent wings unfolding. It banked away sharply just as the Akita flashed under the fallen tree. Moss clods and bark flakes whirled into the air as the animal's broad back scraped the trunk at high speed. Emerging on the other side, the Akita glanced fearfully over its shoulder, eyes tracking the looming enemy. Then, sustaining its pace, it charged off through the forest.

Moonshadow leaned hard to one side in his tree perch, keeping his eyes on the action. Powering into the distance, the beast quickly shrank into a small, erratically turning black figure, the pursuing falcon a tiny flying smudge above it. As they disappeared around the curve of the mountainside, Moonshadow heard another sharp yelp. It echoed through the forest. Despite its size and strength, the Akita Matagi was *really* starting to panic.

He closed his eyes and concentrated on the falcon's vision. The bird relentlessly swooped the distressed dog, herding it downhill into the ruins. Moonshadow nodded to himself as the Akita Matagi ran through another glade of bamboo, then ducked behind a low, crumbling stone wall. Just its ears showed.

Moonshadow released the falcon from his control and swung himself out of his perch. As he dropped to the ground, Snowhawk leapt down from her tree and ran to him.

"Have you stopped?" She peered into the distance. "What if the dog doubles back?"

"I can't afford to keep it up," he told her, already feeling the drain to his life force. "Any long level-three joining wears me out. But don't worry; for now, that dog's spooked. It's gone to ground, so we've bought ourselves some time. Enough, I hope, to throw it off our trail."

Snowhawk immediately turned and started running uphill. "Let's not waste it then!" She glanced back as he followed. "We need to find streams and cross them, so it can't pick up our scent again!"

They dashed uphill through the scattered trees, the jagged rocky outcrops multiplying as they climbed higher. On the crest of a small ridge, Moonshadow's residual beast hearing detected running water. He stopped and signaled its direction to Snowhawk. She skipped along a low, uneven wall of dark granite, leaping from rock to rock, eyes searching.

"Here!" Snowhawk shouted, pointing down. Moonshadow caught up to her. A thin, bright stream bubbled downhill, cutting through the rocks in a series of little waterfalls. They drank greedily, soaked their aching feet in its icy meltwater, then walked uphill in the stream as far as its surrounding rocks would allow them.

Moonshadow and Snowhawk staggered from the refreshing brook. Doggedly they paced up the mountainside until they came to the mouth of a narrow rocky gully. Its floor was flat, covered with a layer of dried leaves. Slanting granite horns rose on each side of it.

"We could rest in there," he ventured wearily. "It's hard to spot from most angles."

"I'm so tired." She stumbled into the gully, sagging to the bed of leaves. "We *must* rest."

Moonshadow nodded, flopping to the ground beside her. He groaned. He felt as wrung out as she looked, and the temptation to steal a small nap felt awfully strong.

He forced himself to resist the idea. He had to stay at least *half* awake.

Quiet minutes passed as they rested, the only sounds their labored breathing and the occasional far-off birdcall. Despite himself, Moonshadow began to nod off.

Until he felt Snowhawk grip his hand. Tightly.

"What is it?" He turned his head and looked at her.

"I don't believe this," Snowhawk whispered. She motioned. "Look. There."

Moonshadow rose up onto one elbow and followed her gaze. His heart skipped a beat.

The Akita Matagi stood blocking the mouth of the narrow gully, watching them.

The dog's chest heaved and there was a patch of dried blood on its back, but otherwise it appeared to have come through its falcon encounter unscathed. Its head was low to the ground, big paws spread, back tensed in a ready stance. From what he'd already seen, if it charged, it could probably reach them before they escaped the gully…especially in their current exhausted condition.

Moonshadow focused on the beast's icy blue eyes. He grabbed Snowhawk's arm. "Look at *that*," he muttered. "I don't like the look of that."

Lips peeling back, the dog showed its massive canine teeth. They were dripping.

"Know what you mean," Snowhawk whispered. "Those teeth are huge."

"Not the teeth," he said quickly. "The eyes." He sensed her look, felt her shudder.

The Akita Matagi's eyes were glowing, lit from within by some strange energy, their blue far brighter than before. The dog relaxed its lips, hiding the drippy canines, but its cold stare never left its cornered targets.

"That's why I couldn't take control of it." Moonshadow started reaching for his hidden sword.

Snowhawk shook her head. "Because somebody else already has."

She flinched as the mighty animal bolted into the gully.

22

DANGEROUS FRIENDS

Private Investigator Katsu trudged up the third flight of narrow dark-wood stairs, his big frame just squeezing between the posts at the top.

Samurai escorts led and followed him. Katsu stepped through a dim porch with a tiled roof and stone walls and out onto the battlements of Momoyama Castle, home of the warlord Silver Wolf.

A gorgeous spring sunset, pink and apricot shades, splashed the waning sky. The sun was behind the high hills, its diffused light still strong and faintly tinged with orange.

"Sunset," the samurai behind Katsu said, "is a precious time of day. It reminds us that every glory must fade and that all things, cruel or sweet, come to an end."

The man leading him grunted in agreement.

"You, sirs, are wise warriors indeed," Katsu said, smiling. He turned his head, admiring the vista. Across the wide moat, the town of Fushimi sprawled over low hills. He nodded at its greatest landmarks. The torii gate near the entrance to town, its modest shrine nearby, the poor street on low ground that always flooded, Fushimi's main temple...*wait*. He glanced back sharply to the left. There were changes he hadn't noticed before. They had moved the sake brewery, once the scene of a fight with the *shinobi* Moonshadow. And that old cable-and-winch system over the moat had been dismantled. Security was tightening. Did Silver Wolf expect a siege?

The samurai ahead stopped, moved to one side, and bowed. "My lord awaits you there, among his archers."

Katsu bowed back. When he straightened up he saw Silver Wolf motioning to him.

He met the warlord where a high parapet jutted out from the castle wall. Along it, samurai archers were undertaking sunset target practice, their proud master looking on.

"I know that *detective* face!" Silver Wolf laughed as Katsu approached. "Always questions, ever the probing mind, huh?" He slapped his visitor's back. "You're wondering what their target is, aren't you? You're curious if I'm bloodthirsty enough to take potshots at my own town."

"Oh, no, great lord." Katsu lowered his head meekly, relying on his skills as a liar. "Simply curious," he chuckled. "While assuming nothing."

Katsu studied Silver Wolf's twinkling eyes and breezy manner. Why was he in such a good mood? For some reason, Katsu found it just as disquieting as the warlord's more frequent state: dark brooding rage. He wasn't sure why. Katsu forced a smile.

His news was going to shatter this contented little atmosphere, that was for sure. He glanced at the nearest archer, then the others beyond him. Once he ruined Silver Wolf's tranquil evening, would they be taking potshots at *him*?

"Go ahead, push between those two archers, see what they shoot at." The warlord bundled Katsu to the edge of the parapet. He felt his broad back muscles stiffen. *A big drop. So far down.* Katsu broke out into a sweat. "Not *that* close, you'll pitch over." Silver Wolf sniggered, dragging him back. Katsu took a deep breath, steadied himself, and looked down.

A rice-straw dummy, in the shape of a slender man, bobbed in the center of the moat. It was pin-cushioned with arrows. More arrows floated around it, along with three bloated dead carp the archers had accidentally killed. Katsu squinted hard. The dummy rose from a single circular wooden float. He frowned at the unfamiliar design.

"I didn't have it made." Silver Wolf smiled, his eyes bright. "It was a gift. From our Fuma allies. A training toy they use, to help *shinobi* learn to kill *shinobi*. On water!"

The warlord took Katsu's wrist and drew him clear of the archers.

"Show this snooper what you can do!" Silver Wolf held his head up. "Begin!"

The archers nocked arrows as one, drew in perfect synchronicity, and fired a tight cluster of arrows. It hissed high into the air at a sharp angle. Katsu frowned.

That vector looked all wrong. They'd miss! Why not shoot directly at the dummy, using line of sight? He watched the arrows soar until they became invisible. Katsu blinked, picking them up again on their way down. Steadily their *hiss* grew louder.

The arrows fell straight at the dummy. It bucked as they made impact. Katsu gaped. Unless he was mistaken, every projectile had found its mark.

Silver Wolf rounded on his hireling. "Each unit in my command is receiving special training, based on Clan Fuma advice. We will be *ready*, and when this is all over, I will be cleaning my claws!" He held up his hands, fingers curled to represent talons.

"My lord will prove invincible." Katsu bowed low. "You are the wind of destiny. Japan will be returned to the Way of the Warrior. I am proud to serve the future Shogun."

"Yes, yes, smooth tongue." The warlord looked him up and down, eyes narrowing. "I know you are... but what brings you back to me now? Your visit is a day early."

Katsu quickly scratched his chin so that Silver Wolf didn't see him swallow. "I have news, master." This was it. He filled his chest, raised his chin high. Dignity mattered, even if death came soon after. Katsu spoke slowly, his tone formal. "I was contacted on the Tokaido, by an exhausted rider. As he had already done, he bade me memorize this dispatch to you. It comes from your task force in the north."

"Might this be... bad news?" The warlord's eyes glowed as if that idea excited him.

Katsu nodded, trying to glean his master's motive. What an odd reaction! Surely the warlord couldn't *want* bad news? He grinned sheepishly as sweat ran down his back.

Silver Wolf examined Katsu's face and sighed. "Speak your news; you are safe."

"Yes, lord. There was a skirmish, fought against a young male and a young female agent of the Grey Light Order, identified by Jiro as Moonshadow and Snowhawk. It took place in a market, in a town north of Edo. One of our bounty hunters, my friend the former sumo wrestler" — Katsu hung his head — "was badly injured."

"How?" The warlord folded his arms. "A sword cut? *Shuriken*? Witchcraft?"

"A collision with a stone well, incited by the youth called Moonshadow."

"Whose head," Silver Wolf said with relish, "will be on show here one day soon."

"Both Grey Light Order agents escaped, heading north. Your task force is in pursuit. More may have already happened, but no further word has reached me as yet."

"Ah, yes. Heading north, to *that* mountain. How fitting that once again, so unexpectedly, blood must be spilled there for my honor to be satisfied." The warlord drew a folded paper from his jacket and held it out to Katsu, who eyed it uneasily. "Here, take it.

In the light of such an early loss, I now order you to transmit *this* to our Fuma friends in the usual way. But with all haste; take a horse, ride to their inn. I prepared this dispatch in case just such news arrived. It's my personal request for them to send immediate reinforcements. It's brief. Go ahead, read it...."

Katsu unfolded and read the message. "My lord... that many? Only *two* hostile agents are on their way to the White Nun!"

"My good detective"—Silver Wolf squeezed Katsu's shoulder with an iron grip—"I've underestimated a Grey Light Order brat before. Not again. This time, we *win*."

Behind the warlord, his archers launched a final precision volley. Katsu heard it hiss into the darkening sky. There was no need to check the results. He trusted their uncanny accuracy. Right now, little else in his world deserved trust.

Not his master, for he knew his master's secret dreams didn't end with crushing the Grey Light Order and taking the shogunate. Oh, no, Silver Wolf would then invade the Korean Peninsula, expanding the empire... and he'd go on expanding it, until he ruled the very world.

And as for trusting his master's new allies, the Fuma... hah! *Never trust a* shinobi.

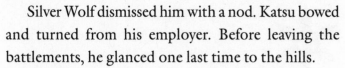

Silver Wolf dismissed him with a nod. Katsu bowed and turned from his employer. Before leaving the battlements, he glanced one last time to the hills.

The sumptuous sunset was over, replaced by the dull haze of twilight.

Those escorts had been so right, Katsu mused. *Nothing lasted forever. Especially not peace.*

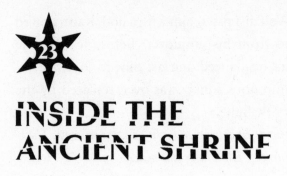

INSIDE THE
ANCIENT SHRINE

I ron lanterns burnt at even intervals along the
dark wooden walls of the old shrine. Shadows
danced across exposed beams on its ceiling.

Its windows were boarded up; the badly worn
matting floor smelled of time.

The building was at least hundreds of years old,
and though it kept out the weather, it was cold and
drafty. How could anyone so old live here willingly?
How did food supplies get up here? Surely no one
from those towns would cross the haunted forest?

Moonshadow looked up from his bowl of ramen
noodles and stared at the White Nun hunched

opposite him. At his side, Snowhawk ate fast, with an almost impolite amount of noise.

Beside the sage sat the Akita Matagi that had virtually captured them and marched them up here. Motionless, the dog stared at Moonshadow, its weird blue eyes boring into him.

Moonshadow looked back to the White Nun. She was undoubtedly the oldest person he'd ever met, and her appearance was distinctive: snow-white hair peeping from the pointy quilted hood she wore; impossibly pale, paper-thin skin; a deeply wizened face; and *red* eyes. It was said that one of Japan's long-dead emperors had been born with such rare features and he had proved a good, wise ruler. Moon-shadow had never seen a human being like the White Nun. Nor one who could—it appeared—stay linked to an animal indefinitely. How did she do that? Why did such a prolonged joining not suck the very life from her?

At their sunset arrival, the pair had made another startling discovery. The White Nun could read minds, or so it seemed. It was disconcerting to say the least, the way she finished sentences each of them began. Moonshadow eyed her uneasily. Could she pick up everything that flickered through his mind? He hoped not. Moonshadow forced himself to concentrate on the generous and satisfying meal she had prepared them.

"Yes, the noodles are filling, are they not?" The White Nun smiled. Her voice was soft, remote.

He grinned back. She had done it again. Moonshadow scooped up a last thick noodle between his chopsticks, fed it between his lips, then lowered the bowl to the stained matting at his side.

He sighed. Since she knew his thoughts, there seemed no point in holding back.

As he met her peculiar red stare, she smiled again. "You want to ask about Motto." She gestured at the beast beside her. "I call him that because *motto*, of course, means *more*, and he's indeed *more* in every way: bigger, stronger, faster, smarter than any dog or wolf I've seen. He's...simply *motto*."

Covering her mouth with a heavily wrinkled hand, she giggled at her own joke.

Moonshadow chuckled and leaned forward, offering the back of his hand to the dog. "Good evening, Motto-San," he said warmly. "You sure scared us back there."

The wolf dog stared at him without expression. Then its lips peeled open. The flash of teeth made Moonshadow snatch his hand back. Motto relaxed his mouth again.

"That's unusual," Snowhawk said thoughtfully. "Animals generally take to Moonshadow—not just the ones he links with, either. Maybe we don't smell so—"

"Oh, no, dear." The White Nun glanced at her only permanent companion. "It's not about you. He's like this because I'm here. He can be much friendlier. But while we're linked and I'm present, I'm afraid Motto-San is single-minded to the point of rudeness."

Staring at the wolflike beast, Moonshadow slowly shook his head in wonder.

"Come now, dear," the sage said gently. "Don't be so amazed that I could control Motto-San over such a distance, call him off you, and have him bring you here unharmed."

Moonshadow blinked, embarrassed. That was *exactly* what he had been thinking.

The White Nun went on enthusiastically. "As young Snowhawk here says, you've always had a strong rapport with animals. I felt it the day I encouraged your selection for training in the Order's orphanage. And there's still more to your special skill than you know. One day, you too will extend your Eye of the Beast powers, just as I have. You'll hold a permanent link with a creature over a great distance, maintaining the bond even when you sleep—confident that the beast will carry out your intentions on its own."

"Great sage." He bowed. "Thank you for this encouraging word. But how do you—"

"All in good time." The White Nun held up a finger. "And yes, as you theorized, it can be almost fatally draining, but once your skills have fully matured…" She sighed. "In any event, it is how I have stayed safe all these years…despite my reluctant involvement, at times, in *shinobi* politics."

Snowhawk spoke earnestly. "Your skills are beyond remarkable, great lady. Not even Moonshadow's august teacher, Brother Eagle, appears to share your level of development."

The White Nun laughed. "You are so sweet, child. And I know just what you recalled while saying that: Moonshadow here…trying to link with my Motto-San." She looked to Moonshadow. "The attempt seems to have made him suspicious of you, but don't take offense. His wariness will pass. Motto-San is a particularly loyal beast, and I'd say he simply disliked another trying to usurp my control."

Moonshadow nodded at her intently. Meeting Motto had been harrowing, all right.

"Of course your attempt to meld with him failed." She leaned forward. "Only one set of very unusual circumstances can break or override my link with him. They are so unlikely, they're not worth discussing."

Motto-San and Moonshadow looked up at the ceiling at the same time. A moment later, a wave of late spring rain began to fall noisily.

"I knew you possessed the Old Country science of insight," Moonshadow said, "but I didn't know you also had this...this ultimate mastery of the Eye of the Beast."

The White Nun smiled sadly. "Child, if all the powers over which I am custodian were known, the Shogun himself would probably want me dead, though I am neither spy nor warrior. I have only ever used my skills personally in self-defense. Even then, with great loathing and *only* to the extent required to save my life."

She thrust a finger at Snowhawk, startling her. "No, it's not therefore pointless power, child! I was put here to teach, never to do. Let others bear the karma of how they use my training. For good or evil, for glory or destruction. No, I know *my* destiny. And knowing it, I must honor it. Such is everyone's ideal path. To know and thus to honor."

"Forgive my ignorant thoughts." Snowhawk dipped her chin. She paused, then thumbed at the ever-watchful Motto. "Heron said you were guarded by a bear."

"I was, and guarded well, for many years. I'd go south each winter and visit a warrior monk I trained on the southernmost island, while the bear slept in this very shrine. But in the end that magnificent beast died of old age. She's buried close by."

To Moonshadow's surprise, she raised one hand and wiped her iridescent red eyes.

"Ironic, is it not, the replacement the *kami* chose for her? A lost or escaped puppy wandering in a forest...that turned out to be a bear-hunting hound. The Satake Clan are clever breeders. Motto-San too has proved a fine protector, as you found out. I can order him to patrol, then turn my mind to other, more pressing matters. Of course, at such times my awareness is somewhat impaired. Hence I could sense your distant approach but not recognize you, as I normally would."

Snowhawk inclined her head and frowned.

"No." The White Nun quickly shook her head. "Don't wonder what those matters are. Too hard to explain to you at this time."

"Forgive me prying then, but was one such task *summoning us*?" Snowhawk gestured at herself and Moonshadow. "That's why we've come. To evacuate you."

"To help you escape the coming attack," Moon-shadow put in keenly.

The White Nun sighed. "Though I *was* expecting to see you someday soon, I did not summon you." She eyed their shocked faces. "But I see that someone did, apparently using me—and this imagined threat—as bait." She closed her eyes for a few seconds. "Yes. There *is* an attack coming. But I am not its target. And had you not come to me, it would have befallen you somewhere else." She raised one eyebrow. "Anyone genuinely out to capture or slay me would risk enraging the many *shinobi*, some of them now clan masters, who I have known, taught, and even healed during—well, at least the last fifty years. Warmongers like to be in control of who they upset as much as they can. They delight in acting as puppet masters, using the people of the shadows against their samurai foes or even each other, but they avoid lighting fires no one can control or quench. No, no, in this matter, I was ever but the lure, and you two the tasty fish, to be hooked and fried, each for a different reason."

Moonshadow and Snowhawk stared at each other. They'd been set up? It was all a ploy?

"So it is now *I* who must rescue *you two*." The White Nun laughed almost bitterly. Beside her, the great dog huffed, threw back its head, and let out a

243

single wolfish howl. Though Moonshadow saw it coming, the powerful bay still made him flinch. The sage glanced at her animal guardian. He quickly lay down, stretching out and resting his head on his enormous paws. Despite the more relaxed position, Motto's eyes stayed fixed on Moonshadow.

"*Me* saving *you* could be difficult." The White Nun sighed again. "Given that I will not kill, your safety may be something I cannot guarantee. Do you not sense why you were each trapped? He wanted *you*, boy, out of Edo so he could take his revenge. They wanted *you*, girl, far from the Grey Light Order's walls so that you may be recaptured."

"*He...*" Moonshadow's face darkened. "You mean Silver Wolf? He's behind all this?"

"I'd rather die than go back!" Snowhawk snapped. Motto half rose, glaring at her.

"You know I won't let that happen," Moonshadow said stubbornly. The dog's head turned at him.

With a knowing smile, the White Nun waved a finger. Motto sank to the floor.

"Let's discuss a thing or two." She bowed her head, and her hands trembled. "Your enemies indeed approach. What a large force they send against only two people! We should leave at dawn, evade them in the forest, get off this mountain as they ascend it. I cannot let a battle take place in or around this shrine. It is holy ground."

"Will we escape them? Is it too late?" There was fear in Snowhawk's eyes.

"Only destiny cannot be escaped," the White Nun said gently. "And fortunately for mortals, destiny is fluid, pliant; it changes with every decision one makes." She arched forward to eye Moonshadow closely. "Mark me then, boy. Some battles, one *must* win alone. Others, the winning comes by learning to accept help, the right help. Even I have learned to depend, at times, on the strength of others. A network of holy men, old pilgrims, passes this mountain regularly. It is they who bring Motto-San and me much of our food, in exchange for healing and counsel." The White Nun tapped her chest. "Oh, I know, it rankles the pride and can confuse the mind, but it's a lesson even the great must learn. Choosing to depend on others can demand as much courage as fighting alone and outnumbered!"

She stared at Moonshadow knowingly. "Leadership, like most things, is about *balance*; knowing when to put faith in a friend." Her red eyes flicked to Snowhawk, then back to him. "And when to trust *your* instincts alone because they happen to be the wisest available. You're young, inexperienced in the ways of the world, that's all. Be patient. In time, you will get there."

He frowned. So she even knew the background thoughts that had nagged him throughout this mission. His uncertainty in his leadership, doubts about the way he'd handled the volatile Snowhawk. Her words were astute and comforting, surely a beacon to follow, but he *had to know* one thing: just how long would it take him to ... get there?

"No one can answer that" — she waved away his imminent question — "because it is unwritten. It depends on you! Besides, you and I have more pressing business. Though you were led here in deception, yet were you meant to come." The sage gestured for Moonshadow to approach. He shuffled forward on his knees, wary of Motto's jaws as he drew right up to the White Nun.

The Akita Matagi's blue eyes tracked him, but the animal stayed still.

"I must pass something to you now," the White Nun said solemnly. "An anointing. It will rest within you, a planted seed, but in time it will grow, helping you take the Eye of the Beast to that ultimate level: long-distance sight control. Be very patient. It will take years. It's the most useful of all powers, I think, though also the hardest to refine. It is the means by which, for a long time, I've watched over you, both in the field and at home."

Moonshadow's mouth fell open. "The cat! The temple cat!"

"My spy." The White Nun flashed a crafty smile. "I chose her to be my eyes upon you and my disciple Heron. She is a true cat, not a spirit creature or a mystic's disguise, but from time to time I watch things through her. When I sense your mind reaching for hers, I step back and release her into your control. I felt you reach for Motto too, back down on the mountain. But if I'd stepped back then and let you control him, who would have herded you up here to me?" She patted her chest. "Yes, there's the cat and Motto-San. Linking thus to two creatures can leave me most depleted, in need of...*sleep* for weeks, though I have grown more skilled over time in managing the energies and delaying such rests."

"But..." Snowhawk gaped. "When you must rest, for *weeks*, who protects you?"

The White Nun tittered. "The snows that seal off this mountain. Yes, children, in winter, I sleep like that bear. Long links can cause an exchange of traits. You will see."

Moonshadow was fascinated. So those animal

residues were only the beginning. "Why, great sage," he asked, "do you care so much about *me?*"

She quickly shook her head. "Not yet, boy. Be patient. It is not yet the time."

"I don't understand," Snowhawk blurted. "The time for what?"

"The time to speak of my debt to his mother." The White Nun pointed at Moonshadow.

Her words tore through him like a fire arrow. Moonshadow felt himself reel where he sat. A matter of some ten words, and his world was turning inside out.

Snowhawk gasped. "His mother?"

The White Nun raised a hand sternly. "No, stay your tongues, do not probe further. We must not speak of this subject until the right time, and only in the monastery in Edo, lest a certain destiny be thwarted." She gazed into Moonshadow's eyes. "Now. Will you, on trust and in faith, even with so many unanswered questions, accept my anointing?"

Feeling that his brain had just frozen, Moonshadow managed only a scant nod.

"Good boy." The sage stared, breathing in and out deeply, just once. "There. It is done. I have just planted in you all that I can. The remainder you must find...elsewhere."

"Forgive my brashness," Snowhawk said impulsively, "but there is a certain blessing *I* would beg for." Her chin trembled. "To rid me of a problem, no, a poison—"

"No, no, no, child." The White Nun sighed heavily. "You would ask me to sweep away the hate and bitterness that fill your poor heart with anger? Only you can do that."

"How?" Tears rolled down Snowhawk's face.

Fixing her with a tender look, the sage spoke gently. "Your enemy told you how."

Snowhawk wiped her cheek and slowly blinked. "Be like the river?"

"Be like the river," the White Nun repeated softly. "Wisdom, child, is where you find it. The one who counseled you thus spoke from a natural gift she truly has; one she might have lived to serve, had her life not begun much as yours did, being orphaned by the hand of bandits, then being raised *shinobi*, made special, made alone...made hard as folded steel! How ironic! Your enemy has yet to master her own rage, believe me, but nonetheless she advised you out of the one place left in her that is not hunter, captor, *killer*. So ignore her deeds, be mindful of her sorrow, and heed her words anyway."

"It's so confusing." Snowhawk shrugged. "I know she spoke the truth, but why—"

"Even the she-wolf shows a trace of tenderness at the sight of an orphan cub." The White Nun ignored the questioning frown on Moonshadow's face and winked at Snowhawk.

Struggling to her feet, the sage turned and made for a thick bedroll under a lantern on the far wall. Motto stood briskly and walked backward at her side, his eyes moving constantly between the two unexpected guests.

The White Nun stopped at the foot of her bed, looking back at them.

"I am empty now. I must grow truly still, withdraw inside my mind's deepest shield to recover my strength. At such times, my life is in Motto's paws, for while resting thus, I can neither sense nor repel any form of attack. But do not fear: if your enemies arrive, Motto will hear them and raise the alarm. So now, both of you, sleep. I will wake you just before sunrise."

Snowhawk eyed the dog as it sat down beside the White Nun's bedroll. "But, apart from Motto-San, you have no maids or servants. Who will first wake *you*?"

The sage batted her strange red eyes. "No one needs to. Though all living things require rest, let's just say I do not sleep in the way of men, women, and beasts."

"I once heard," Snowhawk said, "that there were people who lived without sleep in the ancient days, the Old Country days, in that time before the first scrolls were written. But that's probably just another legend...."

"No," the White Nun said wearily, "we...they... did live that way."

Moonshadow gaped at Snowhawk. *We?* Could it be true? Was the White Nun herself actually *ancient?* Was she—through some powerful lost science—immortal now, perhaps the last of her kind? If she had been alive—even as a child—in the Old Country days, she would now be at least hundreds of—perhaps even a thousand—years old. He stared at her, amazed. Had this frail-looking old lady actually found a way to cheat death itself and live forever?

The White Nun caught his eye and gave a soft groan. "If only, boy, that were so."

The sage stretched out slowly on the bedroll, lying on her side, quickly entering some form of trance. Beside her Motto sat, tireless and vigilant. As they watched, the White Nun's breathing slowed until finally it appeared to stop.

The pair looked at each other, dumbfounded.

Moonshadow shook his head. "She can do all that," he whispered, "but not guarantee our survival.

So much power, yet there are crucial things she refuses to get involved with." He clicked his tongue.

"Is that not proof," Snowhawk replied slowly, "that she truly *is* a saint?"

He tried to ponder her question as he stretched out on his own bedroll, exhausted and eager to let sleep find him. But one thought alone drove all others from his mind.

The White Nun knows who my mother was.

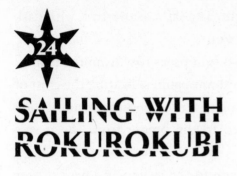

24

SAILING WITH ROKUROKUBI

Moonshadow awoke with a start, the sting of crisp salt air in his nose. He sat up.

It was daylight. He was no longer in the shrine, nor even on the mountain. How?

How did he get *here*? This was impossible. It had to be some test the White Nun had miraculously thrown him into. Was Snowhawk being tested in the same way?

Scrambling to his feet, Moonshadow turned a circle as his head cleared.

He stood on the elevated rear deck of a long, single-masted ship that sat low in the ocean. There was no land in sight. The sky was overcast, with dark clouds on the horizon.

Beside him, two iron poles rose from the planks, and on each, vertical war banners bearing the crest of the Tokugawa Shogun tensed and snapped. A wide white sail fluttered in the breeze from the mast's crossbeam.

Moonshadow ran to the railing and peered over the side. This ship was built to be propelled by both wind and samurai rowers, but there were no rowers. He turned again, eyes hunting quickly. No crew either. He tilted his head, listening. All was silent belowdecks.

"Nobody," he murmured. Great! Moonshadow hung his head. The ship *was* deserted. How was he supposed to get home?

"Is it safe to come down now?" The woman's voice came from the direction of the mast. "Is it over?"

He leapt from the rear to the main deck. "Where are you?" Moonshadow shouted.

There was a long, slow, *swish*ing sound. Then he spotted her, sliding down the mast. A woman in a golden kimono; older than Snowhawk, younger than Heron. Her hair was neatly thatched on the crown of her head in an elaborate highborn lady's style.

Moonshadow stared at her, biting his lip. Was

she the wife of a great lord? Or a dignitary, perhaps? Maybe the ship had been transporting her. Had an enemy found them?

He ran forward and bowed. The lady gave him a stately nod. She must have been hiding up the mast, hanging on to its rigging.

Why? *How?* Did her guards help her get up there?

"It was awful." The woman's pale but youthful face creased. Moonshadow could see terrible memories flickering behind her large brown eyes. "It went after them, moving systematically through every part of the ship." She tightened her kimono around herself. "One by one, they all jumped, or were taken."

"Taken…" Moonshadow repeated, glancing warily over each shoulder. "What was it? What do you mean, *taken?*" He tipped his head, checking in all directions. No. He heard no lurking entity. He also sensed no *shinobi* presence.

"It…it tore them apart." She motioned at him. "That sword on your back won't stop it." The lady hunched sorrowfully. "Many brave warriors died trying to fend it off."

She drew a breath and pointed below the edge of the elevated rear deck.

There, in a dark wood frame, stood a foreign-made

mirror. This imported treasure, the lady's golden kimono, the ship itself, all spoke of money and the highest connections. So this lady *was* a person of great importance. Moonshadow's heart fluttered. What if she was royalty and the White Nun had flung him here to protect her? What an incredible honor!

Beside the foreign mirror stood what the lady had pointed at: an open sliding panel revealing a narrow flight of wooden stairs.

"Please." She wrung her hands. "Go ahead of me, belowdecks, just in case...."

Moonshadow drew his back-mounted *shinobi* straight sword in a flash of steel. "A pleasure, my lady. Please follow at least four paces behind me, for safety."

"Yes, of course, brave young sir." She gestured for him to lead. Moonshadow took four long strides, then motioned for her to follow. He was guarding royalty! Eager, excited, he reached the stairs more than four paces ahead of the lady.

As he raised his sword, ready to descend, movement in the mirror caught his eye.

His gaze flicked to it, and his mouth fell open. He was seeing things. Moonshadow jolted back a pace. That was no normal mirror. It must be bewitched, a haunted mirror!

For in it he saw the lady he protected, but her

neck was elongating, hoisting her head high into the air on an ever-stretching cable of pale flesh.

It was a vision of a Rokurokubi: a fabled, sinister *yokai* that usually pretended to be human before ambushing its prey in some remote forest or lonely field. Using its distinctive anatomy, a Rokurokubi choked, headbutted, or just plain terrorized its victim to death. Moonshadow flinched. Pretended to be human. A lady. Royalty, even.

Then he knew. What he saw was no vision, it was a *reflection*.

He whirled around, bringing his sword up fast. The Rokurokubi's head flew at him, while the neck continued to stretch yet keep its thickness. Its gold-kimonoed body stood rigid in the background. Its womanly face was dark and frightening now, all sharp lines around tiny, cold black eyes. That formerly petite mouth had stretched to three times its width. Shining lips opened, and a single row of oversize human teeth snapped.

Moonshadow ducked and ran below the lunging head and snaking neck. He hopped to one side and turned fast, raising his sword, ready to cut down hard through the neck. But before his blade could fall, the head swung back and hurled itself sideways into him. Moonshadow streaked through the air, crashing to the main deck, sliding and finally rolling to the foot of the mast. He forced himself up quickly, nursing a bruised shoulder.

The Rokurokubi's body held its ground but turned as the meandering neck and bobbing head came after him. Moonshadow sheathed his sword and jumped onto the mast, clamping his hands and feet around it and ascending monkey-style. As he rose level with the crossbeam, something pale swished behind him. He turned his head and saw a thick coil of neck curving away. Moonshadow froze, looking about him in abject horror.

Its neck now elongated to perhaps the length of the ship, the Rokurokubi was steadily winding itself round and round both mast and sail. It was keeping each twist out of sword range, patiently forming a fleshy cage that could tighten at any moment.

Just as that thought struck him, the gaps between the coils of neck began to shrink. Moonshadow jumped onto the crossbeam, drawing his sword.

With a loud *whump*, the creature's head struck his from behind. He sagged to one knee, stunned. The sound of snapping teeth rang loud in one ear. He twisted away, flailing with his weapon. Missed!

Whump, it rammed him again from a different angle. His head ringing, Moonshadow fell forward onto the crossbeam, the sword spinning from his hand.

With a hard sideswipe, the Rokurokubi flipped him onto his back. Wide-eyed and gasping, barely fighting off panic, Moonshadow sat up fast.

The monstrous, scowling head hurtled at him with blinding speed. Before he could react, its massive teeth closed around his bruised shoulder. He struggled, groaned, and threw blind punches. Unperturbed, the Rokurokubi hoisted Moonshadow and then swung him at the crossbeam, headfirst. He winced as the beam's dark wood flashed toward him.

Then the beam went black.

He blinked and turned his head. Everything was now black and he was tumbling, upside down. No, he was still again now, but on his back...and just his shoulders moved.

Moonshadow opened his eyes. Lantern light. Ceiling shadows. Snowhawk was shaking him, her face ashen. He lay on his bedroll, in the shrine, on the White Nun's mountain.

Realizing what had happened, he let out a low moan. *Another* dream attack!

"Thank the gods!" Snowhawk released him and sank back wearily. "The way you were gasping, I thought it was happening again! And it was, wasn't it?"

"Yes! Thank *you*." He patted the back of her hand. "Once more you have saved my life." He peered up at her. "Hey, that's my *second*. There have been no attacks on you. *Why?*"

She shrugged. "I'm pretty sure dream assassins have to focus on one victim at a time, who then gets pursued all the way to death. Encouraging, hey?" Snowhawk paused thoughtfully. "Now I remember: a Death Dream killer must imprint himself onto his target before the hunt can begin.... He has to look at his prey and forge the unseen link... just like *you* with that falcon."

"Imprint? You mean he's already marked me?" Moonshadow blinked. "And I didn't know?" Images flashed through his mind: the crowded marketplace, that odd, confident youth in city clothes, and his bold, peculiar stare. Moonshadow scowled. He *had* felt something then.

"It could have been anyone we passed on the whole journey," Snowhawk murmured.

"It was a guy, a *young* guy." Moonshadow raised his head, touching his neck. "And I'll know him if we see him again, I promise you." He was drenched with sweat. He looked around. The White Nun still lay in her trance, so still she could have been a fallen statue. Motto-San lay beside her, as motionless as if drugged.

Yet his ice-blue eyes remained open, their glow half as intense as when he had cornered his visitors in that rocky gully.

"Why didn't they know I was under attack?" Moonshadow frowned hard.

Snowhawk gave an impatient sigh. "Remember what she said? When she rests, she can't sense or repel any kind of attack. As for Motto-San, she said if your enemies arrive, he'll hear them and raise the alarm. The Death Dream *shinobi* can't be that physically close, then."

Sitting up, Moonshadow ran his hands over his face and through his hair. "Snowhawk," he whispered haggardly, "what if this keeps happening? What chance do I have if it happens when we're separated?"

She thought awhile before answering. "I know enough of this dark art to know there is only one defense during an attack. You must fight, *in* the nightmare, as you would in real life. Fight, and win."

"How?" His mouth quirked to one side at the impractical notion. "When these evil *yokai* invade my mind, I don't even know it's a dream. I'm confused; I think it's real. Anyway, just now, I *tried* to put up a fight. I was nothing against the creature's powers."

"Did you try using yours?" Snowhawk indicated Motto. "The Eye of the Beast?"

"Hah!" Moonshadow rolled bloodshot eyes. "And duel the Rokurokubi with *what*? Irritable seagulls? How about dolphins? I could have watched myself die up on that mast through dolphin eyes." He shook his head. "Because that's *all* they could have done. Watched!"

Her nose creased. She squinted at him. "Rokurokubi? Dolphins?" Snowhawk edged closer and took his face in her hands. She asked gently, "Are you going mad?"

"No." He grinned awkwardly. "In the dream I was climbing the mast of a ship."

"Ah! I see." She nodded. "I'm so tired, I can't think straight." Snowhawk gripped his arm tightly. "Pray if there's another attack, it happens in daylight."

"Why?" Moonshadow scowled. "Can't I just pray there are no more attacks?"

"Listen to me. Though daylight assaults are the most powerful form, they at least begin with the victims knowing they're being dragged into a waking nightmare. That's what the dream assassin sacrifices in order to launch a day attack; the advantage of complete surprise, the confusion a sleeper faces. There's even a reliable giveaway sign."

Moonshadow read the discomfort on her face. "What happens? What will alert me?"

Snowhawk swallowed hard. "You may or may not see your attacker just before the assault begins, but once it does, you won't see anything. You'll go blind."

"Fine, then, if you see me go blind during the day, just grab me, snap me out of it, and—" He saw her shake her head quickly. "What? Why not?"

Snowhawk took a deep breath. "You're better off taking your chances in the dream battle, no matter how scary. Because if you're shaken out of a daylight attack dream by somebody else, you *stay* blind."

"What? And you think I should *pray* for a daylight attack?"

His raised voice brought Motto's big head up. The dog stared at him. Moonshadow held his hands up in surrender until the head sagged down again.

Snowhawk shrugged. "If it happens, Moonshadow, you just have to win! Use your special skill. Find a way! Just remember what I said," she whispered. "Fight like it's real life."

"Real life?" Moonshadow patted his chest, shoulder, and the back of his head. "I feel bruised. So can injuries from these dreams follow you back into real life?"

She nodded gravely. "For both you and your opponent, it can work that way, yes."

He lay back on the bedroll, hands behind his head, desperate to sleep, desperate not to. Snowhawk went quiet beside him. After a few minutes, she began snoring.

Fight like it's real. Some solution. It was impossible. He was going to die.

OF ONE MIND

The four candles lay in a diamond around the scroll of empowerment sutras. Their dancing light threw misshapen shadows up the walls of the Grey Light Order's briefing room. Eagle, Heron, Mantis, and Badger sat facing each of the candles in the *seiza* position, their folded knees pointing at the document in the diamond's center.

"Is everyone ready?" Eagle's eyes flicked around the group. His three companions nodded. "Sister Heron, please tell us exactly what you saw, before we proceed."

Heron gave a seated bow. "This was my dream. In light of all the White Nun has taught me, I do humbly call it prescient." She drew in a breath. "I saw Moonshadow standing at the top of a tall, primitive stone tower. Lightning flashed all around it. A great, colorful serpent climbed after him, winding itself around the tower on its way up." She cleared her throat and spoke softly. "I apologize for the scream that woke you all."

"What of waking riddle phrases? Did one come to you?" Eagle's face softened. "After the scream, perhaps."

"Yes, Brother Eagle." Heron smiled and then answered formally. "As I woke, this formed in my mind: *He will presently taste of future strength, or drown in his enemy's poison. His is not the choice.*"

"Comments?" Eagle paused. "Are we all of one mind in what we make of this?"

"His is not the choice: ours is the choice," Mantis said quickly. "For a change, the riddle phrase's meaning seems almost clear. Our actions here will decide Moonshadow's fate. True, we deployed Groundspider, and we hope he and his team will reach the mountain soon. But more is required of *us*."

Badger nodded. "It has a logic of its own, which I agree implies that *we* must act."

Heron gestured at the document between them. "I thought of this practice at once."

Three heads turned toward Eagle.

"Then we *are* all of one mind," he said. "Anticipating this, I had you, Badger, fetch the empowerment sutras. As it has been a while since their last use, let's recall the custom once more. We will each in turn read a full sutra aloud, one hundred times, at a contemplative pace, while the others focus their minds on Moonshadow, far to the north." Heron, Mantis, and Badger replied as one with a seated bow. Eagle nodded. "Whatever grace or skill from his future he needs to access now, I pray we can trigger it." A grim light flecked his eyes. "Before *our* strength fails."

"It will not," Mantis said defiantly. Heron shook her head. Badger grunted.

"Dawn is close. I will take the first reading," Eagle said confidently. "We'll have a break at sunset." He watched the others. "Unless that seems too great a burden?"

There was a long silence. Eagle smiled proudly, moved his candle aside, and reached for the scroll. It was time to deploy one of the Grey Light Order's most powerful secret arts.

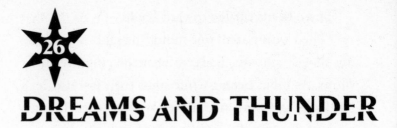

DREAMS AND THUNDER

S nowhawk had suggested they swap their mer-
chant costumes for their night suits until they
had cleared the haunted forest. Moonshadow
was grateful—at last, real freedom of movement
again! His suit was a light blue-grey, hers green-hued.
Both color schemes were popular choices for coun-
tryside and forest stealth operations.

He had left his hood off but tied down his pack
and mounted his sword as if about to scale a castle
wall or run through a battlefield. Anything could
happen now that they had left the shrine. At least it
wasn't raining and they were covering ground fast.

Moonshadow's head twitched to one side. What was that? Approaching thunder cloaked the sound. He dropped into a crouch on the forest floor, angling his head. As the ominous muttering in the sky faded, his mouth fell open.

Leaning heavily on her gnarled walking stick, the White Nun watched him. Moonshadow's eyes closed as he listened.

"One man, moving quickly, climbing directly in our path." He stood. "A scout, I would say. Our other *friends* will be right behind him."

"I can't feel anyone." Snowhawk watched the ridge below them intently. "You know what that means."

"Do not fear *him*," the White Nun said firmly. "And that is all we'll say on the matter." She indicated a new downhill course with her stick. Motto flitted from behind her to gallop along it. "Down that way until we meet the ridge. Then turn east, through the ruins."

Thunder rumbled, closer now. Through gaps in the trees, Moonshadow saw the distant peak of a snow-covered mountain. It rose behind spiky green hills and sweeping folds in the land. He jumped as lightning struck the top of a closer hill. Moonshadow smelled no rain, but greenish, thundery clouds converged on the mountain, thick with hail, lightning, or both.

His mouth went dry. After that nightmare about the Kappa, green-tinged light bothered him. He blew out a long breath, remembering the equally fearful Rokurokubi dream attack. There was a good chance he'd be avoiding ships from now on. Moonshadow set his teeth. What would the next mind assault take from him, burden him with—?

He stopped himself. *Do not fear him.* The sage was right. This game had to end.

"Find me," Moonshadow whispered. "I know you can sense me. Come on...."

Striding ahead of Moonshadow and Snowhawk with surprising vigor, the White Nun followed her dog downhill, nimbly sidestepping rocks and logs as she wove through the forest to the plateau. Moonshadow's forehead creased as he watched her. Such agility!

By the time Moonshadow reached the ruins, with Snowhawk at his side, Motto had stretched out in the shade of a low, crumbling stone wall. The White Nun sat nearby on a curved, mossy log in the shade of a long, high hedge of black-green bamboo. She was hunched forward, head resting on her stick.

"Let them climb awhile, pass us by." The sage gestured at scattered flat stones. "Sit, save your strength. You may yet need it." She looked away, smiling secretively.

Moonshadow scouted the ruins. So this *was* once a small castle. Whoever had destroyed it had done a very thorough job; not one wall had been left intact.

He walked to the crumbling, gap-toothed remains of the outermost wall, once the little fortress's battlements. It was perched on the edge of the plateau. Peering over, Moonshadow caught sight of the haunted forest, almost directly below them. He shuddered.

Pacing back among the drizzled lines of rock, stands of bamboo, and haphazard forest growth where the others rested, Moonshadow sidestepped a rusty, fragmenting helmet. In it was a skull. Moonshadow shivered and looked up. The overcast green sky seemed to be darkening quickly. Was the air growing colder, or was it the scent of death that chilled his veins?

It was Snowhawk's turn to be a mind reader. "This is a most creepy place, even by day." She indicated a black-and-white tangle in a patch of grass between two stones. "There's a pile of charred bones right there."

Moonshadow noticed more signs of a fire-projectile attack. Broken arrows. Boulders and cut stones that were also blackened. Rusting spearheads with cubed charcoal trails behind them. There were even burnt scraps of armor, some riddled with punctures.

The White Nun covered her face with her hands. "They have a right to be bitter, the spirits in this place." She looked up, red eyes tearful. "None were shown the slightest mercy. Not lord, babe, nor dog." Motto stiffened and huffed.

Snowhawk approached the sage. "You brought us here for a reason, didn't you?"

"Clever child." The White Nun brushed her eyes with a knuckle. "Your kind avoids the pages of history, yet in shadow writes them. So remember this place. It was the handiwork of a certain young lord... named Silver Wolf."

Moonshadow's hands balled into fists. "He did *this*?"

"Oh, yes. And simply to settle a personal matter. I wonder how many died, jumped, or, as it ended, were pushed? All over an insult that had passed between two men."

"But this is far from his domain." Snowhawk looked around. "How could he—"

"With the former Shogun's permission." The sage shrugged. "A legal feud. He wiped out the noble family, their castle and servants, their samurai. Then, his precious *honor* not yet satisfied, he let his men loot the fiefdom's two villages that lie to the south. They took everything, triggering the famine, and soon the abandonments began, the very old, the very young...."

"That man's evil stench is everywhere." Moonshadow shook his head angrily and then spat. "In *his* honor!"

There was a loud roar of thunder overhead, and seconds later a blinding flash as lightning struck a tree thirty paces uphill from the ruins. The White Nun stood up. Motto ran to her feet. Another bolt of lightning streaked down into the forest, ten paces closer.

As the second flash's glare faded, Moonshadow squinted uphill. A maple sapling had been set on fire. Movement drew his eye. He flinched. Snowhawk grunted a curse.

Twenty strides to the left of the burning tree stood a line of figures.

"I count *nine*," Snowhawk said quickly, hurrying to his side. Moonshadow glanced at her. She had already—soundlessly—drawn her blade. He nodded grimly. No more running.

The line of figures strode forward, moving downhill in unison. One limped.

Moonshadow studied them as they advanced. Six were definitely men, hooded, armed with back-mounted straight swords. One wore a compact *shinobi* bow and a quiver of arrows. None looked familiar, but all six wore matching forest camouflage suits. He recognized the two-tone maple leaf pattern at once.

No wonder Snowhawk had cursed. The design was Clan Fuma's.

The tallest, strongest-looking ninja among them also wore a *shuko*, an iron climbing claw, over his left hand.

Always a hard combination to fight, Moonshadow thought with a frown: curved claw-blades in one hand, a *shinobi* sword in the other. He'd be a problem.

Moonshadow glanced to the right of the six Fuma ninja. Jiro grinned back at him, hands already gliding into his jacket. Beside the limping gangster walked a beautiful woman in a kimono, fanning herself and gazing at Snowhawk with watchful intelligence.

"That's her," Snowhawk whispered fearfully. "Ignore the face. That's Kagero."

At the end of the line walked a young man. His look was distinctive: makeup, fashionable hair worn long but untied, eye-catching clothes. Armed only with a dagger.

Yes. Moonshadow nodded. *I do remember you.* The market in that first town. The stranger with the bold stare. That feeling, like being struck with an icy

274

wave ... the imprinting! The youth broke into a remote smile. "I am Chikuma." The young man paced directly for Moonshadow, who instantly felt an odd pressure building in his head. "I come to grant your wish."

At least now Moonshadow knew his enemy. He set his jaw. "And I am—"

"Moonshadow of the Grey Light." Chikuma rubbed his hands together as he approached. "And, shortly, my thirty-fifth kill. What do you think of that?"

"I think," Moonshadow retorted, "you talk too much."

Then everything went black. It had happened: he was blind. Moonshadow felt himself freeze with terror on the spot. He heard fresh thunder, followed by the *snick*s of swords being drawn. Then his hearing also faded.

CONFRONTATION

Snowhawk bounded up onto a rock, her head quickly turning back and forth.

Was this what it looked like? Moonshadow obviously couldn't hear her now. She called his name again, but he was unresponsive, motionless, staring off into the distance. Chikuma was the same, a mirror to Moonshadow in stance and expression.

Were the two already battling each other in a dreamscape only they could see?

"Remember," Snowhawk muttered as if Moonshadow could hear her. "Like in real life."

The White Nun hurried to Moonshadow's side.

She stamped her gnarled stick forcefully. "Protect his body," the sage said quickly. "He fights his most dire battle."

Motto sprang in front of the White Nun and Moonshadow in a menacing stance, blue eyes on the enemy ninja.

Hoisting her blade, Snowhawk pointed it at Kagero. "I've decided to take your advice!" she shouted.

Kagero, still in disguise, bowed politely. "Why, thank you. A wise decision." The bounty hunter already held an open fan. Now she produced the other from inside her kimono, flicking it open as she drew it.

"I'll treasure your words." Snowhawk sneered. "The last advice you'll ever give!"

"Oh, don't be like that." Kagero advanced on her. "We're so much alike." She raised the fans, adopting an angular, warlike stance. "People always used to say *I* was beautiful and bad-tempered. Sounds a lot like you, huh?"

Jiro held up a *bo-shuriken* in each hand, edging closer with limping half steps.

The ninja wearing a *shuko* as his gauntlet pointed with it. "Don't forget: we take the girl deserter and the old woman *alive*." Five suited Fuma agents quickly encircled Snowhawk's rock. Their clawed leader cast an uneasy look at Chikuma. Snowhawk followed his glance and gasped.

Like Moonshadow, the youth remained frozen, wide-eyed, face blank, oblivious to the surrounding world. But Chikuma's eyes had changed: their pupils had vanished!

She looked back to Moonshadow. His eyes matched! It was creepy—now only the whites were visible! Snowhawk tensed. Moonshadow and Chikuma *were* locked in combat!

The White Nun stood at Moonshadow's side, clutching her stick with her head down as if praying. Snowhawk briefly considered trying to launch an attack on Chikuma but decided the risk to Moonshadow was simply too great. The Fuma agents would close in, try to stop her. In the process, Moonshadow would either be wounded by them or jolted out of the dream—*blind*.

The head ninja turned back, flicking his head at Kagero as if requesting orders.

Kagero pointed at Snowhawk with a fan. "Go ahead, gentlemen. Wear her down first, then I'll take over." Her mouth warped into a spiteful smirk. "It's really *my* responsibility to get her home alive, but if she won't submit, *barely alive* is also fine." She let out a soft chuckle. "And once we're there, I have so many questions for you, my dear, on behalf of *our* former clan's leadership! You'll talk to Kagero about your new friends, won't you?" She laughed again, this time with unconcealed malice. "Submit! You have no choice!"

They all flinched as lightning struck a patch of weeds near the ruin. A puff of smoke rose from the charred circle it left.

"Submit?" Snowhawk gave a menacing laugh of her own. She felt her eyes glaze over with wrath. "Here's what I say to that, Kagero. I think it a most appropriate answer."

Snowhawk flung her sword point-first at the ground alongside her rock. As it dug in, she dropped to one knee, wrists crossing as her hands flashed into her jacket. Darting back out, her right hand whip-cracked in the air.

Almost instantly a cloud of smoke plumed at Kagero's feet. Snowhawk's left hand reappeared and whipped forward. A curve-bladed Fuma *shuriken* whirred through the smokescreen. As the teeming white cloak enveloped Kagero, she gave a loud shriek.

Snatching up the sword, Snowhawk backflipped off the rock. One of Jiro's black *bo-shuriken* streaked past her. She landed on balance in time to see the head ninja signaling.

Three of his camouflaged agents ran for the White Nun and Moonshadow.

Motto bolted forward and threw himself at the closest one, rearing up and ramming chest to chest, big paws swiping inward to trap the man's arms. The other two agents leapt clear as Motto drove their companion into the ground. Swords ready, they advanced on Moonshadow and the White Nun. The sage raised a trembling hand, then made it a fist.

The pair of ninja stopped walking and turned to glare at each other. Both went into defensive stances.

"Who are you?" one shouted. "What treachery is this?"

"Who am I? *You're* the infiltrator!" his agitated comrade snapped back.

There was a bright flash of steel between them, the ring of impact as one cut and the other blocked. Hand guards locking together, they began to shove each other back and forth. Behind them, Motto released the ninja he had downed, springing away as the obviously shaken man fumbled drawing his sword. His camouflage suit was torn and he moved as if the dog had badly bruised him head to foot.

Jiro ran around them all, his second *bo-shuriken* raised, targeting Snowhawk as she scrambled backward between two piles of crumbling wall stones.

Snowhawk watched her smoke bomb's cloud disperse. Kagero still stood in what had been its center. Teeth set, she pulled a *shuriken* from her shoulder. *A Fuma* shuriken, Snowhawk thought, and smiled. The *shuriken* wound itself was shallow and it barely bled, but as Kagero's fingers probed the new tear in her flower-patterned kimono, she cursed wildly.

The bounty hunter's face shifted, her true appearance breaking through the *shinobi* illusion. A more sharply lined countenance locked fiery eyes on Snowhawk.

"Congratulations on that lucky throw! Savor it while you can! Because before I am done with you, little squirrel," Kagero growled, "you will beg Lord Hachiman for death!"

Snowhawk swallowed. Lucky throw? That smoke-bomb-and-*shuriken*-combination trick was one of her best moves! And since combat fatigue reduced throwing speed, she'd cunningly used the ploy as an opening attack, striking while she was still fresh. The trick would have killed any other opponent outright. But not Kagero! Snowhawk shook her head. Apart from inflicting a pathetically minor wound, all she'd done was make her enemy angry. Great! Now Kagero would fight even harder. Snowhawk eyed the bounty hunter's furious expression, her hateful eyes.

She frowned thoughtfully. Kagero would fight harder, yes, but maybe not better.

Part of the White Nun's counsel came back to her. *Your enemy has yet to master her own rage.* Snowhawk's eyes lit up. The infamous Kagero was an amazing fighter, but was rage the untried gap in her armor? How ironic. Snowhawk sighed. Anger had proved *her* greatest weakness too. If she was to attempt the impossible—defeating Kagero—she'd *have* to control it now, even when provoked.

Victory would belong to whoever could be the most like that river. Would it turn out to be Kagero—or her? The Fuma, her childhood, all those dark and bitter memories! She had to get past them, or she stood no chance. But even now, life-and-death situation or not, *could she do it?*

Snowhawk set her jaw. Failure was not an option. Others were counting on her! She looked protectively at Moonshadow. Riling Kagero right here would put him at terrible risk.

I must lead them away, thought Snowhawk to herself. Lead them away from Moonshadow so he has a fighting chance against Chikuma. As long as they don't take me alive, I don't care what happens. Grimly, she half smiled. A simple enough plan. Make the rest of this wolf pack give chase and draw them off the White Nun too. Then bait Kagero!

She cupped three Fuma *shuriken* from her holsters, then threw each hard and fast.

The first flew at the claw-handed head ninja, who was trying to pacify the two the White Nun had tricked into fighting each other. Missing its mark, the *shuriken* struck one of the confused fighters in the neck. The ninja shouted in alarm, then crumpled. The man he'd been struggling with flinched, suddenly recognizing his leader. The White Nun's influence over them had run its course.

Snowhawk took a pace backward. Even with *one* down, the odds remained *nasty*.

She lobbed the second *shuriken* at Jiro, forcing him to duck and shearing off a matted lock of hair near the crown of his head. He straightened up and swore at her.

The third *shuriken* she thrust at Kagero, but the experienced agent, despite her wound, was ready this time, and she blocked it with one of her war fans. With a *clunk* and a flash of iron spokes, the throwing star wheeled to the leaf-strewn ground.

Kagero stared at the *shuriken* she had pulled from her flesh, then looked up. "You are Grey Light now, yet you use Fuma-designed *shuriken* to battle us?" Her face swam with barely controlled fury. "An insult! I am a professional. You just made this personal. Get her!"

Spinning about, Snowhawk broke into a hard run, her eyes on the area uphill where the lightning struck most often. Hard footfalls pounded the ground behind her as she dashed between two gently swaying stands of bamboo and out onto open ground.

Be careful what you start, Snowhawk told herself.

She hurdled a log, sidestepped a rain-cut trench, and glanced over one shoulder.

The fallen ninja lay curled up, staunching his fast-bleeding neck wound.

But apart from him and Chikuma, every other enemy was now right behind her.

28

NUMBER ONE TARGET

Silver Wolf awoke with a start and propped himself up on one elbow.

He had told his men he was going into his bedchamber to sit and meditate, but he suspected that at least his sharpest guards, the father-and-son bodyguard team, knew the real reason. He had spent most of the night wide awake, pacing his audience chamber, scheming. Today, a dull ache had steadily grown in his head, and he'd felt the need to try to sleep it off.

On entering this, the innermost room of his castle's keep, he had hung a simple, ink-brushed portrait on the wall, one that had been relayed to him on Katsu's orders through a chain of agents in the field. Then, sagging backward onto his futon, he had fallen asleep at once. He was unsure for how long, but it was still daylight outside.

Now all trace of his headache was gone, and he felt strangely alert. He found his eyes drawn to the rectangle of handmade paper dangling below the wall lamp's iron bracket.

The warlord stood up and stared at it with a dark, sullen expression. The crude portrait showed a long-faced youth with an ample head of dark hair, tied back in a single tail. The boy's eyes were sharp, purposeful, his nose long, lips thin, chin pointy, and face free of scars.

"I have never seen you," Silver Wolf muttered, his chest immediately heaving with anger, "but now I know you, Moonshadow of the Grey Light. Do you still live?" He glanced at the diffused glow coming through the oiled paper squares of the sliding screen. "Or have my allies done their job by now"—his voice built into a roar—"and taken your stinking little head?"

Silver Wolf dropped to one knee, one hand burrowing between the futon and the tatami beneath it. He sprang back to his feet and his arm streaked forward, fingers aligned, pointing at the picture. Polished steel caught the light as it whirled through the air. A low *thud* followed. Silver Wolf blinked at the picture, then flashed a maniacal grin. His small samurai-style throwing knife, made from the same folded steel as his swords, stuck from the picture's grim face, right between Moonshadow's eyes.

"Yes!" Silver Wolf's stare narrowed with sustained hate. "A good start, but not enough!" He twisted to the sword rack at the head of his bed, snatched up his long sword, and drew it from the scabbard. Hurling the scabbard to his futon, Silver Wolf rushed the picture, *hakama* trousers rustling as he sped across the room. He swung a blindingly fast cut downward at the face, stopping his whispering blade's tip a finger's width short of the paper.

The sliding door to his bedchamber flew open. His father-and-son bodyguard team appeared around it, faces wary, hands ready on their undrawn swords. They glanced around the room, frowned, then stared at the warlord with baffled expressions.

After studying his master's incensed face and drawn blade, the older samurai waved his son away and bowed low. A shrewd light came on in his eyes.

"Forgive the intrusion, my lord. We were overcautious; we did not intend to disturb your practice."

"Get out!" Silver Wolf stood, hands and sword

trembling with fury, his unblinking eyes on the samurai as he bowed again and closed the door.

The warlord looked back at the picture. His eyebrows fell and mouth twisted as he drove the tip of his blade through Moonshadow's cheek and into the wood behind it.

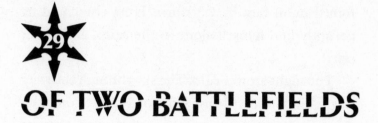

29

OF TWO BATTLEFIELDS

Moonshadow felt his body start to relax as the silent blackness thinned.

At first he made out only shifting shadows, heard just one sound, a distant owl's call. Then abruptly he found that he could see and hear properly again.

But not, he realized at once, the sights and sounds of his actual life.

He looked around, turning a slow, wary circle. Was he simply turning inside the dream? Or did his body rotate now, out in the real world?

This *had* to be a dream, a daylight mind attack,

forced upon him by Chikuma. How else could he abruptly find himself alone in the ruins, and under *stars*?

The night air was cold. The sky through the trees starry and still, with no signs of thunder or lightning. Far up the mountain, a wolf howled, then its whole pack joined in.

Moonshadow paced through the ruins, looking around. Yes, he *was* alone. An urge came to him. A prompt to go to that wall on the edge of the plateau, to look over as he had before.

"No," Moonshadow said instinctively, "I won't." The urge repeated, more insistent now. He steeled himself against it and felt its strength quickly halve. Then it was gone.

"Well," he said to himself, "that wasn't so bad."

Twigs snapped at the other end of the ruins.

Muffled footfall, then a *thump*. He turned fast, eyes hunting for the source of the noises. Louder snapping, closer. Moonshadow gripped the jacket directly over his heart.

An awful, now familiar feeling spiraled through him, growing stronger with each passing moment. It made his breathing accelerate, his stomach knot.

Something genuinely terrible was approaching. He had no idea how he knew, but he was utterly certain of it. He stepped up onto a cracked boulder, peering through the stunted trees and scattered rocks in the ruins. There, staying in shadow: a figure. Female?

It was weaving toward him in the dark, approaching with skittish, disturbing bounds and lunges. Every movement was too fast, too sharp, impossible, yet on it came. Moonshadow swallowed. It couldn't be human. Not even a *shinobi* could move that way.

His right hand flew up, fingers stabbing for the grip of the sword on his back. They closed around air. Moonshadow shuddered deeply.

His sword was gone.

Ahead of him, whatever was coming let out a long, slow *hiss*.

Snowhawk looked back downhill. In the heart of the ruins, Chikuma and Moonshadow faced each other, stock-still as before, eyes open, pupils gone. The White Nun hovered at Moonshadow's side, her eyes closed. What was she doing? And where was Motto-San?

Movement between two of her pursuers drew Snowhawk's eye. She saw the huge animal charging up the hill, teeth bared, and it made her sigh grate-fully. The White Nun would not kill with her awe-some powers, but nor would she abandon her companions to battle these fiends alone.

Snowhawk's seven attackers encircled her; Mr. Claw and the remaining hooded Fuma ninja, the limping Jiro, and the relentlessly scowling Kagero.

Raising a *bo-shuriken*, Jiro leered. "Time you started walking like me!"

He drew back his hand and tensed for a powerful throw, but just on the point of release Motto crashed into him from behind.

The *shuriken* whizzed wide and stuck in a slim young maple tree. Snowhawk watched Motto tram-ple the gangster and push him along the ground. Ignoring his wild punches, the dog rammed Jiro into a roll with its head and then bit its screaming target.

She marveled at Motto's enthusiastic attack. So, animals instantly hated Jiro too.

"Get this thing off me!" Jiro wailed as Motto clamped his wrist and started dragging him away along the forest floor. "Iiiii-eeee…" The gangster's screams rose to a high pitch. "Don't let it eat me!"

"Everyone has their problems," Kagero sniffed, eyeing her bloodied shoulder. "This kimono was expensive!"

"Enough delays," the leader snapped at his men. "Take her *now!*"

He stood back as his four remaining underlings ran at Snowhawk. They formed a diamond around her and began edging closer, shuffling warily, swords held overhead.

"Help me, White Nun," Snowhawk whispered. "This is too many, and too close..." *If you let me live out this day*, she vowed silently, *I* will *cut the hatred from my heart. I will show respect for this second chance that destiny has given me and—*

The ninja wearing a bow and arrows flinched and started looking in all directions. "How?" he addressed his sidekicks. "She's not supposed to have invisibility skills!"

All four hooded agents began turning twitchy circles, the typical *shinobi* response to a threat or mystery. Snowhawk inclined her head at their odd behavior.

What was this? They were acting as if she were no longer there.

"It's a trick! It's that demonic White Nun!" Mr. Claw called. "*I* can't see the girl either now!" He glanced downhill over his shoulder and then glared at Kagero. "Are you *sure* we can't just kill that old hag?"

"That path," Kagero said coldly, "you will go down no farther. Just do your job!"

Sounds came from the distance: Jiro squealing, Motto's growls and jaw-snaps.

"Close in, then!" the chief ninja commanded. "Listen for her!"

Snowhawk held her breath. The four encircling Fuma ninja cocked their heads.

"She *is* gone," the archer muttered. "No, wait... I hear her heartbeat!"

Snowhawk winced, her eyes darting between the men. Which one would attack first? Whoever it was, this was going to hurt.

"Idiot!" Another ninja pointed through the trees. "There, *there* she is!"

"So!" the nearest agent said, peering into the forest. "She's learned eye trickery!"

Compulsively, Snowhawk turned and looked, along with her enemies. Her mouth twisted in wonder. She saw herself, obviously just as they did, running away through the forest, vaulting fallen trees and rocks. Smiling in awe, she checked downhill.

Beside Moonshadow, facing the immobile Chikuma, the White Nun pointed uphill with her gnarled stick. Thunder rumbled above. Snowhawk held her ground as the four ninja tore past her, one

brushing her jacket with his elbow. Their clawed
leader followed. The pack wove away through the
forest, accelerating, chasing the second Snowhawk.
Unslinging his compact bow as he ran, the archer
among them made ready to shoot.

The real Snowhawk quickly glanced around. Flashes
of sheet lightning lit the green clouds overhead. Far
away downhill, Jiro scaled a maple. Motto circled it
ardently.

Only Kagero had stayed where she was. Snowhawk
eyed her suspiciously. Could this veteran *shinobi*
see her, the real her? Was the bounty hunter adept
enough to neutralize certain of the White Nun's
skills? Kagero wasn't even watching the departing
ninja team. If she wasn't fooled by the illusion, why
had she not alerted the others?

Kagero stopped fidgeting with her kimono's
shoulder stain and tensed her war fans. "There." She
gave Snowhawk a superior glare. "Let the gullible
stretch their legs, believing the old sage's trickery.
Not all of us are so easily fooled! Now we can be
alone, just you and me. You're *my* prize and I don't
want any disputes about who earns that bonus!"

"In case you hadn't noticed"—Snowhawk gestured downhill—"I'm hardly alone and at your mercy."

A wolfish *yike* came from the foot of Jiro's maple.

Kagero and Snowhawk both turned to watch the tree. Jiro slid down its trunk. Motto scampered away, tail between his legs. He hunched his great back, big head turning hard to one side as he snapped at something.

Kagero laughed as the dog fled through bamboo toward the remains of a wall. Then Snowhawk saw the *bo-shuriken* sticking from the Akita Matagi's shoulder. She covered her mouth with one hand as the sight needled her heart. It felt so wrong that he should be hurt in any way. True, Motto-San was an animal warrior, but he was also an innocent, caught up in a human conflict, controlled by the wills of others.

Whimpering, the mighty beast ran behind the wall and out of view. The White Nun stared after him. Had she lost control of Motto now? Could she heal his wound?

"How sad. I know just how the poor creature feels." Kagero pouted. "And I have you to thank for it! Now, what were you saying? You're hardly...alone?"

Running forward energetically, as if her shoulder wound suddenly meant nothing, Kagero hacked with her fans in a double slash across the front of her body. Snowhawk bolted clear, springing backward high into the air, turning as she descended.

Kagero accelerated after her, closing the gap

between them with astonishing speed. As Snowhawk landed in a crouch and turned to roll evasively, the tips of a fan swished above her scalp. She gasped as a severed lock of hair fell, twisting past her face.

Snowhawk bounded to her feet, turned fast, and struck hard with the side of her hand at Kagero's wrist. Kagero snarled, but instead of dropping her fan, she spun on the spot with great force, slashing for Snowhawk's neck with her second fan's spokes. Snowhawk threw herself back, and the fan's iron tips grazed the collar of her *shinobi* suit. Her eyes widened with alarm. That was far too close—*twice*! She cartwheeled away, gained a secure footing, then jumped hard. A heartbeat before she soared clear, she heard Kagero's labored breathing right behind her.

Gliding above the ground, Snowhawk realized her mistake. She'd forgotten their battle in the corridor of the inn! Kagero was just too good at close-quarter fighting, so had to be kept at a distance! Snowhawk quickly hatched a new plan: once she landed, she'd jump again, keep moving in a random pattern, stopping only to let fly with her *shuriken*. . . .

The ground rushed up, looking solid and even, but as she landed, one foot struck a pit under the forest's thick carpet of leaves. Snowhawk stumbled and fell.

She twisted quickly onto her back. Kagero, air-borne, was coming for her.

Snowhawk dug into her jacket, fingers probing fast into one holster, then the next.

Empty. No more shuriken. Snowhawk cursed and waited for the end.

30

A FEAST FOR YAMAMBA?

Moonshadow crouched, peering over a low wall as the thing came toward him through the starlit ruins. It paused, letting out another long *hiss*.

Its strange energetic flitting carried it from a patch of shadow into an open expanse between lines of stone. All at once he could discern the creature properly.

Moonshadow shuddered and checked again for his sword. Still missing. He *was* unarmed.

Unarmed and facing the most malevolent of *yokai*. A Yamamba.

Yamamba were cannibal witches. They usually dwelled on mountains and lured their victims into caves or huts, where they killed and ate them. This one had a rotting half-skull of a face, hawkish talons, and long, twig-strewn hair. Its gaunt body was draped in a torn kimono that revealed decomposing flesh over sunken ribs. It was alive, yet not.

Moonshadow struggled with a deep urge to run screaming in terror as the Yamamba approached, peeling back lips to show bright yellow dagger teeth.

"Teeth," Moonshadow muttered. "Why are there always teeth?"

Moving with frenetic, sudden motion, the Yamamba darted at him, avian claws slashing downward for his head. He hurled himself back from the wall. The talons dug into the stones with a puff of rising white powder. Moonshadow twisted around and sprinted away through the ruins. He looked up for a high tree he could jump at to escape the awful thing, and then glanced back. What if, given those claws, it could climb?

He resumed scanning the tall trees and then froze, distrusting his eyes. What was *that*?

A strange golden ribbon, of steam or smoke perhaps, was snaking through the clear night sky from the south, twisting, surging forward like a tentacle above the trees.

Was it all part of the attack? Surely nothing to do with that Rokurokubi and its ever-stretching neck? Moonshadow fought to still his thoughts. A fresh instinct spoke to him. Unlike the earlier impressions, this directive didn't make him afraid.

Go to it. It looks for you.

He heard a scraping noise right behind him. It was all the push he needed. Moonshadow bobbed forward and ran, weaving past rocks and trees, eyes on a bald spot just uphill.

The golden ribbon's tip was descending there; he would meet it head on.

As Moonshadow closed with the spot, a sharp *hiss* behind him warned that the mountain witch was in close pursuit. Talons swiped noisily, fanning his back with shock waves of displaced air.

He forced more speed from his legs. *It* closed in on him.

Grunting with effort, he charged for the tip of the shimmering golden tentacle just as it brushed the forest floor. Stumbling, Moonshadow rolled into the glow's center, regained his feet, and looked back. The Yamamba had stopped. It seethed with malice, cuffing the air wildly with its talons, hissing but coming no farther, unwilling to enter the golden light.

Moonshadow felt the ribbon bathe him in a strange, nourishing heat. He opened his hands, closed his eyes, let it wash over and through him. Like the volcanic water in the monastery's bathhouse, this golden glow brought calm and flooded him with awareness.

He blinked. He was suddenly aware of something, but what? Moonshadow stared at the Yamamba. That was it: he could respond, strike back, he didn't have to hide in here, nor run from the creature. But respond how?

"You already know," Moonshadow said aloud. "Fight, exactly as in real life."

A third time he checked for his sword, confirming that it had indeed vanished. Moonshadow patted his clothing for *shuriken* and smoke bombs. Nothing. He took a deep breath and focused on the enveloping golden light itself. *Show me what I already know.*

Immediately a new urge, strong and lucid, told him what to do. He went with it.

"Whatever you gave me," Moonshadow shouted to the White Nun he couldn't see, "help me skip ahead with it...just this once!"

Moonshadow reached out with his feelings, try-

302

ing to sense the wolves he had heard earlier. He felt nothing, no impressions, no tremors in his hands. As he persisted, the golden light around him began to fade. *Why?* Moonshadow wondered desperately. Had it failed? Or was its job already done? Had he received something? Absorbed new knowledge?

As he watched, the last smoky wisps of the golden glow evaporated.

The Yamamba cocked its head sharply and started forward, taloned fingers working excitedly. Moonshadow looked down at his own hands. Tiny tremors shook them. He started to grin. Had he just forged that link? He thought of the wolves and willed his command to them: *Assemble and defend.*

But had they heard it? Would this work?

With a loud *hiss*, the witch rushed him.

Evading with a fast cartwheel, he watched the Yamamba fly past him, snatching at the air. It roared with fury as he landed on his feet and pushed off into a run downhill.

He wove between the trees and rows of bamboo and charged back down into the ruins, a great weariness now tugging at him from within as he ran. Branches and leaves flicked up behind him as the witch gave chase, closing at phenomenal speed.

Suddenly he was hunched and panting at the edge

of the plateau, the crumbling old battlement wall beside him, the black drop yawning beyond.

The Yamamba advanced, holding its arms wide to block his escape, talons outstretched, flicking ominously. Its teeth meshed, then parted, and a low, crackly voice that didn't sound even remotely female came from its throat.

"Young flesh!" it croaked. "I gloat, I gloat!" It bounded toward him, rubbing its hands together, teeth chattering as if rehearsing a series of fast, tearing bites.

Moonshadow looked uphill. What had come of his joining? His *supposed* joining? He was running out of options fast. Full of dread, he glanced over the old battlement wall.

Rather than let the witch eat him, he could choose to jump, but what was down there? In the real world, the haunted forest of the abandoned. In this mindscape, maybe even worse horrors. A powerful urge to leap rolled through him. Then an instinct spoke from within.

You have been helped, it said, *but only you can do the rest. Only you can find the courage to stand your ground. It is a choice, and lies beyond any magic or science. Courage to stand. To wait, to trust.* He swallowed hard, struggling to obey the inner prompts. *To take a differ-*

ent kind of leap. A harder leap. Only you... if you can find it in you. It was his own voice, the speech of his highest, wisest self, the sum of everything his teachers had imparted to him, and more. But it wasn't the only voice tugging at him.

The conflicting urges battled in Moonshadow. He felt sweat roll down his temples.

Just jump and take your chances; anything has to be better than facing those teeth unarmed.

No! Stand your ground, wait, trust, and if you have no choice, fight bravely.

Moonshadow stared over the edge, heart pounding. "Help me, White Nun," he began, then stopped himself. "No, *I* must do this."

His right hand became a fist topped with white knuckles.

An urge tore through him, almost swamping his will with its power. *Just jump, now*, it said. Moonshadow felt his foot slide forward for the edge. "No," he grunted.

Jump. It is your destiny.

He forced himself to recite the words of the *furube* sutra, the anchor of calm in every *shinobi*'s life. "Gather, tidy, and align your ways, for they bring karma." Moonshadow wrestled against the dark urge, pushing out the stabilizing words, "Cleanse

305

any lies made this day, scatter not…one…grain of life…."

To save lives, save the others, you should jump, the opposing voice nagged.

"To end this path in happiness," Moonshadow willed himself to say, "seek peace within your mind…."

Only one thing will bring you stillness and peace. You must jump. So jump!

"Never!" He felt a nauseating wrench, then a tearing sensation deep in the pit of his stomach as he hurled off the compulsion like a poisoned cloak. Grinding his teeth, Moonshadow snatched at his courage and pushed himself back from the edge of the abyss. He turned his head, scowling and resolved. *This* was his choice. He would fight and win, or fight and fall. *For glory or destruction!*

Moonshadow rounded on the Yamamba as it closed in confidently.

He raised his hands into a combat stance. He was unarmed, and even his special skill might have failed, but he would go down fighting.

The creature rushed him, claws raised. Moonshadow evaded with a sideways bound, then leapt onto a nearby rock. As he caught his balance and turned to face his opponent, the Yamamba bolted at

306

him, its torn kimono rustling. The witch hacked for Moonshadow, talons descending hard in an angular stroke that swished with unnerving speed.

As he somersaulted from his perch, there was a loud *smash*, and the rock shattered into a pile of rubble. Landing beside it, Moonshadow quickly turned and drove his strongest side kick into the Yamamba's sunken ribs. But the kick's impact surged back through Moonshadow, rebounding with tremendous force. He reeled off balance and fell to the ground.

Moonshadow stared, wide-eyed, up at his looming foe. Well, *that* really worked. He grimaced. What had he just felt? Did this creature have an invisible shield? Witchcraft indeed!

The Yamamba gave a long, triumphant *hiss*. Hunched over, arms spread wide, it stalked toward him. Its teeth gnashed, claws worked busily. Moonshadow back-rolled, rose into a combat stance, then edged away, desperately trying to come up with a new tactic.

His eyes flicked to the rubble near his feet. He had no *shuriken*, but he could try...*this*!

He dropped smoothly to one knee and scooped up a fist-size rock. Springing up, he lunged forward and hurled it with all his strength at the witch's head. With impossible speed, the Yamamba brought up a claw and deftly cuffed the spinning missile straight back at him.

Moonshadow saw it streak for his forehead. He ducked breathlessly and felt the rock flash through his tail of hair. With a loud *whoosh* it vanished into the distance.

"Yes," the witch croaked ominously. "Yamamba play. *Then* Yamamba eat!"

Moonshadow backed away, chest heaving. It was hopeless—the monster was invulnerable. Very well then! He stopped, raising his hands, tensing them like blades. He *would* die fighting.

If only, he thought wistfully, *the Eye of the Beast had worked on* this *battlefield!*

Moonshadow stood tall, holding his head up. The creature advanced, talons twitching.

Then darting grey movement broke the stillness of the ruins.

From all directions wolves converged on Moonshadow and the witch. Fearlessly the animals surrounded the Yamamba, barking and baying. Moonshadow broke into a wide, hopeful grin.

Time for tactical control! But what should he make them do? Mantis's wise words came to him at once: when dealing with a strong enemy whose limits are unknown, play it safe, test his stamina, wear him down.

Harrow and tire! he silently commanded. The animals began taking turns leaping at the witch, jaws snapping. Despite her formidable appearance and powers, the creature appeared immediately intimidated.

Two more wolves appeared out of the forest, taking a shortcut along the battlement wall to join the fray, flashing past Moonshadow as if they couldn't see him.

The agitated Yamamba swung back and forth, talons raised protectively.

Moonshadow stared at his tenacious wild defenders. He had called to them, linked with them, and now ran their coordinated attack. What had that golden ribbon done to him? He narrowed his eyes as the truth struck him. It might have boosted his strength, but it had not made the final leap for him; nothing could. It was his own boldness that was challenging the tide. Moonshadow shook his head at the hissing Yamamba. Would his four-legged allies prove enough? The biggest animal, probably the pack leader, bounded in front of him, growling at the witch. The wolf had suffered an injury. A small dark length of broken stick hung from its bleeding shoulder.

A dream animal with a wound the witch didn't give it? What could that mean? As Moonshadow stared at the bloodied stick, his conversation with Snowhawk in the shrine came back to him.

"So can injuries from these dreams follow you back into real life?" he had asked.

"It can work that way, yes," she had answered.

Or the other way around! Moonshadow grinned. Despite being trapped in this daylight dream attack, he was thinking strategically now. What he saw reflected something taking place in the real world. In the real battle!

In the field, in action, Eagle had always reminded him, protect your allies at every chance, invest in their safety, and the reward may be your own life saved.

Moonshadow scrambled forward and yanked the giant thorn out. It spun to the ground. The powerful animal flinched, then lowered its head and stalked up to the hissing Yamamba.

Moonshadow bit his bottom lip as the pack leader and the witch squared off, each looking set to spring on the other.

What he had just done should trigger some outcome in reality, out in the real battle.

But what?

The four candles had burnt out around the scroll of empowerment sutras.

The room was dim now, lit only by diffused daylight.

Eagle, Heron, Mantis, and Badger still sat facing the candles in the *seiza* position. Badger was open-mouthed, eyes bulging. The scroll he had been reading from only seconds earlier was trembling slightly in his hands. He had been near the end of his turn at reading a sutra, then a remarkable event had silenced him in midsentence.

They were all quiet, stunned into awe and wonder by what had just happened.

A tangible sense of life force, of ki, had steadily built in the room, in the very air itself, over the last hour. At the height of its rise, a spherical glow, golden at first, then green, had lit the center of the room above their heads, and at its core, a faint image of a wooded mountainside had flickered for half a breath. A jagged bolt of lightning had flashed through the center of the image, and then it had vanished with a sharp crackle, snatching the power from the air as it went.

Now the four stared, blinked, and licked their lips

uncertainly. Badger cleared his throat and glanced around but didn't resume reading.

Finally Eagle took a deep breath and broke the silence. "Heron," he said hoarsely. "We *all* saw that, right?" She gave a haggard nod. He sighed with relief. "What did it mean?"

Despite her exhaustion, Heron smiled broadly. "I think it worked."

31
TURNING TIDES

T hunder cracked hard overhead, and two jagged bolts of lightning lit the forest in quick
succession.

With his teeth, Jiro pulled at the last knot on his
bandage until the torn strip of jacket almost hid his
mangled hand. He muttered a curse and raised a
throwing knife in his good fist.

Snowhawk saw the *bo-shuriken* rise but knew she
couldn't keep her eyes on it. Jiro, as always, was a
hazard, but Kagero, circling her and swinging wildly
with those fans, was the real problem. What other
tricks did she have up those loose silk sleeves?

Kagero ran at Snowhawk, bringing the fans close together, peeping through the gap between them. Snowhawk lunged with the tip of her sword between the paper triangles. Kagero changed her footwork, turned her arm and shoulder hard, and used one fan's iron spokes to parry the blade aside. She dropped into a crouch and rolled along the ground, slashing with the fan tips for Snowhawk's ankles. Snowhawk vaulted over the attack and landed on Kagero's shoulders before springing off into a somersault. She hit the ground with well-spaced feet and turned smoothly, raising her sword.

"Nice trick," Snowhawk panted. "Pity you weren't just a little fast—" She cried out as an impact from behind drove her chest forward, snapping her head up. Sinking to her knees, she clawed for the arrow in her back with gritted teeth.

"Pity *you* weren't a little more observant." Kagero gave her old innkeeper titter.

Painfully, Snowhawk seized the arrow's thin bamboo shaft and with a hard grunt snapped it off. She looked in all directions through watering eyes. If she lived, the arrowhead itself could be dug out later, the wound seared with fire. She'd been through all that before. For now, the iron tip had to stay where it was, blocking the flow of blood so she could fight on.

Snowhawk cursed her own carelessness. She had forgotten a most basic rule of open combat: always know what's going on behind you. The five ninja must have returned! She snorted bitterly. Would she live to receive a well-deserved lecture from Brother Eagle? A penalty she'd happily endure! But the gangster's taunting snigger warned Snowhawk that her beginner's mistake was about to bring far worse upon her.

A *bo-shuriken* wagged in Jiro's hand. "Well, why waste this on you now?" He grinned. "You're already one shot down, Snowhawk, right?" He guffawed at his own joke.

Snowhawk raised her sword painfully as the Fuma ninja, back from their fool's errand, surrounded her. She peered downhill, eyes frantically hunting for the White Nun. The sage was hunched on a stone, her stick sagging. She appeared exhausted. There was no sign of Motto. Snowhawk swallowed hard. Had the noble beast fallen?

Desperate thoughts assailed her. She knew her own fate; they wanted her alive. She'd have to deal with that later. But if Moonshadow did not somehow rejoin the fight within the next few minutes, he would most certainly be killed or blinded right in front of her. Even if left alive, how long would a blind *shinobi* last—one who had already made himself at least one vengeful warlord enemy? She ground her teeth. This was it. From so far away, that very foe, the blood-crazed Silver Wolf, was about to get even.

What if she offered to cease fighting, surrendered herself to the Fuma in exchange for them letting her companions go? As if in reply, lightning struck a stunted tree nearby, setting it alight. *Exactly*. She hung her head, nodding. What mad optimism caused *that* idea? Had she really needed a sign? Make no deals. They'd still slay Moonshadow. So what to do? Brother Mantis, her favorite Grey Light trainer— apart from his endless karma talk—sung the praises of surprise at every chance. *Never underestimate it*, he loved to tell her. *Surprise is the number one tactic for turning the tide during combat. Try to employ it*, he'd added earnestly, *before you run out of stamina*.

Well, she was wounded, demoralized, and almost out of stamina, but Snowhawk felt she could still offer the Fuma one last surprise. She rallied herself for a final charge. Springing up with a yelp, she dashed for the ninja between her and the burning tree, scything the air with her sword, forcing the man back until he felt the heat and had to jump away. She tried to accelerate, preparing to leap the fiery tree and lead them off again. Something flashed into the corner of her vision and she raised her sword at it. With a resounding *clang*, the *bo-shuriken* glanced off her blade, its rounded club end striking her temple.

Her sword tumbled to the ground beside her as she dropped to her hands and knees. Disoriented, Snowhawk smelled burning pine, heard Jiro's victory howl, saw stars.

What chance did she have now?

A low, powerful form thundered past her. She shook her head hard and looked.

Motto-San, the *bo-shuriken* flicking up and down in his shoulder, was charging downhill, ignoring the ninja, Jiro, and Kagero. The claw-handed Fuma chief signaled quickly, and his archer nocked an arrow. Snowhawk scrambled across the ground and snatched up Jiro's last *bo-shuriken*. The archer drew and took aim at Motto. With a snarl, Snowhawk hurled the black throwing knife at him. The ninja ducked, aborting his shot.

Weaving among the bamboo and the ruins, Motto charged straight for the Fuma dream assassin.

First Jiro, then the five ninja, and finally Kagero grew transfixed. Eyes still watering with the pain of her arrow wound, exhausted and out of ideas, Snowhawk welcomed the pause.

Just before Motto reached Chikuma, the

bo-shuriken came away from the dog's shoulder and fell spinning to the ground.

Snowhawk squinted. Strange, it had looked as if something had plucked it out.

Chikuma's eyes were open and he appeared to remain in his trance as Motto slammed into him. The Fuma assassin reeled, barely keeping his balance on stiff legs as the Akita Matagi bundled him, one hard shove at a time, to the old battlements.

Ignoring Snowhawk, Kagero and the ninja started running downhill, with Jiro in a limping trot behind them. Snowhawk sneered, wiping her running eyes. They'd reacted too late. That dog would knock their friend off the edge before they could stop him.

With a final growling chest ram, Motto sent Chikuma flying sideways against the crumbling battlement wall. He struck it hard, making several loose stones tumble over the edge, then flopped helplessly into a gap, limp as a cloth doll.

Turning to face the enemies approaching from uphill, Motto spread his paws and growled. His bared, dripping teeth warned not to advance on him or Chikuma. The dream assassin dangled from the waist up through the gap in the low wall. His head and upper body's weight threatened to drag him over, into a plunge to the haunted forest below.

"Stop, all of you!" Kagero ordered. "Don't try anything. Someone's controlling that beast, and if we move on it, it'll nudge him over!" The line of attackers froze.

"The White Nun?" One ninja pointed at the sage, still hunched on her stone.

"It must be her!" Kagero snarled.

The White Nun raised her head and stared at the attackers. "Indeed?" She gave an enigmatic smirk. "How little you know!"

Moonshadow swayed on the spot, snatched a deep breath, then covered his face with his hands. He groaned, shook his head, and peeped between his fingers. As he took another deep breath, the pupils of his eyes reappeared.

Snowhawk used her sword to force herself up into a wobbling stand. Despite the pain in her back, she grinned. That tide might just turn now. She was almost combat useless, but they had no plans to kill her anyway. And *he* was awake!

Moonshadow lowered his hands, looked around, quickly sized things up, and ran to Chikuma. Motto skipped away from his prize but kept glaring at the foes looming uphill.

Shaking his head again, as if throwing off the last tendrils of sleep, Moonshadow stood over his unconscious enemy. Snowhawk felt tension surge through her stomach. What was he going to do? Would he push him over? Hold him for ransom? She watched Moonshadow snatch for the back of Chikuma's colorful waistband. She held her breath.

With a strong wrench, Moonshadow dragged Chikuma back from the edge. Once the assassin was safe, Moonshadow dropped him in a crumpled heap and stared uphill.

"Let the karma of his death be *yours*!" he shouted at his shocked enemies. "Not mine!"

The White Nun stared at Moonshadow for a lingering moment and then gave a single firm nod.

Snowhawk blew a long breath between her pursed lips. *Scatter not one grain of life.* It was humbling to see the sutra lived, before her very eyes. She, who had been so eager to kill! Moonshadow had honored their code admirably. If only Mantis had been here to see that.

Snowhawk silently chided herself. She had some work to do to follow Moonshadow's example, but at least now she knew it. That in itself was a healthy sign. With newfound clarity she reaffirmed the way to defeat Kagero: the assassin's buried anger—like Snowhawk's—was a serious flaw just waiting to be exploited! Snowhawk gave a steely nod.

Wounded or not, she was about to exploit it. *Here I come, Kagero*, she bristled.

She saw Moonshadow studying her, taking in her injury. Then his eyes tracked along the line of ninja to Jiro and the bounty hunter. Snowhawk gaped. Was he about to—

Drawing his sword deftly, he broke into an uphill run.

Moonshadow was back!

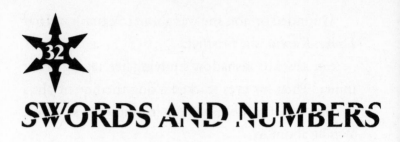

SWORDS AND NUMBERS

Moonshadow charged at Jiro, who turned and started to run away. He then changed direction suddenly to attack the claw-wielding ninja.

The Fuma warrior drew his sword, and he and Moonshadow traded cuts and blocks until Moonshadow was forced to evade the sideswiping *shuko* claw, its iron prongs missing his arm by less than an inch. Moonshadow broke off his attack and ran sidelong across the mountainside, past clumps of black-green bamboo, until he was directly between two of the Fuma ninja.

They saw an opportunity and rushed in from both sides at once. Snowhawk broke into a wily smile. Just as Moonshadow had hoped. The ninja had thought they were springing a chance trap, but Moonshadow had set them up, baited them, so he could employ one of his favorite strategies, one that Mantis had developed.

With a steely ring and the flash of a blue spark, Moonshadow caught the descending blade of the ninja in front of him with his own sword, letting his weapon absorb and redirect the incoming strike's force. Like a coiled snake turning, Moonshadow's blade brushed his foe's aside, snapping around to strike the opponent in the center of his forehead. The man obviously wore a metal guard under his hood, for it *thunk*ed as he stumbled back a pace. Turning like the lightning that had strafed the forest around them, Moonshadow surprised his rear opponent, slashing downward fast and grazing the man from his shoulder to his hip. As the ninja bellowed and collapsed, Moonshadow pivoted back just in time to cut down the stunned enemy in front before the man could recover his poise.

Mantis called that set of moves *zengogiri*—it had featured in his half-finished dueling manual. Snowhawk nodded with admiration. It was the fastest, fiercest technique one could use to drop two foes converging from front and back.

Also the riskiest. Moonshadow had pulled it off.

As Moonshadow ran for Kagero, Snowhawk squinted at the two downed men. Their wounds were long but shallow, intended to immobilize but not to kill.

Again, Snowhawk decided, Mantis would be so proud.

With an angry thunderclap low overhead, the lightning strikes intensified, jabbing the mountainside around the ruins like silver spears. The bamboo seemed to sweat, and the humid air suddenly felt thick, hard to breathe. A blinding bolt of lightning clipped the edge of the old battlements.

For the first time, Motto was frightened by it. He cowered, then ran to huddle at the White Nun's feet. Snowhawk bit her lip. Was that a sign that the White Nun was out of power for now?

She turned anxiously as Moonshadow engaged the bounty hunter, advancing on Kagero with his sword pointed at her throat.

The remaining ninja and Jiro circled Kagero and Moonshadow, the gangster holding up a *bo-shuriken*.

"That thing comes anywhere near me," Kagero

snarled out of the side of her mouth, "and I'll form my own alliance with Moonshadow to take *your* head, gambler!"

Jiro lowered his *bo-shuriken*. "Be like that then," he grumbled. "He's all yours!"

"You won't defeat him, Kagero!" Snowhawk called. "He's as strong as you and, besides, fate's on his side because he walks a true Way, lives by a code!" She pointed confidently. "Not like you! You know what's right, even offer wisdom, but in the end, hatred drives you! *Be like the river?* What a joke, coming from you! From Kagero, the sword that can never be sheathed!"

"Fickle brat!" Kagero's face darkened, and her eyes seethed with black rage. "How dare you lecture me like this! When it comes to anger, we are the same, me and you: *tiger and cub*!"

"Not anymore!" Snowhawk stuck her sword in the ground, then stared at Kagero. "I turn from that path!" She gave a sly, provocative smile. "After all, who wants to be the next *you*?"

With a shriek of fury, Kagero strode for Moonshadow. "Cruel-mouthed little squirrel!" she fumed at Snowhawk. "I'll make you pay for that—by killing your champion in front of you!"

Snowhawk bit her lip. Well, she'd done it, she'd tapped Kagero's anger, incited her to recklessness, and it was up to Moonshadow now. Could he really defeat this veteran killer? Snowhawk believed him strong enough, but Kagero had a huge advantage: experience.

Quickly Snowhawk prayed that Kagero's pluming wrath alone would dictate her moves.

Snowhawk stared at Moonshadow anxiously, willing him to hear her thoughts. *Whatever you try, try it fast*, she warned him, *before Kagero has a chance to calm down!*

Kagero locked her fans out at the ends of her arms. She whirled, advancing on Moonshadow with astonishing balance as she rotated and dodged obstacles on the forest floor at ever-increasing speed. Lightning struck the ground only paces from Moonshadow, making Kagero bound to one side. Seizing on the distraction, Moonshadow cut her off with a speedy leap and then lunged with his sword. Kagero's fans flashed together around the advancing blade, and Snowhawk heard a dull *clank*. She stared, wide-eyed, as the two combatants froze.

Moonshadow was leaning forward hard, arms stretched, sword extended between the fans. Was it wedged or frozen by a *shinobi* blade-paralyzing trick?

Did Kagero know that one? She too was immobile now, glowering at Moonshadow.

Kagero let out a long wail that reminded Snowhawk of a kitten mewing. Her fans glided apart, one cut deeply between its iron spokes. Snowhawk's eyes hunted for Moonshadow's sword tip. It had pierced Kagero's arm on the opposite side to her shoulder wound. Moonshadow withdrew the blade and jumped back.

Her reckless fury draining away as pain took hold, Kagero whimpered and sank to her knees. She dropped the fans and cupped her bleeding bicep. Her head flicked up at Moonshadow, then she turned and scowled at Snowhawk. It was there, in her eyes: *defeat*.

As Snowhawk looked back, her face involuntarily softened. Now, to her surprise, she actually felt pity for Kagero. The woman had lived by illusion, misdirection, and bluff. She'd cleverly fooled the world into believing her invincible; yet she'd also wound up fooling herself.

"You wretched brats!" Kagero spluttered. "No respect for your elders!" She caught the claw-handed ninja's attention. "What are *you* waiting for? Three of you are still standing! Take him! Move, or are you afraid of him now?"

They quickly surrounded Moonshadow. He raised his chin and sword together defiantly.

"I don't mind these odds at all," he said, smiling. "Who's going down first?"

Snowhawk heard a twig snap, far off in the forest. Then another. She turned her head, listening carefully. Closing footfall. Someone was ascending the mountain and tacking this way. No. Several of them! They were being openly noisy, so maybe it was a party of samurai. She swallowed. Silver Wolf's men? He was taking no chances with his revenge! What if he was leading them himself? Would she and Moonshadow be thrown from the mountain, like that poor clan he wiped from history? Would they be tortured first?

One by one, the three remaining ninja, Jiro, Moonshadow, and then Kagero, all looked. Only the White Nun ignored the sounds. She stood stiffly, head bowed, one hand over Motto's bleeding shoulder.

Figures came into view, weaving quickly through the trees. Snowhawk focused on them, and her heart sank. These were not samurai. More ninja. More *Fuma* ninja.

Six *more* enemies, armed and hooded, their faces bound, all in the same maple-patterned forest suits. Two were enormous. Three were archers. It was overwhelming; these *were* hopeless odds.

The enemy reinforcements, seeing combat already

under way, fanned out fast into a huge containment circle around everyone but the White Nun and her wounded dog. Snowhawk grunted. She had to get to Moonshadow, help him, stand with him, even if…

Plucking her sword from the ground and leaning on it like a crutch, she began taking painful steps in Moonshadow's direction. He saw her coming and launched himself into a high, powerful jump, landing at her side. He looked her over, wincing at the arrow wound in her back.

Somehow she stayed on her feet, tears of pain running down her cheeks. With a sob of agony she put her throbbing, bleeding back against Moonshadow's.

They raised their swords as their foes formed a new inner circle around them: Mr. Claw and his two henchmen, the grinning, triumphant Jiro, and behind them Kagero, smiling wickedly.

Farther off, six new attackers waited for their opportunity. There was no way out.

Her throat began to close up. This time they had been outwitted, and the end was truly upon them. Silver Wolf had proved cunning and hateful enough to cover all the angles. His vengeance would now see Moonshadow's annihilation and her capture, misery, and death. Snowhawk glanced downhill at the White Nun with pleading eyes. Sensing it, the sage looked up. An enigmatic smile broke her heavily lined face. Snowhawk tried to read the expression. Was that sorrow? Indifference? Or was she hiding something?

"I…I'm sorry I've been so foolish," Snowhawk said quickly to Moonshadow, her chin trembling.

"Forget it." He shrugged. "I'd already be dead—*twice*—if not for you! Please forgive my confused leadership!"

"No, no, despite me, you made the grade, you really did." She sniffed. "And I hope in whatever life we get next, that we…"

"Wind up as best friends again?" Moonshadow flashed a smile. "I just prayed the very same thing."

A growl came from the storm overhead. Snowhawk's eyes flicked up. The green ceiling of clouds was thinning. No lightning had struck in the last few moments. She cursed. With the storm waning, there'd be no more using its random flashes to advantage. Then she laughed bitterly, long and low. How ridiculous. It was futile to keep grasping for some tactical escape. *Nothing* could save them now.

It was Jiro who felt compelled to shatter the new silence with a near-hysterical cackle of joy. The gangster held up his bloody, bandaged hand, face glowing as he anticipated his—and Silver Wolf's—imminent revenge.

"Perfect timing! Welcome, gentlemen!" He looked over his shoulder at the reinforcements, beckoning with wounded fingers. "What a pleasure this is going to be. And why make it hard?" He turned, leering at Moonshadow. "Everyone! Kill *him*!"

THE GREATEST GIFT

J iro squealed and buckled to the ground, his bandaged fist flailing. Moonshadow gasped at the *shuriken* that had bitten into the gangster's hand from behind. It was not a Fuma throwing star but one of the simple, cross-spiked Iga-Koga design.

Clutching his wound, Jiro squealed with pain and distress, rolling in the leaves.

Moonshadow's eyes flashed to the apparent leader of the new arrivals, a big man drawing his sword. "For the Grey Light!" the guy shouted, and at once Moonshadow knew him.

The other five agents unsheathed their weapons. Groundspider led them forward.

Moonshadow also recognized the strapping figure beside Groundspider. The freelancer they'd met on the mission to Lord Akechi's secret meeting in Edo! He gently elbowed Snowhawk, then indicated the man. There was no need to say it: good thing she *hadn't* killed him!

Kagero's eyes flicked straight to Snowhawk's. "We'll meet again." She smiled. "Your business with the Fuma isn't done... nor with me!" She nodded to the claw-wearing ninja, then shouted, "Jiro, fool! Get over here!"

The *real* Fuma agents who could still stand scurried into a cluster around Kagero, one of them dragging Jiro behind him.

"What of Chikuma?" said Mr. Claw, peering downhill.

"Leave him," Kagero snapped, "like the wounded. Let our enemies here save Clan Fuma their work!"

With pained, deliberate movements, her hand went into her jacket. The *shuko*-wearing ninja leader did the same. Groundspider held up a fist, and his circle of advancing warriors froze. Kagero and the Fuma around her quickly stroked the air, hands flashing.

A chain of smoke bombs went off before them. Each cloud expanded fast, the staggered white eruptions meshing to form a dense, high wall of smoke.

"Down, everyone!" Moonshadow yelled. "Beware of *shuriken*!"

He hunched low, supporting Snowhawk, who ground her teeth and cursed.

"Nobody move!" Groundspider called from somewhere beyond the smoke. "Defense only!"

With a stubborn *hiss*, the last smoke bomb gave out, and the white cloud quickly thinned and broke apart, wisps drifting through the clumps of bamboo. As the final shreds of it lifted, Moonshadow stared at the spot where Kagero and his other enemies had just stood. *Nothing*. His eyes narrowed. The Fuma must have helped the bounty hunter and Jiro jump away, then run, well beyond the smoke screen. Still clutching Snowhawk, he turned his head. Where were they hiding? They couldn't have gone far, not yet.

Groundspider ran up to him, sheathing his sword. His men did the same.

"What are you doing?" Moonshadow frowned. "You're not going after them?"

"No. We're to let them go!" Groundspider signaled to his troops. He pulled down his face-binding and chuckled at Moonshadow. "Don't stay wound up, kid. This really *is* a rescue mission! We're not to engage them." His eyes darted to Snowhawk. "But I see you already have. Snowy doesn't look too well." He turned and motioned for the battlefield healer among his men to come and deal with Snowhawk.

She looked up at Groundspider with glazed eyes. "I'm still strong enough to flatten you if you call me Snowy again."

Groundspider smiled down at her with genuine concern. "*That's* a good sign."

"How did you get here?" Moonshadow asked as the healer eased Snowhawk from his grip, lowering her gently on her side into the pine needles and leaves.

The big agent shrugged. "We stole a cavalry unit's best horses. They're all tethered downhill. I have a seventh warrior guarding them. Our fast way home!"

Moonshadow gaped. "You did *what*? You robbed a daimyo?"

"Oh, don't worry, he's just some minor lord, and anyway, he'll blame the Fuma. We made sure one of his experienced guards saw these." Groundspider tugged at his uniform. "Pretty good, hey? Badger had these made a year ago after I captured that Fuma spy in Kyoto, you remember, the one who took poison before we could interrogate him?"

"You told me about it." Moonshadow nodded. "But I was a no-name, not an agent then."

"Yeah, well, I guess that just by wearing his clan's only forest suit design, he gave us precious information after all. I was wondering when we'd get a chance to use these. Badger was originally thinking infiltration, but today they also made for a nice ambush!"

Moonshadow could not disguise his amazement. "And that...that was all *your* idea?"

"Sure." Groundspider frowned indignantly. "Why not?"

"That's...brilliant." Moonshadow grinned. "They tricked us with a false message, but you turned the tables back on them with false Fuma ninja. And laying blame on them while getting such good horses..." He laughed, then gave a massive sigh of relief.

Groundspider shoved him, making him wince from many bruises. "Quit acting so surprised, kid. It's not like I used an Old Country skill. You want to know the truth? Most people just don't use the greatest gift they've been given. So happens that I do, that's all."

"Which gift is that?" Snowhawk called skeptically from the forest floor.

"Imagination," the White Nun's voice answered, her tone emphatic.

Beaming, Moonshadow turned around. The sage looked utterly wrung out. Nonetheless, she had managed to sneak up on them all.

"Am I not right, Brother Groundspider?" The White Nun smiled knowingly. "Is the answer not *imagination*?"

The big *shinobi* bowed low in deference. "Yes, indeed, great sage."

Moonshadow shook his head, astonished by it all.

Groundspider straightened up and gave him an even harder shove. Moonshadow groaned.

"See, kid? Imagination. Don't you know *anything*?"

34

A FINE PARADE

Katsu sniffed the air as he was escorted through the immaculate garden to the main courtyard of Momoyama Castle.

A dour-looking samurai who never spoke led him across a small wooden bridge that forded the garden's spring-fed stream. Beyond it, Katsu slowed at a stone lantern under a maple tree. He studied the maple's invigorated leaves, green and flushed with life. Spring was waning, Katsu thought. The first hint of the coming summer's humidity tinged the air. Soon the last wave of spring rains would give way to the typhoon season. Some said there would be earthquakes this year. Upheavals of a man-made kind concerned him far more. What would his volatile, changeable master do on hearing his latest report? Slay him where he stood? Pay up happily? With Silver Wolf, either was possible.

Gesturing edgily, the silent escort led him through a narrow stone corridor. It opened onto a wide, packed-grit courtyard crowded with samurai. Hundreds of them.

Rows of armored men stood proud and silent, faces full of resolution. Swords curved from their hips, spear blades rose in neat gleaming lines from their shoulders. War banners fluttered overhead to identify each of Silver Wolf's units. Katsu smelled sweat and ambition even before he saw the warlord in his brilliant red armor, pacing up and down before his troops, a riding crop under one arm.

Silver Wolf stopped before one stocky samurai whose face was badly scarred. The extensive, ugly wounds looked quite old. Fire? Katsu wondered. Clamping a gauntlet on the man's shoulder, Silver Wolf engaged the surrounding ranks of warriors.

"This samurai once saved my life!" he shouted. "Are each of you as much a man?"

He paced on, chiding a tall spearman for his passive facial expression. "I want you to terrify my enemies, not lull them into sleep." Silver Wolf laughed. "Work on that face!"

Katsu swallowed, intimidated by the atmosphere of warmongering. Military musters, like mock battles, were supposed to be held only with the Shogun's knowledge and blessing. He couldn't imagine Silver Wolf respecting either. The lavish parade so unsettled Katsu, he failed to see his grumpy escort urging him forward.

Just as he noticed the samurai gesturing and scowling, Silver Wolf himself called Katsu's name. Forcing a breezy look onto his face, he paced quickly to his master. Katsu bowed low and received a loose nod in return.

Silver Wolf led him along the front line of samurai. Each warrior they passed watched Katsu closely, openly disdainful of the commoner beside their lord. No sudden moves, he reminded himself: many overzealous veterans sliced first, investigated later.

"Inspiring, are they not?" Silver Wolf watched Katsu's face as he put the question to him.

Fortunately, Katsu was ready with an irresistible lie. "Breathtaking, my master. On seeing them when I first entered, I was deeply moved. The keenness of their devotion to you struck me at once. These magnificent warriors will not fail you, no matter what."

The warlord nodded slowly. He flashed a crafty smile. "But some others have?"

Katsu put his hands behind his back to hide his shaking fingers. "About that"—he drew in a slow breath—"it is now my unhappy duty to report."

Silver Wolf's face betrayed no reaction as Katsu summed up the debacle on the mountain of the White Nun. It was, he admitted, a rather sad damage report and not much more. He told of Jiro, injured worse than last time, taking permanent damage to one hand. The supposedly invincible Chikuma and several other Fuma *shinobi* defeated, abandoned by their own people, presumably now to be hunted and killed for failure. It seemed that executing such sentences doubled as training exercises for the Fuma's more successful agents.

The warlord shook his head at the account of Kagero's defeat and flight with two wounds. His eyes narrowed as Katsu reluctantly admitted that, to round it all off most miserably, Snowhawk and Moonshadow remained alive and at large.

"From what I've heard of the actual combat," Katsu finished nervously, "we may have overestimated Kagero, but underestimated...Moonshadow." He winced as he said the name. "I'm told it was *he* who meted out the decisive wound."

"Moonshadow." Silver Wolf mouthed the name with loathing. "So where is he now? Perhaps resting at the Grey Light Order base in Edo." His voice grew cold with menace. "Or perhaps he's up on that roof"—he pointed angrily—"about to hurl a bomb at me!" He watched Katsu sweat and squirm, then threw back his head and laughed. Silver Wolf raised one finger, and the whole courtyard of samurai joined in, guffawing along with their master. Of course, they had no clue about what was so funny.

Katsu blinked at the ranks of hardened soldiers, then smiled sheepishly at their warlord. Silver Wolf made a gesture in the air, and as one the whole army fell silent.

"That, Katsu," he said, "is *real* power. Years from now, you will tell your children of the awe you felt at seeing it." He patted his hireling's shoulder amiably. "Yesterday I might have been so offended by your news as to have taken your large head. But not today. Not after the letter I just received, which bore an update on what you've told me. An update showing that both my wrath *and* my money proved well-aimed arrows after all!"

"An update?" Katsu asked through dry lips. An update had saved his life?

Silver Wolf nodded. "Before dawn today, a black

message arrow, a Fuma trademark, landed right here where we stand. The battlement night watch saw no one."

"What...what did it say, lord?" Katsu asked guardedly, his eyes narrow.

"It seems the Fuma want this Snowhawk back quite badly. Who knows why? They also want their defeat on the mountain avenged. I sense they are enraged at having to hunt and slay one of their most special assassins for failure." He smiled. "It's perfect! Come, Katsu, you're a detective. Tell me what this all adds up to."

"Lord..." Katsu faltered, too scared to venture a theory. "I am not really sure."

"The Fuma, just as I'd hoped, have at last grown *angry enough*, the way I had to at the upstart Shogun. My plan has worked! Don't you see? I *never* intended, of course, to complicate my relations with the shadow clans by actually capturing that weird old crone of a sorceress, the White Nun. Hah! That would be political suicide for one who deals with *shinobi* so regularly these days. And I didn't care whether the Fuma actually retook their runaway agent or killed Moonshadow for me just yet. I was never worried about *that* for a moment! When it comes to feud and vendetta, in truth, my fury has its patient side."

Katsu watched Silver Wolf produce a folded letter from his belt. Handmade black paper. The words *Great Lord Silver Wolf* were brushed on it in white ink.

Holding up the message, the warlord laughed self-importantly. His men watched him, eager for their cue, but this time he didn't signal them, so they all remained quiet.

"Behold, proof of the value of patience! Clan Fuma, as I prayed, have declared, according to ancient *shinobi* custom, Twilight War against the Grey Light Order."

"Twilight War?" Katsu gaped. "What does that mean?"

"Secret but *total* war, with no possibility of truce." Silver Wolf sniggered. "Winner takes all. No mercy. No terms of surrender accepted. I *like* this tradition!"

"Then, not only Moonshadow but all those with him," Katsu mused, "will die at the Fuma's hands. You need do no more for now."

"Exactly." The warlord's eyes glowed. "Mark my words: early in this Twilight War, his young head will go chattering into the dust! I have just pitted two great shadow armies against each other and made the Fuma the instrument of my rage. Once the Grey

Light Order falls, who will save the Shogun from us? There will be no lasting *age of peace* in my Japan. Not while I live. There will be a revival of the old ways, the settling of some scores, then...conquest!"

"A golden age, my master," Katsu said, forcing a smile and hiding his thundering heart.

Silver Wolf turned to his army. "What *is* life without war?" The rows of warriors erupted into cheering, each man hoisting his weapon or shaking a gauntleted fist.

THE PERFECT NAME

Moonshadow crept slowly behind Snow-hawk, watching the bobbing pole-lantern in her hands light the start of the next row of shelves. She stopped, winced, rubbed her back.

As they crept deeper into the Grey Light Order's labyrinthine archives, past musty lines of maps, scrolls, and flip books, he realized he felt vulnerable. They were unarmed apart from these lanterns. They wore only plain indigo house kimonos, no armor, and this little mission could turn crazy again at any moment, as it already had, out in the gardens. He scowled at the fresh monkey bite on his hand. Saru-San would pay for that later.

"Can you see them?" he whispered.

"No." She spoke without hushing her voice. "But I can smell them." Snowhawk rounded on him. "Before we go on, what really happened to you back on that mountain?"

"I think the White Nun's anointing was accelerated somehow, just for a moment, by what Heron and the others sent me from back here. In the dreamscape it was a golden ribbon, but it was actually strength or understanding... I don't know. Under its influence, I too could suddenly link to beasts over a distance. When I tried to do so in the hostile dream, out in the real world I guess I took control of Motto... right when I needed him."

"The White Nun said only a set of unusual circumstances could break or override her link with him, remember?" Snowhawk frowned. "I'd say you experienced them."

"Well, I won't experience such power again for years." He groaned. "I've tried since our return, but I can't repeat it, that long-distance linking. It was there for a flash, like one of those lightning strikes, then gone again." Moonshadow then made a resigned face.

"There!" She held up a hand. "That way! I can smell them…on the move again."

They slunk down an aisle with great vigilance, as if hunting an armed intruder.

"When we parted on the road home," Moonshadow whispered, "where did Groundspider escort the White Nun to? I saw her whisper to him, then they rode off slowly." He blinked. "I couldn't believe it when I first saw her climb up onto that horse's back. She's just incredible."

"Incredible or not, Heron told me she was hiding out at some temple with a group of warrior monks she trusts." Snowhawk inclined her head. "Why did she insist we bring Motto-San back here? His injuries were half healed by the time we made it home. He could have gone anywhere with her."

Moonshadow saw her smile at her own use of the word *home*. "She told me on the road that she's broken her link with him now," he said solemnly. "He's not here to be her second set of eyes in Edo."

"Why then?"

"She told me a new animal guardian was being guided to her. Destiny, of course. She also said we needed Motto-San here."

Snowhawk put one hand over her heart. "What could that mean?"

"With someone from another world, who can say? The White Nun seems to want him with me. Within an hour of her telling me that her link with him was broken, he nuzzled my hand for the first time. I think she knows something.... Maybe we're *really* going to need him." Moonshadow raised his lantern and peered upward, sniffing the air. "Still, I wish she hadn't sent for Heron at once. I know she feels some urgency about Heron's further training now, but…"

"Thanking Heron a thousand times didn't feel like enough?" Snowhawk grinned.

"No! And there's someone else I should thank," Moonshadow said thoughtfully. "*You.* It's been two months since we met, and in that time, you've taught me heaps." He saw her surprised expression. "No, it's true. You've backed me up through…what, fifteen missions now? Shared your knowledge of the world with me. Even helped me get to know myself better." He paused reflectively. "And there's special power in that. Power to grow and improve, or even just to brace up and…keep going when one must!" His face abruptly darkened. "Spring is waning. Brother Eagle fears that by summer, things will come to a head between Silver Wolf and the Shogun. Outwardly, Japan's at peace, but that's about as real as one of Kagero's smiling faces."

Snowhawk nodded. "I feel that pressure building too. The Shogun knows Silver Wolf plots against him. One of them must act decisively soon. If the Shogun delays, Silver Wolf will either launch an open war, or make his next move using *shinobi*. If it's open war, the Shogun can field a vast, loyal samurai army. If it's *unseen* war—" She stiffened with resolve. "Then Silver Wolf and his Fuma goons have to get by *us*, right? And whatever he tries, we'll be ready!"

"Only if we first survive *this* risky mission." He laughed. "Finding that dog before Badger slays us all."

"I told you." Snowhawk instantly mimicked Badger's dry, scholarly tone. "Don't look for the dog. Look for the monkey. The cat is following it, and the dog is trailing the cat. I saw them come in here, in a beast string, moving just that way."

Moonshadow clicked his tongue. "If they keep fighting, Motto-San will tear his stitches again."

"Wait a moment." Snowhawk prodded his arm. "The dog is Motto, the monkey is Saru, so when are you going to name the cat?"

"Not you too!" Moonshadow hung his head, thinking a moment, then said impulsively, "Fine, from now on, she can be known by what she does. She is the White Nun's Edo *banken*. So there you are:

350

the cat's name is officially Banken. Ban-ken. A watcher."

"I like it." Snowhawk giggled. "But I can see now that my non-*shinobi* schooling, whether at cruel hands or not, went further than yours."

He lowered his lantern, face clouding with suspicion. "What do you mean?"

Snowhawk wagged a finger. "I'll tell you only if you promise first not to change your choice. I know how sneaky you can be." She creased her nose impishly.

Moonshadow hesitated, muttering, and then gave her a single, firm nod.

Snowhawk chuckled. "*Banken* means watchdog, not watcher."

Moonshadow turned away, cursing. "I can't *believe* you just tricked me into keeping that," he muttered.

Snowhawk smirked. "I can." She threw back her head and laughed heartily. "Anyway, I love it! A cat named *Watchdog*! Only you could have a cat named Watchdog! Perfect!"

"Don't give me a hard time. I'm … I'm still tired from the road," he said defensively. "Tired … and preoccupied!"

She saw the look on his face and turned serious at once. "What's on your mind?"

"Two things," Moonshadow spoke earnestly. "First of all, it was disturbing, wasn't it, being pursued, town to town, then into the wild? As *shinobi*, we're not used to that, I guess. It's *we* who pursue, hunt down objectives, steal or kill, and then simply vanish. I think this mission made me realize, for the very first time, why ordinary folk fear us so much." He shrugged.

A look of dread sheened her eyes. "Get used to it. I know my former clan. I may need to forgive them, but they don't war in time to *that* drum. Brother Eagle is *so* right! What we just survived"—Snowhawk heaved a knowing sigh—"was only the beginning." She eyed him closely. "What's the second matter bugging you?"

"Learning to let go of something," Moonshadow replied. "The same lesson you had to learn on our journey. *Be like the river. Just flow on.* All that stuff."

"I don't understand. You don't have a problem with"—she looked momentarily embarrassed—"with unforgiveness leading to *hate*."

"Maybe not," Moonshadow said slowly. "But I have a massive problem with *patience*." He frowned hard. "Snowhawk, the White Nun knows who my mother was. Or who she is, if she still lives. Yet for now, with my country and my liege lord in so much danger, and the only family I've ever known standing between Japan and a new civil war, the truth about my mother has to wait. The urge to discover more is strong. But for a time at least, I must simply ignore it."

"Such a heavy burden." She shook her head, marveling. "How will you cope?"

"With your help"—he smiled—"I'll learn to fight my impatience, do my duty with all my heart, and simply put my trust in fate. Then, I believe, in time I'll be rewarded, guided to the truth, perhaps even to *her*. It won't be easy, I know, but I *must* hold that course."

"Listen to you! This tough last mission has changed us both," Snowhawk said firmly. "Do you have any idea what you sound like now?"

"No." He blinked warily. "Like…a little Mantis?"

Snowhawk shook her head, giving Moonshadow a proud smile. "Like a proven leader."

✦ Glossary ✦

Akita Matagi or Akita: Pronounced *ah-key-tah mah-tah-gee*. A tough, intelligent, wolflike dog. Originally bred from Japan's ancient Matagi native hunting dog in the Akita region of Japan, according to some historians, by samurai of the Satake Clan. Matagi originally hunted wild boars, elks, antelope, and the huge Yezo bear. Nowadays called simply Akita, these dogs are fast, agile, and, despite their gentle temperament, fearless when hunting or defending their human family.

Bo-shuriken: Pronounced *boh-shoo-ri-ken*. An iron or steel throwing knife with a double-edged blade at one end, a tapering handle, and a circular threading eye—also a miniature club—at the other. Of the many *shuriken* designs used by *shinobi*, it is the hardest to throw, as it is not star-shaped but linear. The threading eye enables it to be incorporated into traps or attached to a rope or chain and then whirled. See also **Shuriken**.

Daimyo: Pronounced *die-m-yoh*. A member of the Japanese aristocracy and a powerful feudal lord owning a fiefdom of land. The title can be translated as "a great name" or "one who aspires to something better."

Edo: Pronounced *eh-doh*. The city also once called Yedo and now known as Tokyo. It was the Shogun's chosen capital and is now the capital city of Japan.

Fuji: Pronounced *foo-jee*. Japan's highest mountain, considered sacred.

Furube sutra: Pronounced *foo-roo-beh soo-tra*. Literally "The Shrugging Off" or "Shaking Off." An ancient saying or prayer, recited by *shinobi* each dawn and dusk, and just before going into action. It was intended to clear spies' minds of distractions, calm them, and ready their skills.

Hakama: Pronounced *ha-ka-ma*. Traditional Japanese clothing that covers the body from the waist down and resembles a wide, pleated, and divided skirt but is actually giant pleated trousers. A traditional samurai garment worn over a kimono, originally by men only.

Hour of the Rat: Prior to the arrival of a Western timekeeping system, Japan marked time by dividing each day into two parts: sunrise to sunset, and sunset to sunrise. Each of these periods was then broken down into six shorter divisions, roughly two hours long in modern Western time. These twelve sections of the day were identified using the animals of the Chinese zodiac. The Hour of the Rat was approximately 11:00 p.m. to 1:00 a.m., kicking off a cycle of two-hour time segments named in this order: Ox, Tiger, Hare, Dragon, Snake, Horse, Goat, Monkey, Rooster, Dog, and Boar.

Iaido: Pronounced *ee-eye-doh*. The samurai art of sword-drawing and dueling, which features about fifty different *waza* (techniques) and reached the peak of its development around five hundred years ago. Different from Kendo, which is a full-contact sport. Modern students of Iaido use steel swords in wooden scabbards and wear the traditional clothing of medieval samurai. Iaido takes many years to master. To this day, the art's world titles are held in Japan, on a mountaintop near Kyoto, before a Japanese prince. Author Simon Higgins has competed in this event as well as in Australia's national Iaido titles. Many such old Japanese arts, including the tea ceremony and ikebana, were not referred to as a *do* ("the way of…") until they became popular and their teaching practices were formalized.

Iga: See **Koga**.

Kami: Pronounced *car-mee*. The Japanese term for objects of awe or worship in Shintoism, Japan's oldest (and native) religion. Though sometimes translated as "deity" or "gods," this is not strictly accurate. "Spirits" may be a safer way of describing the Kami, who can be "beings" but also simply forces of nature or "living essences."

Kappa: Pronounced *kap-pah*. A *yokai* and water monster featured in Japanese folklore, sometimes depicted with a turtlelike beak. The Kappa is said to love cucumbers. The top of its skull is supposedly shaped like a bowl and filled with water. Signs warning children to "beware of the Kappa" still appear beside many Japanese rivers. See also **Yokai**.

Karma: Pronounced *car-mah*. The Buddhist philosophy that states that deeds or actions create cycles of cause and effect. Thus, good thinking and good deeds produce good outcomes, now or at some time in the future.

Ki: Pronounced *kee*. The life force common to all living things. Internal or spiritual energy, which in traditional Asian martial arts is harnessed to increase a warrior's power and stamina. Using ancient sciences like sight joining can quickly deplete a *shinobi*'s ki.

Koga: Pronounced *koh-gah*. Like Iga (pronounced *ee-gah*), a name associated with a mountain region of Japan in which "shadow clans" trained highly skilled contract spies and assassins whose powers of stealth and disguise became legendary. Author Simon Higgins visited a preserved three-hundred-year-old Koga ninja house that features a display of weapons and tools and, beneath a trapdoor, an underground escape passage. It stands near Konan railway station in farming country outside the city of Kyoto.

Kunoichi: Pronounced *coo-noh-ee-chee*. Traditional term for a female ninja. Certain ninja skills, in particular those associated with using poisons or forcing one's target into a hypnotized state, were associated primarily with female *shinobi*, though a minority of male spies also excelled at them. See also **Ninja** and **Shinobi**.

Kyogen: Pronounced *k-yo-gen*. A popular Japanese school of theater that has existed since at least the fourteenth century. Kyogen plays are usually short, slapstick-type satires that poke fun at religious rites or feudal lords regarded as buffoons, or offer humorous versions of folktales. Human, animal, and even god characters do quaint, unexpected, or ridiculous things, sometimes reflecting the politics of the time when the play was written.

Moonshadow: See **Tsukikage**.

Ninja: Pronounced *nin-jah*. Alternative term for a *shinobi*. Some scholars believe this term emphasizes their role as assassins, whereas *shinobi* is more general, implying the inclusion of scouting and spying roles. The combined *shinobi* combat arts were sometimes called *ninjutsu*, as *jutsu* means "art" or "technique." Shadow clans had many methods and weapons in common, but distinctive practices, clothing, and gadgets also evolved among specific groups. See also **Shinobi**.

Rokurokubi: Pronounced *roh-koo-roh-koo-bee*. One of the many Japanese *yokai*. Rokurokubi initially look human and unremarkable, but their necks can magically elongate. They can also disguise their faces, all in order to deceive and then frighten or attack mortals. See also **Yokai**.

Sake: Pronounced *sah-kay*. Japanese for "alcoholic beverage," it can refer to alcoholic drinks in general but usually refers to the traditional Japanese drink made by fermenting polished rice. Though often called "rice wine," sake is actually brewed and so is really more like beer than wine.

Samurai: Pronounced *sa-moo-rye*. A member of the ruling warrior class; a warrior in a warlord's service.

-San: The *a* is pronounced with a slight *u* sound, as in *sun*. An honorific attached to a person's name to show one is addressing the individual with respect. It can be taken to mean "Mr.," "Mrs.," "Miss," or "Ms."

Saru: Pronounced as it reads. Japanese for "monkey."

Seiza: Pronounced *say-zah*. The traditional (floor or mat) sitting position of the Japanese. The legs are folded, back kept straight, palms rested on the thighs, and one literally sits on one's heels. Difficult at first, the body adapts to it within a few months. It is likely that *seiza* was also used in ancient times to refer to the familiar cross-legged seating posture used during meditation.

Sekigahara: Pronounced *seh-key-gah-hah-rah*. A town in the Gifu Prefecture of modern Japan. Back in 1600 it was a village near which Tokugawa forces won a decisive victory against their rivals. Though not the last conflict fought in the period, the battle is generally held to mark the end of the lengthy civil-war era and the birth of the long-lasting Tokugawa Shogunate.

Shinobi: Pronounced *shi-no-bee*. Also known as *ninja*. Those adept at spying or covert scouting. Some *shinobi* were also hired killers. They were trained in a wide variety of secret and martial arts, said to include combat with and without weapons, acrobatics, the use of explosives, poisons, traps, hypnotism, and numerous forms of disguise. Some of the most effective historical ninja were women who went undercover inside well-guarded fortresses, successfully stealing information or carrying out assassinations. See also **Ninja**.

Shogun: Pronounced *show-gun*. Abbreviated form of *Sei-I-Tai Shogun* ("barbarian-subduing general"). The ultimate commander of the Japanese warrior class who, prior to 1867, exercised virtually absolute rule (officially) under the leadership of the emperor, who was in fact a figurehead only. Many warlords aspired to seize or earn this auspicious rank. In Moonshadow's time a member of the Tokugawa family was the Shogun. See also **Sekigahara**.

Shuko: Pronounced *shoo-koh*. Iron claws worn on the hands to assist climbing. *Shuko* were used, usually along with *ashiko* (foot spikes), to scale walls and climb up trees, cross icy surfaces, and even during combat.

Shuriken: Pronounced *shoo-ri-ken*. Circular or star-shaped throwing knives, usually black and made in ingots or from thin sheets of iron. They could have four, eight, twelve, or more points. Each "shadow clan" or spy group used their own distinctive style or styles of *shuriken*, though some also adopted designs created by their rivals or enemies. Thrown over arm, they were aimed for soft points such as the throat, eyes, or temple. Their tips could be poisoned or flecked with a powerful sedative if the target was to be taken alive. Any *shuriken* wound disrupted and weakened an enemy. See also **Bo-shuriken**.

Sumo: Pronounced *soo-mo*. An ancient Japanese form of competitive wrestling where opponents try to force each other to leave a circular ring or touch the ground with anything other than the soles of their feet. Sumo is steeped in ritual and custom. Wrestlers are selected for size, power, and speed and are specially fed and trained. To this day, sumo wrestlers are lauded celebrities in Japan.

Sutra: Pronounced *soo-tra*. A "scripture" of the Buddhist faith; teachings that were sometimes chanted or recited to focus and empower the devotee. See also **Furube sutra**.

Tanto: Pronounced as it reads. Perhaps best described as a dagger. Up to thirty centimeters long, *tanto* are shorter than both the long and short swords worn by samurai. Samurai women often wore *tanto* for self-defense.

Tatami: Pronounced *tah-tah-mee*. Usually translated as "folded and piled," tatami are traditional Japanese flooring mats, made of woven soft rush straw and packed with rice straw. Tatami are often bordered by brocade or colored cloth. Until the seventeenth century, few non-samurai enjoyed tatami; the lower classes instead placed thin mats over dirt floors.

Tetsubishi: Pronounced *tet-soo-bi-she*. Also known as *makibishi* or (in Europe) caltrops. Sharp, usually triple-spiked foot jacks made from a rare seedpod, iron, or twisted wire. The jacks' tips were sometimes flecked with poison. They could be painted to blend in with reed matting or a polished wooden floor. Able to penetrate sandals, *tetsubishi* caused unexpected injuries, stopping or slowing a pursuer.

Tsukikage: Pronounced *skee-car-geh*. A 470-year-old sword *waza* (technique or set of skills) of the Musou Jikiden Eishin-Ryu school of Iaido, the art of the samurai sword, after which, in keeping with *shinobi* tradition, our hero was named. The Moonshadow technique employs a low, delayed turn, then rising at the attacking foe and executing a crescent strike at their raised forearms. This combination block-and-cut is followed by a push, then a step, after which a fatal single vertical cut is unleashed. The characters making up the technique's name can be translated as "moonshadow." See also **Iaido**.

Yamamba: Pronounced as it reads. In traditional Japanese ghost stories, a witch, living in mountains, who lures men into her hut or cave and eats them. Naturally, Yamamba can disguise themselves, but their real appearance is generally terrifying.

Yokai: Pronounced *yo-k-eye*. Apparitions, spirits, imps, and demons of Japanese folklore. They vary from terrifying ghostly monsters to cute and amusing sprites who want to be friends or offer help to humans. Most *yokai* were originally specific to regions, landmarks, or particular activities. They are often depicted in art, songs, folk festivals, and plays.

Zengogiri: Pronounced *zeng-go-gi-ree*. A *waza* still learned by many schools of Iaido, designed to enable a swordsman to overcome two simultaneous attackers, one coming at him from the front, the other from behind. Though this technique was actually devised and spread much later in Japanese history than the Tokugawa era of Moonshadow, in the story Mantis is identified as the originator of the *waza* and author of a dueling manual. *Zengogiri* is regularly displayed in modern Iaido competitions, and author Simon Higgins has performed it twice in the art's world titles in Japan.

The Moonshadow stories are fantasy tales set in a romanticized historical Japan. Though they reflect certain key events of the early Tokugawa era and include many facts and details about the sword art of Iaido and Japanese warrior culture in general, they remain adventure yarns, not histories. Despite the many liberties I have taken, I hope these stories inspire readers of all ages to investigate the saga and customs of fascinating Old Japan, a world that still has so much to teach us.

My heartfelt thanks to my multitalented wife, Annie, for her great ideas and fantastic support in developing the Moonshadow tales. My gratitude also to Anita Bell, another creative polymath, for her guidance, business savvy, and insight. A very special thanks to the amazing *kunoichi* of Clan Little, Brown, especially Alvina Ling, Connie Hsu, Maria Mercado, and Barbara Bakowski, whose powerful talents steered these stories to a whole new level. Moonshadow and I are in your debt. My thanks also to Catherine Drayton for her brilliant representation and astute ideas.

A warm thanks to my kind friends "Iron Chef" Hibiki Ito, his generous wife, Yoko, and to tea person and *tokonoma* advocate Margaret Price, for all their wonderful support and knowledge. A special tribute to a resident of Japan, Dr. Glenn Stockwell, Kancho (Chief Instructor) of Seishinkan Iaido Dojo, for his expert coaching and for so devotedly preserving the beautiful Iaido of his teacher, Kimura-Kancho, in the twenty-first century. My personal gratitude also to Yasuhisa Watanabe, Fuku-Kancho (Deputy Chief Instructor) of Seishinkan Iaido Dojo, for translating the *furube* sutra and leading me to sites of historical significance to *shinobi* culture while in Japan. My thanks also to Yasu and to instructors Matt Andrew and Nathan Nilsen, and to my friend Nobutaka Tezuka of our Tokyo dojo, for training me in Iaido. To any readers wishing to learn or know more about this graceful five-hundred-year-old art, please visit this website:

www.seishinkan-iaido.org

✳ About the Author ✳

Simon Higgins's employment history reads like a novel. He's worked as a disc jockey, laboratory assistant, marketing manager, and even as a monster on a ghost train. He also spent a decade in law enforcement as a police officer, a state prosecutor, and a licensed private investigator.

Simon is proudly a student of Eishin-Ryu Iaido, a 470-year-old style of swordsmanship that prizes traditional techniques and medieval samurai etiquette and courtesy. He has trained in Japan and participated in Taikai (contests) before His Imperial Highness Prince Munenori Kaya. Simon placed fifth in the 2008 Iaido World Titles, and in 2009 he was awarded a black belt by masters from the All Japan Iaido Federation.

As well as conducting professional development sessions for educators, Simon explains his work, demonstrates Iaido, and runs writing workshops for kids and adults, in Australia and overseas.

www.simonhiggins.net